Flavors of Gray

A Murder Mystery Amateur Sleuth With A
Past

Jodi Walter

THIRTEEN PAGES

To my past self,
You were never given anything you weren't strong enough to handle and overcome. At the time, it was extremely over-whelming and difficult. But without all of those experiences, you never would have discovered your inner strength and power that has led you to the wonderful life, people and experiences you now can enjoy to the fullest!
I Love You!

CHAPTER 1

THE GARAGE LAY DARK and silent.

In one small corner to the left sat a heavy wooden trunk, bolted to the floor. A door across from the trunk opened, and warm yellow light flooded into the cavernous space, driving away the shadows. Dusty boxes and old equipment from past projects sprang into view, all of them sandwiched around a beat up '98 Toyota pickup. The door slammed shut once again, letting the shadows resume their rightful reign.

Next came the sound of footsteps, confident and swift, navigating the pitch black with an ease that revealed many years of maneuvering. Near the middle of the room, unseen hands pulled the low-hanging cord to turn on a dim light. The sound of footsteps resumed once more and then stopped as they reached the trunk. Those hands stretched forth to lift the trunk's lid, and the person pushing it upward struggled a little to move the ancient wood. The rusted metal hinges creaked loudly in the room's eerie quiet. The smooth gloves that concealed those hands did nothing to make hoisting that trunk's lid upwards easier. A dull thud reverberated through the room as the wood came to rest on the wall behind it.

The ventured inside the trunk, pressing a hidden button set on the side wall. There was a click, then the bottom of the trunk loosened. It was pulled upwards, and those hands fetched a vial filled with liquid. Carefully, as though carrying dynamite, the hands closed the lid again, and the sound of the heavy footsteps returned. The cord was pulled on the light once more, allowing the garage to plunge back into total darkness. The liquid shone clear and amber as the door on the far side of the room opened and light peeked around it. After the door closed, the garage returned to the deepest darkness again, as if it had never been disturbed.

CHAPTER 2

CHRISTIE WATCHED THE YOUNG man cross his arms to cover his chest and turn up his nose at her.

"I have nothing to say to you," he stated.

He was looking at the walls, at the table, at the floor, at his own lap… at everything except her. She weighed her options. It was almost six in the evening, and she had already had a long, hard day. Her patience was long expired, yet she'd still been holding it together pretty well through the entire interview. But the boy was a pompous brat, someone who had no regard for officers of the law—and definitely no regard for human life.

He was being interviewed as a suspect in a hit-and-run case. He was sixteen, drove a Mercedes that cost the salary of two police officers combined, and had the ingrained arrogance of a fifty-year-old businessman who had never been denied anything his entire life. Christie had been planning to continue the interview until he cracked under the pressure, but the longer she watched that smug confidence settle into his features, the more her own patience waned. She tried again.

"Where were you on Wednesday evening, Mr. Brooks?"

The boy rolled his eyes, a smirk tugging at the corner of his lips.

"Detective, you're wasting your time. I didn't do anything," he emphasized in an infuriatingly condescending voice, gesturing at his watch.

That was the last straw for Christie.

"Fine. Let me tell you something, then. On Wednesday evening, at four thirty p.m., there was an accident in the parking lot of the Hudson Yards shopping centre."

The boy's smile faded a bit as the realization struck that she wasn't buying his show of innocence or ignorance.

"A young lady named Ashlie—you know, your girlfriend—was hit by a car, which then sped off."

Christie looked away from the papers before her and up at him. "But those are all details you already know, right, Mr. Brooks?"

The boy shook his head quickly, nervously.

"No. I have no idea about that." There was a slight waver in his voice now. That smug surety was gone.

"So, you didn't know that your girlfriend has been in the hospital because of an accident?"

He hesitated. Christie could see him calculating his next move. His pupils were flitting wildly left and right like malfunctioning lasers.

If he says 'yes', he'll be proven a liar, and then we can question him about everything else he's just said. If he says 'no', we can ask him more about his girlfriend. But dammit, he still could lie his way out of those questions.

The boy squinted at her. "Hospital? No, I don't know anything about that. Is she okay?"

Christie didn't bother responding to his feigned concern. She paused for a moment, then looked down at her notes again.

"Well, that's interesting because we have CCTV footage of you and your girlfriend arriving together at the mall. Then, approximately 45 minutes later, we have you driving out and hitting her on the way before fleeing the scene. I guess you must not have realized that it was her you hit. I have to admit, though, I find that strange. I mean, you both had just gone to the mall together, and then you left without her. How would you explain that, Mr. Brooks?"

The boy's eyes widened. All the colour drained out of his face. Christie watched sweat gathering on his brows and thought he might pass out from shock, considering how ghostly pale he looked. But that didn't happen. Instead, the boy did what many other criminals did once they realized the net had descended on them and they were trapped. He channelled his shock and fear into anger.

The boy jumped to his feet. Pointed at her, with a single accusatory finger, and stuttered, "Listen here, you little *bitch*."

Christie didn't flinch.

"I don't know what you're talking about, and I won't let you taint my reputation! Defamation of character is punishable by law!"

Christie nodded. "Except that it's not defamation because we have your face and vehicle on video, fleeing the scene—which is also punishable by law."

The boy's mouth fell open, and he began to tremble, his hands balling into fists. Christie swallowed, still maintaining her cool but wishing that Jed was in the room with her. Even though this case didn't need his expertise, he would have intervened the second the kid jumped to his feet and started insulting her. Christie looked the boy up and down, determining that he was not a physical threat to her. He was as scrawny and thin as sixteen-year-olds could get.

"Listen here, you!" Now, he was full-on yelling and seemed about to lunge across the table with his fists flying. "Do you know who my father is? How dare you threaten me with false claims! If I want, I can have your head on a plate by tomorrow... all the heads in this goddamned station!"

Christie heard the door open behind her, and then Jason was moving toward the boy, pinning him to the floor and forcing his arms behind his back, while the boy screamed madly.

Finally. Took him long enough to get in here.

"Mr. Brooks, you are being charged with attempted murder with a deadly weapon, fleeing the scene of a crime, and we have just added menacing an officer of the law to your charges." Christie closed her folder of papers and picked it up. "I'll see you and your father in court."

As he climbed into the Jeep, Jed put his foot down on the brake and started the ignition. A rush of cool air came pouring out of the vents, and he sighed, sitting back in his seat. He ran a hand across his face before shifting into drive, leaving the premises of the prison to go back to work.

Visiting prisons was never an easy part of the job. No matter how many times he went, it never failed to shake Jed up. Regardless, he always showed up for duty and, in fact, always showed up early. He had just met with a new client. The man had been incarcerated for seven years, after being involved in the robbery of a specialty liquor store as the getaway driver.

The good news was that the man's seven-year sentence was coming to an end this week, and he had expressed interest in receiving addiction counseling so he wouldn't end up in the same position down the road. It was why his warden had contacted an addiction rehab facility, who had then contacted Jed. Always interested in helping people with their sobriety, Jed had agreed to work with the man and had been excited to meet him.

In situations like this, though, excitement could not be allowed to outpace caution. Jed never quite knew what he was getting into when he went to a prison to meet with a potential client. Sometimes, the incarcerated person made false promises to pursue therapy so they could reduce their sentence and be out on the streets earlier.

Then, there were other times when the person was genuinely interested, but once they were released, the inexorable tug of their old life proved impossible to resist, and they ended up caught in those same vicious cycles of crime and addiction. For some people, however, an unbreakable determination not to return to the darkness they had just come out of turned them into a better version of themselves.

This man, Jeff, seemed to fit into that last category. He had greeted Jed with a smile and had shaken his hand. They had sat down to have a brief chat about what Jeff's hopes and expectations would be going into the therapy process, and there Jed had gotten another surprise. The man hadn't been unrealistic at all in his expectations and was extremely humble. That was rare to find.

I've been in prison a long time. Seven years. I could have gotten married, had three kids, and started working on my own business or bought a house. I just wasted a lot of time. I'm not expecting this therapy to cure me overnight, and well, since I just wasted seven years of my life inside these walls, I'm committed to putting in the work and the time to make sure that I recover for good. Man, it's the least I can do after all this time I've wasted. I can't get those years back, but I can make sure that I never have to waste that same amount of time—or more—again.

Jed smiled to himself as he coasted down the street, heading back into the city to his office to continue the rest of the day's work. Jeff the kind of client he so loved working with—the ones who were self-aware, who could see the error of their ways but needed help to break through their fog of the addiction. They were people who were not afraid to ask for help.

Jed took a moment to reflect on his own past and what had led him to where he was now. What could have been different for him? How could his life have been better if he had just asked for help? Even though he knew better than to invalidate the magnitude of emotional distress he had been experiencing at that time, and how isolating that experience and those drugs had made him feel, he wondered if the trajectory of those experiences might have been different. Jed had reached out for help prior to that, but he hadn't been truly ready to make any changes yet. He'd still been stuck in the throes of addiction, unable to face, let alone change, anything at that point. It was the avoidance phase, where drugs were used to dull everything so he could just escape. He knew all too well the individual needed to be ready and committed to make the needed changes, or no amount of therapy would work.

If that had been different, Jed might have actually listened to what his therapists were saying. Maybe he could have enjoyed his mother's company instead of wreaking havoc on both their lives and making her afraid of him. He might have started recovery before he almost died from multiple overdoses. He might have committed to being clean earlier. Jed tapped on the steering wheel as he waited for the light to change from red to green. A lot of things could have been different, and he knew that. The decisions one should have made were always clearer in hindsight. But the reality was that his addiction had played out exactly how it had needed to for him to end up in this position, helping others through their addictions.

And it was the same thing for Jeff. He had to go through seven years behind bars, spending all that time constantly evaluating his life, evaluating his actions, and regretting his decisions, to get to the point he was at now, where he was finally ready to let go of alcohol for good. Jed was going to do everything in his power to support Jeff so that he could succeed.

CHAPTER 3

BACK AT HIS OFFICE, Jed took a pause before his final client of the day to call Christie. Their retreat was coming up. Chief Lucas had been so pleased with his and Christie's performance as partners on their first case and the execution of the stake out with the five officers that led to capturing Hugh that he had organized a team retreat. The chief had shared that he thought it would be a good idea to have the takedown team of officers bond more with Jed and Christie, hoping there could be a closer-knit collaboration between them—a taskforce unit. It was going to be hosted by the deputy police chief, Aaron Ryans, whom Jed had met on several occasions. For now, though, he just wanted to check in with Christie.

"You know, Detective, I've been thinking about that ice cream parlor we went to a few weeks back." Jed leaned back in his chair, his feet up on the desk. It was Friday, three weeks after they had closed the first case they'd worked on and solved together. He was hoping to wrap up the week with some ice cream with his work partner. He grabbed a bottle of water.

"You know, Jed, I've been thinking that I should ask you how you've been doing since we wrapped up the case."

Christie spoke carefully, tenderly. "You haven't seemed willing to talk about it, and I've been trying to give you the space you need. Don't you think it's time to let me in just a little bit?"

Jed's hand paused midair with the bottle held in it. Water sloshed around aimlessly inside it.

"I think it's very endearing that you are so worried about me, Detective." He cleared his throat and straightened up a bit, placing the bottle back on the desk. "But I really have been doing okay. I've made journaling a larger part of my routine, and working out also has been giving me some dedicated time to focus on my thoughts and really examine them so I can best support myself emotionally. If you're worried that I'm falling to pieces, I'm not."

The line was dead silent for a few heartbeats.

"I'm happy to hear that you aren't falling to pieces." Christie's voice was oddly flat.

Jed's eyes narrowed, and he could feel himself sliding into therapist mode. He tried to rein it in. Now was not a very good time. The golden-hour's sunlight was streaming in through the large windows, dipping the entire office in shades of soft, buttery yellow. And below the office, the city was full-throttle. Cars and pedestrians cluttered the roads in a spill of bright colors, moving constantly back and forth. Jed was watching them, feeling the gears in his mind turning.

"I sense you've resigned yourself to giving up on the conversation and moving on. Has my resistance to sharing how I feel made you feel alienated somehow?"

Christie sighed. It was a long and weary sigh. "Yes, Jed. It has."

Her matter-of-fact tone made him frown even more. He looked down at his desk for a moment. He really had been doing well since they last spoke about the case and had been doing even better in recent days, considering how it had ended.

For the first few days afterward, Jed had struggled to separate himself from that series of events. Although he knew that what had happened wasn't his fault, for the first three or four days, Jed had been riddled with self-blame. The gnawing feeling had filled his insides like a horde of carnivorous locusts, robbing him of sleep and causing vivid nightmares the few times he did manage to doze off.

Somewhere during the fourth day, his routine for processing his thoughts and holding space for his emotions had broken through the fog bogging him down. He wasn't the one who had murdered those homeless men. Hugh was. There was no way he could have known what Hugh's plans were.

Jed had replayed their interactions over and over, from the first time Hugh had knocked on the door and entered his office to introduce himself to the last time he saw him in the investigation room at the police station, snarling about how glad he was that he had killed those three men. He had scoured every conversation, every time he had sat across from him, and every step they had taken as they walked down the streets of Manhattan together.

There had been nothing that could have tipped him off. If Max hadn't helped him piece the clues together, he would have seen all of Hugh's slip-ups as completely harmless. It was frustrating how he could read people and relationship dynamics so clearly with his clients and friends, but when it came to his own life, he felt completely blind.

There was also nothing he could have done about Ethan. As painful as it was to accept, Jed couldn't have helped Ethan if he hadn't known he was struggling. He didn't even know whether he *had* been struggling or not. He still didn't have an answer for the young man's death. Pain ripped through his heart afresh, and he winced.

"I'm sorry I've been shutting you out so much. I don't want to add my struggle to your plate. I've worked through my feelings about both Hugh and Ethan, and I've come to the conclusion that there was nothing I could have done. That doesn't make things any easier, but I think accepting it is, at least, the first step to healing the gaping hole in my heart."

On the other end of the line, at the station, Christie paused what she was doing, her hands hovering between her body and the mini fridge where she was about to grab a bottle of water. That must have been the first time she had ever really heard Jed open up about how he was feeling after their case had ended. She had witnessed his break down after they'd discovered Ethan's body and had seen a sliver of the pain in his features when they had proven Hugh to be the perpetrator. Since then, radio silence. He hadn't brought it up at all. Now, to hear him say there was a hole in his heart made sadness settle into her stomach. She realized just how much she didn't know about Jed. "See? That's the first time since the case ended that you've admitted to me that this whole ordeal is hurting you. I feel awful."

Jed's brows furrowed even more. "Why do you feel bad?" he asked with hesitation, unsure if she would think it was a silly question.

Christie stared at the phone. "You just think that I completely don't care about you, don't you?" Her voice was low and hurt, like tiny fragments of shattered glass. "Jed, we've witnessed and worked on four murders. We apprehended your colleague as the perpetrator for three of the four, you lost one of your previous clients during the case, and throughout the entire ordeal, you remained fully focused on my emotional well-being. But you haven't let me near enough to you to even try to help."

Jed struggled to find something to say but couldn't. His mind whirred, but nothing popped up, no words which would be appropriate for this situation. He pressed a hand against his faintly throbbing temples and wondered if it wasn't time to go back to the cabin. His emotional burnouts were getting more and more frequent.

"You're right," he finally managed to muster.

15

"Is it intentional?" Christie asked.

"Is what intentional, Detective?"

"You're keeping the hurt to yourself. Do you not want me close to your heart?"

Jed's jaw tightened immediately. That was something else he had been working on over the last weeks while they had both been laying low, trying to recover from the case and get their wits about them. He had settled back into his routine of seeing patients and taking calls. He'd been trying to keep his feelings under control. Now, hearing her ask that question in a soft, sad voice threatened to undo the restraints he had built in his heart and unleash the flood of feelings he was trying to conceal.

Christie continued, "This is hard for me to say, but I feel a bit abandoned. I mean, you've helped me with all my emotions, but you don't let me help you with yours. And I know that just because you've helped me, it doesn't automatically mean that I have the right to demand access to your heart. But the lack of reciprocity makes me feel a bit like one of your clients instead of your partner. Will you let me in?"

The way his heart opened up at her tender question was enough to take all the air out of Jed's lungs. It took everything inside of him to stifle the gasp he was holding in. His chest physically hurt from her words. He couldn't respond—he was far too busy trying to pull himself together. Every ounce of his willpower was directed at not outright responding with, *If I let you in, I'll never release you.*

"Jed?"

He didn't respond.

"Are you still there?"

"I'm here."

The desire to let her know how he felt was overpowering. "I'll let you in, Detective."

Christie stared at the floor in front of her, warmth spreading through her chest. She wasn't sure if her ears were deceiving her, but his voice had changed. The way he'd said 'Detective' just then was different from the way he'd said it a few moments prior. It was deeper, huskier than she had ever heard it.

"Thank you. At the very least, I can offer you unlimited hugs," she said.

Jed clenched his jaw so tight that he was sure he would end up with a tension headache before he could make it home in the evening. His nostrils flared.

"I'll take advantage of that," he whispered in a slightly breathless tone.

"The hugs, you mean?" she asked, though she wasn't sure why.

Now, Jed was sure she was just trying to do him in.

"Are you offering something else for me to take advantage of, Detective? I'm sure we could figure something out." His voice was normal once again, or at least as normal as it could be under the circumstances. That teasing edge he sometimes employed with Christie had returned as well.

Immediately flustered by thoughts of the handcuffs she had found in his room, Christie shook her head before remembering that he couldn't see her. "I mean… maybe the occasional additional advice?"

Jed gave in to the smile that was pulling at his lips. She sounded the way he felt—flustered.

"Then I'll take that, too."

He looked up over at the clock across from his desk. It was nearing the time for Max to call, the perfect time to close his call with Christie before his lips betrayed him.

"How did your case end up?" he asked.

"It was gleefully uncomplicated and was wrapped up yesterday—except for the part where a sixteen-year-old boy threatened me, saying he could have my head cut off and presented to him on a plate if he wanted."

Jed's eyes narrowed, that aggressive protectiveness flaring within him instantly. "What?"

"Yeah. And that was before he tried to come at me during the interview." Christie laughed.

Jed did not laugh. He was the furthest thing from amused. He knew Christie could handle herself. Still, he wished he had been there to protect her. He reminded himself that he could trust the other officers to keep her safe. That was their job anyway. He exhaled.

"I am glad to know you are safe. I need to run now before you get me in trouble, Detective. I have a client call soon.

We'll talk about ice cream and that case of yours very soon, and I'll see you at the retreat this weekend."

After he'd ended the call, Jed stared down at his lap for a long moment before sighing aloud into the room. With the retreat fast-approaching, he really needed to begin his own packing and make damn sure that he brought the *right* clothes with him. If Christie was able to stir up such an intense tornado of emotions within him just through the phone, then what would it feel like to be in close proximity to her during the entire retreat? One thing was definitely certain.

He would not be taking any sweatpants.

Jed spent the next few minutes staring out the windows again, waiting for his office phone to ring. Now that the murders from the previous case were over, he was more relaxed about Max's safety. Of course, he was still eager to get Max off the streets and into a better environment.

With Ethan's passing, Jed was now even more determined to get Max into rehab. The situations weren't exactly the same. No two situations ever were. Ethan was older and had been through rehab, seeming to be on the right track, when someone took his life. Jed was haunted by the uncertainty of whether Ethan had started using again. The common denominator between the two was substance abuse, and Jed was still incredibly uncomfortable with Max living on the streets amid gang violence and gangsters that hated him.

His phone rang. Right on time.

"Mr. G, what's up?" Max sounded excited, like he had just received some good news.

"Well, someone sounds happy." Jed chuckled. "Mind sharing the good news with me?"

"Oh, you know, I'm just chilling, lettin' it do what it do. You know how it is." Max laughed briefly, but Jed saw straight through it. That was the first time in a while that Max had evaded one of his questions so pointedly.

"Got any exciting plans for this weekend?" Jed asked.

"Shanice and I are going to see a movie tonight—catch a vibe, feel nice."

"Oh, well that does sound exciting. Is it a special occasion?"

"Nah, man. I just gotta make sure she don't forget how good she got it, you know what I'm saying, Mr. G? She's a catch, so I gotta make sure these other guys know that she's my girl. Take her out, treat her good, call her every night, you know what I'm saying?"

Jed nodded along as he made some notes. Before he could respond, Max cut in again.

"So, Mr. G…"

This time, there was a mischievous edge to Max's tone. Jed braced himself.

"Yes, Max? What's on your mind?"

"You've got a girl?"

Jed's hands froze, his pen in the air. Was the universe conspiring against him?

"No. I don't."

"C'mon man. Quit playin'."

Jed frowned. Surely, Max wasn't trying to imply that Jed looked like a womanizer.

"Why not? What's so hard to believe?" He tried to remain cool, but his voice was tinged with curiosity.

"I've seen the way you look at that girl you're always with."

Jed's hands stiffened again. Ah. Now he was sure the universe was conspiring against him.

"I'm not sure what you mean," he managed.

"Yeah. I would say that, too, if I was you," Max drawled with a chuckle. "But like I said, I seen the way you look at her. You got it bad."

"Which girl are we referring to, exactly?" Jed asked, a tight edge to his voice.

Max was not bluffing. "Brown hair that looks gold in the streetlights, brown eyes, good deal shorter than you are, slim but still oh so curvy. Always wearing navy cargo pants? Ringing any bells?"

Images of Christie filled Jed's mind, and his jaw tightened again. He forced himself to release the tension in his body and open up to the conversation.

"A few. What about her?"

"Who is she? Isn't she your girl?"

If he was the least bit honest with himself, Jed didn't want to answer Max's questions. What he wanted to do was bang his head against his desk.

"No—she's a colleague," he answered with ease, sure that would put Max off the scent.

Max burst out laughing. "A colleague?" he said between gasps. "You expect me to believe that shit? You really think I'm stupid, don't you? Nah, Mr. G, you trippin'."

Jed closed his eyes for a moment, willing himself not to laugh—or start crying.

"Why do you think she's my girl, Max?"

"Like I said, the way you look at her. You look at her like you've never seen a more beautiful girl in your entire life. You got that look in your eyes that make women go weak in the knees and shit. Real poetic and shit."

Jed sighed to himself, realizing he was failing at diverting the conversation, and Max burst out laughing again. The boy laughed for so long that Jed found himself smiling, too.

"So, when are you gonna tell her how you feel?"

He may as well give in to the conversation, Jed realized. "I have no such plans."

Max chuckled. "Yeah, that's because you haven't seen how she looks at you."

Jed's pen was hovering yet again as he stared at the receiver. He didn't know whether he had the heart to ask Max what he was talking about. More importantly, what he *did know* was that inquiring any further would go against his code of professional conduct.

"Did you just call to discuss my love life? How are things with you?"

"Yes, I called to discuss your love life." Max gave a roguish chuckle. Jed shook his head.

"Why don't you come into office since you've been keeping track of where I am? We can talk about my love life even more in person."

"I think you should tell her how you feel," Max spoke, his voice suddenly turning serious and throwing Jed off guard.

Jed sighed again, and Max's laugh returned.

"I'm sorry for laughing at you so much, Mr. G." He didn't sound sorry in the slightest.

"I don't mind," Jed answered. "I've never heard you laugh this much before. I enjoy hearing you happy. Maybe I should let you laugh at my love life more often."

"I appreciate that, Mr. G. I've been doing good, though. I'm still trying to give it up for real, you know?"

"Yes, I know how hard it is to fully let go. You've been doing well and have been making good progress so far. Have you been trying the reward system I recommended?"

"I mean, yes and no," Max confessed. "Sometimes... I don't know about bothering with the reward because I feel like I'm rewarding myself for something I should be doing automatically, you know? For something that everybody else does naturally."

"Different things are hard for different people, Max. You shouldn't measure what you deserve to give yourself based on what everyone else is giving themselves."

"Words of wisdom," Max answered, and Jed could feel his smile through the receiver.

Max was in his usual spot, in the old oak tree in his girl-friend's yard, perched high up in the branches and looking out over the city. This time, instead of the usual blunt, he was holding an energy drink.

"I don't want to beat a dead horse, Mr. G, but why haven't you told her?"

Jed paused for a moment, eyes furrowing with amusement. "I've always found it kind of funny how people say 'I don't mean to do something' and then do or say the exact thing right after they say it."

"Yeah, that's my bad," Max apologized with a grin.

"It's okay," Jed told him, smiling. Then he sighed, running a hand through his hair. "I haven't told her because I guess I'm scared."

"What? You? Scared?" Now Max's voice was incredulous. "I don't believe that for a minute. Come on, man, stop playin'."

Jed shook his head. "You asked me why, and there's your answer."

Max hummed to himself. "Whatever, man."

It was quiet for a moment on the line.

"Have you made the move to see your mom yet?" Jed finally asked.

"No." Max's reply was deadpan. "I told her she needs therapy before she can talk to me anymore. She's off her fuckin' rockers is what she is."

Jed's brows raised. Max? Telling his mom to seek therapy? Wow. That was a huge development.

"I tried talking to her last week, and she's on the same shit she's always on," he continued. "Started trying to gaslight me about me talking to my dad and shit. I'm not dealing with that shit no more, man. Either she gets therapy, or she leaves me the absolute fuck alone."

"I'm proud of you for setting that boundary for yourself. It takes a lot of self-awareness and bravery to recognize when people around us are repeating patterns of behavior that will put us into harmful situations."

"Yeah, man," Max sniffed once, paused for a moment, and continued in an even tone. "Nothing I say gets through that skull of hers. I see the way my girl's parents act with her, and I can't even imagine how a parent could intentionally hurt their own kid. And I already know what you 'bout to say. 'She's probably not doing it intentionally, and she's operating out of her own trauma, blah blah blah'."

Jed grinned at Max's elaboration of what he thought Jed's response would be. It was kind of funny, but he focused on the rest of Max's explanation.

"But she's not. It's intentional. And you wanna know how I know it's intentional? I asked her. I *asked* her. I said, 'Why do you behave so aggressively toward dad?' and I was listening to her, just waiting for the opportunity to catch her in the fuckin' act. You know she said to me? She said he deserved to lose his child because he left her. I ain't never heard anything more insane in my whole fuckin life, man. She confessed she didn't want him to have a relationship with me because he left her. How much of a narcissist do you have to be to want your child to suffer? She's insane! She needs to go to rehab—not me."

"Well," Jed began. "You definitely did a good job of assessing the situation and coming up with a plan for finding the information you were looking for. How did you feel when your theory proved to be correct? Did it hurt?"

Max was silent. Jed took the opportunity to make some notes about what Max's perception of his mom's mental condition.

"Yeah." Max's voice was small. "It hurts."

Jed felt a heaviness pressing into his heart for the young man. He couldn't imagine how agonizing it must be to watch your own mother betray you. On the other hand, he didn't need to imagine because his father had done the same thing to him.

"I'm sorry that your mom chose herself instead of choosing to protect you and help you foster a good relationship with your father, even though they split up. You didn't deserve that, and you definitely didn't do anything to cause it. I'm glad that you and your father are now on good terms, though.

Have you spoken to him recently? Have you tried telling him about what you're experiencing with your mom?"

"Yeah, we sat down earlier this week and had a talk about the whole situation. I could see the disappointment in his face when I told him what she said. But I don't even think he was disappointed for himself. His disappointment turned into pity real fast. Then he started going on about how sorry he was that this happened the way it happened and that I ended up on the street. I asked him 'was that why he left', and he looked confused."

"Did he eventually answer?" Jed asked.

"I had to rephrase the question. What I was wanting to ask him was whether he left because my mom was a raging fucking lunatic."

Jed swallowed a wild bray of laughter that suddenly surged up within him. Max had this incredible way of putting a lot of passion behind his words, and the way he emphasized 'lunatic' was way funnier than it should have been.

"Well? What did he say?"

"Man, come on, what you think he said? Of course that's why he left. He didn't wanna admit it—tried to be nice about it. He said they thought about things differently and saw things differently. I told him he could have just said she was batshit crazy, and I would have agreed."

Jed was writing things down as fast as he could.

"And you know what he said to me? He said he didn't wanna talk bad about her. Can you imagine? He's concerned about not saying the truth about her, while she trashes him every chance she gets with lies on top of lies on top of lies. And she thinks I'm gonna meet with her? She is out of her mind. I'm not going nowhere."

In his spot in the tree, Max was fuming. His grip on the can of his drink tightened.

"Do you think she will commit to going to therapy?" Jed asked, curious to see if Max had any hope that his mom would have a change of heart if she sought help.

"I mean, I'm in therapy, and I'm getting better. So, anything is possible. But it's only gonna work if she wants it to work. And I don't know if she values me enough to do that. She only thinks about herself as far as I can see."

"Well, time will tell whether she will decide to go through with it or not. And you have been doing well and making great progress. I'm very proud of you. Have I told you that lately?"

Max was quiet for a moment.

"No. You haven't."

"Well, I'm very proud of how far you have come, Maxwell. You've grown in so many ways."

"How have I grown?"

Jed looked at the receiver for a moment, realizing the silent plea in Max's otherwise casual question. He paused his note taking.

"You've gotten bolder, and you've made a decision to change for the better. You've been consistent in working toward that. You've let go of a lot of those violent tendencies you had when we first started these sessions, too—being overly defensive, lying, hanging up out of anger. You've gotten more playful, you laugh more, you're spending more intentional time with your girlfriend, you drink energy drinks instead of smoking weed, you climb trees instead of hanging out in abandoned buildings, and you go to the park instead of getting into fights with gang members. You've also shown an impressive amount of self-awareness and emotional intelligence for someone your age. It really is quite impressive."

"You really think that?"

"I do. I think you're making incredible progress, and I think that you're on the right path to your recovery."

"I appreciate that a lot, Mr. G. I really do." Gratitude welled up within Max, and he closed his eyes for a peaceful moment, letting the cool breeze waft through his hair and gently rustle the tree's leaves.

Jed glanced at the time. Though he had gotten Max a cellphone more than a month ago, the boy still tended to limit their call times to much less than the allotted hour Jed reserved for him. Their calls had lengthened though, from the original ten-minute limit they had to abide by because of the payphones Max used to call in. Now, they were up to fifteen minutes on his cellphone. Jed let Max lead with extending the call longer and longer as he got more comfortable.

"No worries," he said. "I'm always happy to affirm you. Did you wanna talk about anything else? Any thoughts, concerns, feelings?"

"You should tell her." Max repeated, and now there was no mischief in that voice, no teasing. Just honesty.

CHAPTER 4

THE WORKDAY HAD ALMOST reached its end, and Jed was practically soaked with exhaustion. He had attended to each of his clients with such focus and energy that now he felt its consequences finally emerging. His eyelids were leaden and sore, and his limbs were much the same. There was a gentle throbbing on the left side of his head and an uncomfortable tingle in his lower spine. The message was clear: his body was begging him for some relief, and Jed would give it what it wanted soon. Hopefully, the retreat would serve as the reboot he needed.

One deputy chief, five officers, one detective, and one investigative therapist—six men, him, and Christie.

He'd been doing a good job of keeping his apprehensions about that situation to himself, at least in his own estimations. He'd had a hard time sharing the nickname he was fond of using for her with another officer a few weeks ago, so Jed didn't know how he was going to tolerate watching the men flirt with her throughout the retreat—especially since he knew Jason was going to lay it on heavy. Maybe some kind of miracle would happen and allow for the retreat to end early? Maybe he could pretend to get called in for something important?

That would have to constitute a lie, and Jed didn't like lies, or lying. But, if it all got too intense, he would have no choice. It was the least he could do not to torture himself. It was either succumb to an incredibly difficult emotional situation or tell a white lie and vanish to avoid it.

He picked up the phone and dialed a number by heart.

"Mom," he said when she finally answered on the fifth ring right before the voicemail.

"Hi, Jed. Is everything alright?" His mother, being his mother, immediately picked up on the most minute of changes in his voice and was immediately alerted. "You sound stressed."

"I am. Very stressed. Remember the retreat I mentioned to you earlier this week?"

"Yes, I remember," Laurie answered as she sat down in front of the fireplace. It was getting colder and colder these days. Fall was beautiful, but it really was low on her favorite list because it led into her least favorite season—winter. She hated the biting chill that accompanied it, that chill which settled deep into your bones and refused to leave. "Did something go wrong?"

"Not yet. I anticipate there'll be a lot of flirting. The police officers, I mean. With Christie. If it gets too unbearable, I'll call you and pretend you have an emergency so I can leave."

"Jed!"

Jed winced at his mother's surprise. "I know, Mom. But I won't be able to handle it if they flirt with her really intensely."

"Aw, Jed."

"And I don't know what I'd do if she reciprocated," he finished, feeling a terribly painful constriction in his chest as those words registered. He hadn't thought about that possibility before, ever, but now he truly considered it. What *would* he do if Christie reciprocated? Even imagining it made him nauseous.

Jed took a deep breath. His heart now hammered inside his chest. His blood fizzed through his veins like charged battery acid. The retreat no longer loomed in the future as an uncomfortable social gathering. Now, he saw it dressed as his worst nightmare, a nightmare in which he would constantly get to witness his partner and friend being approached by other men, receiving their disguised affection.

And perhaps she would reciprocate.

Jed inhaled another sharp, shaky breath.

"Your feelings for her seem to have developed quite a bit," Laurie mused.

Jed shook his head, forcing his lips into a smile but managing only a sick grimace. "They have, much to my chagrin. I don't know what to do about them. She is my partner."

"Oh?" Laurie had never heard Jed talk about this before.

"Yeah. Usually, I'm just super curious about the woman… and it dissolves at that point. I don't tend to get further than that. I realize some glaring issue that would make a relationship improbable and it just… fades."

"But this one hasn't."

Jed laughed. It was a sour, bitter sound. "It hasn't. After curiosity, there's this period where I always want to be around the woman. It's the same with new friendships, I've realized."

"Oh! It's interesting that you noticed the connection between friendships and romantic interests—that they develop similarly, I mean."

Jed nodded. "Yeah. Noticing attachment patterns is kind of my thing, you know?"

Laurie laughed. "Yes, that's part of your job, and you're very good at it. Do you think you'll get to that stage with Christie? The attachment."

Jed closed his eyes. "I'm not sure, Mom. I'm not sure. All I know is that I am completely overwhelmed by feelings of adoration, grief, and jealousy right now." He sighed. "And then even more grief."

"Maybe it's time to tell her how you feel?"

Jed's exasperated sigh must have been loud enough to be heard in the hallway outside his office.

Laurie teased him a little. "Not what you wanted to hear?"

"Not what I wanted to hear. I feel like it's too soon. My feelings are really unstable right now, and I couldn't possibly pour the responsibility for my heart not breaking in two onto her. It isn't her responsibility. It's mine."

"That is true, Jed, but telling her you like her isn't the same as giving her responsibility for your heart. That's just you expressing your feelings."

"Yeah. I guess so," he muttered, unconvinced.

The silence stretched between them.

"I don't even know how I would say it if I was given the opportunity."

"Oh, Jed," Laurie laughed. "You've always been good with your words. You don't need to worry about that."

"You flatter me too much, Mom."

They laughed together.

After the call ended, Jed found himself lost in thought once more. Two people had told him in the same day that he should confess how he felt to Christie. The universe, was it conspiring against him? Or was it trying to help him? The sound of his desktop's notifications pulled him out of the reverie.

Sitting upright, he pulled his chair closer to the desk and opened his inbox. It was an email from the chief, confirming their rooms and other information for the three-day retreat. He would be in room B. Jed started to pack his belongings away.

CHAPTER 5

AFTER TAKING A SHOWER and completing his morning routines, Jed picked up his duffel bag and his backpack, checking everything over to make sure he wasn't about to forget anything. Items in hand, he bid a silent farewell to his apartment and headed downstairs to his Jeep.

It was almost 6:00 a.m. when he pulled out of the parking garage and onto the streets of New York. He hadn't bothered to make breakfast this morning, since he knew he would be in a hurry to pack his things, prepare his apartment for departure, and then get to the Airbnb on time.

In the mornings, his usual routine was simple—wake up, head to the gym, get back home, take a shower, and get ready for work. Today, he had woken up an extra hour early just to make sure that he would be on time. He had put off his packing until this morning, as opposed to coming home last night and trying to pack on a Friday night while exhaustion was kicking his butt.

The nine-hour long sleep last night had wiped away the exhaustion but not his nervousness. No, that beast had reared its ugly head even more enthusiastically this morning. He was positively anxious. The thought of being cocooned inside a strange place with Christie and six other men was unpleasant no matter how he looked at it. And being a therapist, Jed had tried to look at it from as many angles as he could. Each had left him with a palpitating heart and twitchy fingers.

His stomach grumbled as he pulled up to a red light. He needed to stop and get something to eat. The easiest option would be to head to the coffee shop where he could buy his morning coffee and get a breakfast sandwich, and that sounded as easy as anything else. He wasn't very picky with what he had for breakfast.

Apart from his protein shake after his workout every morning, he wasn't a heavy breakfast person. In the coffee shop drive-thru, his phone pinged. It was a message from Christie.

Hey Jed, what room or you assigned to? In case the team building gets too intense, and I need to sneak into your room to talk in the evening.

Jed chuckled, sensing some of his unease fading. He definitely hadn't seen that coming. She was full of surprises these days. He liked it. It kept him on his toes. After making his order and heading to the pickup window, he typed out a response.

My room is B. How about you? And you can sneak into my room anytime, Detective.

Jed snuck a quick bite of his ham and cheese sandwich as he drove along then heard another message come in. At another stop light he knew would be red for a long time, he picked up the phone again.

My room is A. I wouldn't want to take advantage of you as my friend just because you're a therapist—but I do get a sense that you enjoy psychoanalyzing me.

Jed gave Christie a call instead of continuing to text while he was driving.

"Detective?" Jed led as Christie picked up the call.

"Hey, Jed," Christie responded.

"You know you have my ear and my shoulder anytime you need me. You know that I find you very fascinating."

Christie laughed, her nerves prickling. In the living room of the Airbnb, she scratched the back of her neck. Her Uber had dropped her off at the retreat a few minutes before.

"Thank you, Jed. I appreciate that. Maybe this retreat will finally be the time where I make some real progress or whatever you call it in therapy."

"Yeah, we'll see about that, Detective."

Christie laughed yet sounded a bit sleepy, like she had either just woken up or hadn't slept well.

"Did you sleep well?" Jed asked.

The last time they had spoken about her sleeping habits was when he'd been at the cabin, before they had cracked the case.

"Um," she started, "I—I mean, I slept probably for half an hour before I ended up waking up and not being able to get back to sleep. It was just one of those nights."

"Half an hour?" Jed asked incredulously. "That's absurd. Have you tried sleep meditations? I know that's completely cliché and you're probably tired of hearing that, but many of my clients find them extremely helpful. I can teach you a few different ones."

Christie sighed, and Jed immediately knew what that meant.

"I have tried them," she said. "I've tried everything, actually—except the pills. I've tried the meditations. I've tried listening to brown noise, and white noise, and pink noise, and green noise—the whole rainbow spectrum, in fact. I've tried changing my diet, I've tried not using my phone before bed…"

Christie laughed, but Jed could hear the strain in her voice.

"It must be exhausting, literally and figuratively, to continually trying to fix your relationship with sleep and have nothing work. I'm sorry that you haven't found a solution yet. Maybe you should consider getting sleeping pills from your doctor?"

"Yeah, that's the next option, I'm afraid. But I'm hoping some kind of miracle will happen because I'm not really enthused by the prospect of having to take pills just to sleep. I hate the idea of being reliant on something. Though, constantly being exhausted sucks. It affects everything. I'm also more of a night owl than a morning person, so staying up late and then not sleeping when I try to, really can bite me in the ass sometimes. It also comes with the territory. Whenever there's a crime scene, I'm there. Doesn't matter if it's at 9 p.m. or at 1 a.m..."

"I bet it's hard," Jed agreed with sympathy.

He was one of those people that had never had trouble either falling asleep, sleeping for long periods of time, or staying asleep throughout the night. And he counted himself extremely lucky. Sleep was one thing that was non-negotiable as a human being. Sleeping, eating, drinking water, and human connection were his version of the basic needs. You could live in a house, under a tree, in a tent, deep in the woods in a house made of sticks, or in whatever sort of shelter that you could find; you could make it work. Though the quality of that shelter would have an impact on your quality of life, Jed thought his four basic needs were the true non-negotiables. He was working from the perspective of someone that worked with the homeless. His clients who lived on the street often complained more that everyone ignored them and walked by than the fact that they didn't have a dedicated home.

Sure, being homeless could be extremely dangerous and extremely difficult, but they could get by sleeping in abandoned buildings and parks on benches, as long as they were out of the rain and spared the elements. But that they were invisible to everyone who walked by, that's what Jed noticed seemed to sting them the most. It didn't help that they were also three- to four-times more likely to die prematurely. He wished more of the general population understood just how lonely they were—and how at risk.

"Maybe two nights away from home will help you relax enough to sleep. Let's hope it does. Speaking of 'away from home', are you already at the Airbnb?"

"Yeah. I got here about two minutes ago. I know it's early but... I mean, I couldn't sleep. I thought I might as well just get up and get ready and make my way here."

Jed nodded. "Well, I'm on my way. So, I'll see you there shortly. I'm about three minutes out."

Christie nodded. "Okay," she said, "I'll see you then. We can go looking for our rooms so I can figure out how far I'll have to sneak in the night when everyone's sleeping."

They both laughed before ending the call.

As Jed continued his drive, he thought more and more about Christie's situation. There weren't very many things that one could try to do to fix a situation where their sleep was being affected. You could, like she had already done, try meditations, try delving into the world of broadband noise, try all the teas and herbal brews that people recommend you drink before bed, cut out the blue light...

Otherwise, there weren't many options. You just had to sort of lay awake all night and hope to fall asleep. That was only considering the physical things, though, Jed realized as he merged into a new lane and sped up to climb to the correct speed limit. Subconscious fears were also a huge contributor to poor sleeping habits. Remembering that Christie had mentioned her parents had passed away in fire, Jed wondered if that could have something to do with her insomnia.

Fear was a very subtle thing, at times. In some moments, it could be a literal monster standing before you and preventing you from doing anything short of stepping out of bed. It could fill you up from the insides as completely as a bucket was filled with iced water. It could paralyze your limbs and leave you in a permanent state of indecisive terror. It could take everything away from you, even your ability to make decisions.

Sometimes, however, fear acted in a completely different way. Sometimes, it was the most subtly poisonous presence in your life, its existence so sly you never even realized it was there, spreading its destructive venom into every part of your being. Sometimes, people suffered terribly, and for long periods of time, simply because they were unable to realize that it was fear which was plaguing them. That was how insidiously deceptive that little emotion could be, wreaking havoc inside you whilst making you think that everything was alright.

As he turned into the driveway of the Airbnb he would spend the next three days at, Jed looked around while he searched for a place to park. The building was pretty big. It was a standalone home, which was rare in New York City. This Airbnb was on the outskirts of the city where real estate was more affordable, and he had noticed an abundance of individual homes as he had driven up the street toward his destination. The architecture was reminiscent of oriental influences, and the roof was a dark maroon color, while the exterior was soft white with trim the same color as the roof around all the windows and doors. The lot it was on was also just as well manicured as the building itself. There were bushes along the full length of the house and flowers planted in between. He got out of the Jeep and went to the back seat to take out his bags before walking to the door.

Here goes nothing, he thought.

After knocking at the door, he stood waiting. For a moment, Jed wondered whether anyone would have heard him since the house was so massive. And shouldn't he just walk right in? It was an Airbnb, not a friend's house. Then the door opened. It was Christie.

"Hi, Jed," she greeted him with a smile.

Jed's heart was pounding. He didn't know why. His palms were beginning to sweat even though he had just stepped out of an air-conditioned car.

"Detective, it's good to see you." He mirrored her smile as he stepped inside and closed the door behind him.

"It's good that you're early."

"Oh?" Jed replied, looking around.

"It's good that you got here before everyone else. I was hoping we could settle in together before the onslaught."

Christie grinned and Jed returned that grin, wondering for the first time if things wouldn't turn out as bad as he had thought.

There was a short hallway that served as an entryway, with a console table and large round mirror to the left, before the house opened into an expansive living room that led into the kitchen and a dining area off to the right.

Wow! This place is bigger than it seems from the outside.

Christie led him into the living room, which was beautifully decorated with two identical white boucle sofas and an accompanying accent soft pink leather couch.

"This place must have been a fortune to decorate," he mused.

Christie nodded, her ponytail swishing around the back of her head. Jed fought back another smile and tried to keep his eyes on her face, where they belonged. It took considerable effort.

"Yup. It's beautiful. Chief Lucas must be thrilled with your performance, Jed," Christie replied with a laugh.

Jed shook his head with a half-smile. "Says the lead detective who solved the case."

"Says the investigative therapist who cracked the case," Christie fired back.

Jed raised his hands in mock surrender, chuckling.

"Alright, alright. We both did a good job, and we both solved the case," he relented.

He looked around at the rest of the room. There was art on the walls, plants in the corners, and the sunlight streamed in through the windows.

"Did anyone else arrive yet?" he asked, looking down at Christie, who had just pulled the hair tie out of her hair to let brown curls fall down around her shoulders.

"Hello? I hear talking!" Aaron, the deputy chief, walked around the corner and waved to them. "Jed and Christie. Of course. Always early!"

They all laughed, and Aaron came forward to shake their hands. He was a short man, around 5 feet 4 inches tall, and older than them both, at around 50. His brown hair was streaked white all throughout. He was much shorter than Jed and was built with all the clear signs of well-earned, rugged muscle. It was clear that this man had taken pride in his fitness in his youth and continued to do so. He was wearing a simple silver wedding band. Jed noticed it as Aaron stretched a hand out toward the long hallway to the right of the door.

"Let's find your room so you can get settled before everyone else arrives."

Jed and Christie nodded, turning to follow Aaron down the hallway that led past the kitchen to the other side of the building. They checked each door, all the way to the end of the hallway, and found an assortment of letters, from H through to K. At the dead end at the end of the hallway, Christie stopped abruptly and turned around to find Jed leaning against the opposite wall. Aaron held a slightly puzzled look to his face.

"Well, I guess that means it's on the other side of the building, so let's check there," Aaron resigned, turning to head back up the hallway. Christie followed suit, and Jed kept up the rear.

They all walked back toward the front door and down another hallway just off the entryway to the left, the sound of their footsteps muffled by the carpet. This hallway was decorated similarly to the rest of the spaces they had seen so far. Artwork hung in light oak frames, plants were placed on alternate sides of the passage at varying intervals, and sunlight lit up the corridor.

Christie stopped dead in front of a door that said 'A&B'. She was uncomfortable. Even though he knew she had every right to be, the realization hit Jed in the gut like a punch from a boxing champion. They had been assigned the same room. But *why* had they been assigned the same room? That didn't make any sense. Was it a setup?

No, of course it's not a setup, his inner self was quick to reply. The chief wouldn't do that. In fact, the man had no idea how Jed felt about Christie. If he did, Jed would definitely get a stern talking-to about professional boundaries and why they shouldn't be crossed—and about fraternizing with colleagues. Jed already constantly had these concerns at the forefront of his thoughts whenever he interacted with Christie.

That meant it had to be a mistake. There was no way this was on purpose, especially not since the Airbnb was so large inside and had more than enough room for all of them to have a comfortable stay.

"Check to see if it's just one room, Jed. If it is, then we'll have to move Christie into a room further down the hall," said Aaron.

Jed opened the door, pushing it wide. It led into a secondary hallway that turned into another passage, much shorter than the one they were in. To the left of the passage was another, smaller entry space with a table and a mirror, and ahead of them were two more doors, next to each other.

"I think we've found our answer," he said.

Christie and Aaron followed him past the console table and toward the two secondary doors.

"It's a dual suite?" Christie asked, confusion clear in her features.

"That's what it's looking like," Aaron answered. "They'll probably have a connecting door that you both can lock from either side, so you should be good to go to use these rooms."

The sound of his phone caught his attention, and he thrust his arm into his pocket to retrieve it.

"Sorry, guys. I'll have to take this, but you can get settled in."

Aaron rushed back down the hallway to answer his call.

When they were alone, Jed looked down at Christie for a long moment before turning wordlessly back to the doors. He reached for the door on the left with an 'A' on it. It opened easily, and they both peered into the room. It was a large space, separated into a sitting area with a small lavender loveseat, a workspace fitted with a desk and chair, with a queen-sized bed at the far end of the room. Jed gave a low whistle.

"This is huge."

Turning, he moved over to the other door marked with 'B' and pushed it open.

He came face-to-face with a massive king-sized bed that had a four-post frame.

"There's no way…" he began.

Christie burst out laughing behind him. "Looks like the people who decorated this room know your style."

Jed turned to look at her in the doorframe as she laughed. "Making jabs at me, Detective? Alright, I'll allow it." He turned back to look around the room. "But this room is enormous, too."

"Yup," Christie agreed. "They look about the same size."

There was a sitting space to the right of the door, comprising a small three-seater leather sofa in a rich shade of dark brown. Next to that area was a door Jed figured led to the ensuite bathroom. On the left wall of the room was a closet and another door that made Jed frown. If he were to guess, he would wager that it led to Christie's room.

"Hm. Here's the connecting door to your room." He set his bag on the sofa and walked toward the door next to his bed.

Jed twisted the knob with Christie peeking around him from behind, and sure enough, it led into the bedroom next to his. Pulling back, he turned to look at Christie, amusement tugging at his lips. "What are the chances the chief did this on purpose?"

Christie laughed and shook her head. "Slim to nil. Lucas is like a father to me. He'd probably pass out if he knew we made some of the jokes we do."

That tickled a laugh out of Jed as well, and Christie grinned, pleased with herself.

"I'd say that's a fair wager." He was looking down at her. "What are the chances he'll pass out if we call him and let him know?"

"I'd say 50/50."

"Well, it's up to you and me, Detective. What's the decision?"

Christie shrugged. "I don't think it'll be a problem to stay in these rooms. Would you rather move?"

"I think I'll be just fine either way. I'm more concerned about you being comfortable."

"We are both adults; I think we can handle it." Was it his imagination, or were Christie's cheeks turning slightly pink?

Jed grinned down at her, crossing his arms across his chest. "Sounds like you're planning to leave the connecting door open. Since you can 'handle it'," Jed teased.

Christie froze, and the reddish tint on her cheeks deepened.

"Anything you want to tell me, Detective?" Jed probed teasingly again.

Christie recovered her wits. It took her about two seconds. "Oh, baloney," she replied, rolling her eyes.

That made Jed laugh even harder. "I'm just kidding. You can leave it open if you like or bolt it from your end."

"You're not going to bolt your side?" Christie asked as they headed out of the room and back to the living room.

Behind her, Jed shrugged. "No. I don't mind having you in my space. As long as you're comfortable, I'll be fine."

They were both silent as the current room situation played inside their minds. They made their way back down the hallway to the living room, then sat down in unison. Christie on the white sofa with Jed across from her on the pink leather one. Pieces of Aaron's words could be heard from down the hall, where he was still on his call. Christie suddenly smiled.

"Pink suits you," she said.

Jed raised an arm and held it next to the sofa. "Does it really?"

Christie nodded. Jed hummed. "Perhaps I should look into buying some pink clothing."

A beaming grin spread across Christie's face. "You think so highly of my recommendations?"

Christie thought she saw Jed's gaze darken a moment before he responded, "I do."

CHAPTER 6

THERE WAS A KNOCK on the door right then, and the sound of talking erupted outside. Christie looked at the door, then back over to Jed.

"We're not alone anymore. Brace yourself. They can be rowdy."

"Noted."

Jed got up and walked to the door. Taking one last deep breath, he opened the door, breaking the comfortable rhythm he and Christie had established over the past twenty minutes. Five men, all with bags, stood there. Three of them arguing amongst themselves.

"I told you to be ready by seven, Jason. You always do this."

"Oh, come on," Jason said, glaring at the man next to him. "We got here, didn't we?"

Jed watched the interaction play out before the men realized the door was open and turned to look.

"Jed!" they erupted.

"Boys," Jed nodded as he grinned back at them. "Come on in."

They managed to start bickering about being late again as they clunked around and knocked into the console table. They all greeted Christie, who waved from the sofa, and then Jed showed them down the hallway on the right, where their rooms were located.

After they disappeared into the passage and greeted Aaron with rowdy excitement, the noise of their talking faded. Jed sat down opposite Christie again and sighed.

"What's the matter?" Christie asked.

Jed turned to her. "I'm going to miss being alone with you. Now I have to share your attention with six other men." He grinned. "I'll just have to compete and outdo them all."

Christie laughed as the five officers entered the living room and made their way over to the sofas. Exactly as Jed had expected, Jason headed straight for Christie and sat down next to her, a smile on his face. Jed had sat across from Christie, deciding it was the neutral thing to do.

"Man, I'm hungry," one of the men, wearing black cargo pants and a black hoodie that he had pulled over his head chimed.

"Carter, you're always hungry!" Jason crowed.

"Says the guy wearing the neon green shirt that says 'Where's the food at?' on the back," Carter fired back.

"Hey! You just don't know how to appreciate real art," Jason retorted as he lifted his chin.

"And I suppose you know what art is?" That was from a tall, blond man with blue eyes named Derek. He was wearing light blue denim jeans, a white button down with long sleeves, and a wedding band.

"Jason wouldn't know what art was if it hit him in the face," Carter responded, laughing.

"Exactly. I don't know when he suddenly became an art expert," Derek shrugged.

Jason rolled his eyes. "Shut up."

"Okay, but like your shirt is the least artistic thing I've seen all year," added another, shorter blond man who wore a pink sweatshirt. His features were the most youthful of the group, and the white band t-shirt peeking out from under the hem of his sweatshirt was tucked into gray cargo pants. Jed recognized him from their stakeout as Joseph.

Everyone burst out laughing at that, and Derek shook his head.

"Poor thing," Derek laughed. "He's confused."

"You guys are so embarrassing," Graham announced, rolling his eyes.

Jed looked over at the short, gruff man that had finally added his two cents. He noticed that Graham had the build of a wrestler, and his arm was covered by a tattoo sleeve. Graham's black, long-sleeved button-down was partly rolled up below his elbows and tucked into black dress pants, semi-hiding the tattoo. Derek rolled his eyes at the man's comment.

"Here comes Mr. Killjoy himself—give it up for Graham, everybody," Derek proclaimed as he stretched out his hand in Graham's direction.

The other three men all clapped, and Jed snorted at their antics. With his arms crossed, he shook his head. Watching the dynamics of a group of people was one of his favorite pastimes, and just by how they dressed and handled themselves, Jed had a decent understanding of their personalities.

"The chef will be here soon to start preparing lunch, and we're supposed to start activities afterward," Aaron called out as he walked back into the room.

Carter, who had made the initial comment about being hungry, nodded gratefully. Aaron joined the group, sitting down on the other side of Christie as he read something on his phone.

"At least somebody cares about me!" Carter cried.

Everyone chuckled.

Silence prevailed after that. For a few moments, there was a tense, pregnant silence, waiting to be broken any second by seven guests gathered in the room. Finally, Jason was the one who spoke.

"What's it like being a therapist?" Jason directed at Jed after. "Do you just like... get paid to psychoanalyze people?"

Jed switched his gaze from the checkered pattern in the carpet to Jason. He noticed the unsure smile on the man's face.

"Yes."

"Uh-oh," Carter murmured with mock urgency. "We're all in trouble!"

The group laughed.

"Yeah, you are," Christie added.

Jed narrowed his eyes at her from across the room and laughed a little. "Whatever do you mean, Detective?"

"Oh, so he psychoanalyzes you, too?" Carter cut in.

"Yup. I'm used to it by now," Christie answered, grinning.

"Holy shit! We really are in trouble," Derek groaned, genuine horror spreading across his features.

Jed chuckled, but on the inside, his radar was going off. Could he trust these guys? Since he'd lost Ethan and Hugh had betrayed their friendship by turning out to be a murderer, Jed had become a lot more suspicious of the people around him—especially the men. Jed had always recognized that he had a harder time connecting with men than with women.

"Well, I'm sure I'll be fine," Jason said with confidence, puffing out his chest. "I have nothing to hide."

Jed merely raised a brow. "People who make declarations like that always have things to hide. They think the declaration throws people off their scent because people tend to believe what they hear without thinking too much about it." Jed looked down languidly at his watch, as if he was bored.

"Oooooh. Shots fired!" Derek crowed, looking over at Jason. "Come on, Jason—get him!"

Jason scrunched his brows together into a slight frown. Jed met his gaze and just shrugged.

"Oh, so you think you're going to analyze me and figure out my secrets, huh? Well, you're wrong!" he challenged.

Jed laughed softly. "Yeah, okay. Whatever you say."

Jason's mouth fell open, and Joseph, Derek, and Carter burst out laughing. Christie reached across and patted Jason's hand in sympathy.

"It's okay. There's no escape," she said.

Jason looked over at her and then smiled. "You're lucky she interjected on your behalf," he told Jed.

"Or what?" Jed asked, his brow raised again.

"Oh!!!" Derek cried out as he jumped to his feet. "He's got you, Jason. Don't let him talk to you like that!"

Jed laughed. "You guys are an interesting bunch, that's for sure."

The group chuckled and settled into a comfortable silence again. Then there was a knock at the door, and Derek went to answer it.

"The chef has arrived! Everybody, this is Chef Joel!" Derek announced as he entered the room a few moments later with a man at his heels. Cheers went up from the group.

The chef was a tall, dark man whose long hair hung braided behind his neck. He was wearing a pair of dark jeans and a black t-shirt that rested snugly on his lean frame. As he walked into the room, his lips parted into a merry grin, and his eyes twinkled mischievously. The cheers multiplied when the men saw him.

"I hope you're all ready for lunch! We've got baked chicken, pork, and burgers on the menu!" Joel called to the group as he made his way to the kitchen.

He donned an apron, and soon, the smell of bacon, cheese, pork, and chicken filled the living room. The aromas of the blends of spices that began to fill the house made Jed feel at ease and happy. The smells were familiar to him, somehow.

After gorging on a mouth-watering lunch buffet consisting of baked chicken, pork, and burgers, the group reclined in their chairs for a couple of minutes, letting the wonderful food settle in their stomachs. Then, the group started their team-building activities. This was a bit tough because most of them felt stuffed from the meal, which made them more inclined to take a nap. But eventually, they got into a good rhythm with the activities. The group spent the rest of the afternoon and into the evening going through a series of introductory endeavors that Aaron conducted. When Jed had initially reviewed the agenda for the weekend, he'd noticed that the first day's projects were essentially all the same.

They would introduce themselves in a variety of ways. The agenda had four prompts. *If you were a house, what kind of house would you be? What's the biggest lesson you learned about life in college? What's your favorite part of your job? Share something about yourself that you think would surprise the group.*

At the end of the evening, as they went their separate ways after a hearty dinner that consisted of roasted lamb chops and grilled salmon served alongside baked potatoes and a garlic butter dip, Jed remained seated on the couch. Their break in activities gave them some free time after to explore the property or relax after the first day of the retreat. After dinner, they gathered back in the sitting room where they had started off the day and continued some conversations. Slowly, one by one, they excused themselves to go back to their rooms or walk outside until it was only Jason, Christie, and Jed left.

"Goodnight, Detective," Jason said as he offered his hand to help Christie to her feet.

Jed swallowed. She hardly needed help to stand from the sofa, but Jed had noticed that Jason sought out physical contact with those around him. During their sessions, he'd occasionally bumped fists with the guys or thrown his arm loosely around one of their necks. It was one of the ways he sought out connection. And watching him run his thumb across the back of Christie's hand, Jed stood to his feet and stuffed his own hands into his pockets as he walked out of the room. He couldn't exactly blame Jason either. Who wouldn't want a connection with a beautiful, career-driven, intelligent woman like Christie?

After Jed had taken a long cold shower and changed into comfy clothes, he sauntered over to the connecting door and knocked, hoping she was in and wasn't still talking to Jason where he'd left them earlier.

After a few moments, the door opened.

"Good evening, Detective."

"Hi, Jed. You sound so serious. Am I in trouble?" Christie's brows were pulled together, and she looked adorably confused. Jed shook his head 'no'.

"You wanted me to let you in, right?"

Christie's mouth opened and closed. Was he about to open up to her right now?

"I do." She finally answered.

"Come over. Let's talk. After all, that is why we are at this retreat—to get to know one another better."

Christie's mouth was about to fall open again, but she managed to control herself just in time. Her heart was pounding, and though she had showered mere minutes before, her palms were beginning to feel clammy.

"Okay."

She stepped into his room, the smell of his cologne filling her. It smelled like the most luxurious scent she could imagine.

Something about Jed had changed since she'd seen him earlier in the evening. It was subtle. It wasn't his mood; he still sounded just as pleasant and approachable. It was his tone. He was asking less questions and was now more dominant, in the sexy, *Do what I say* way.

Behind Jed, Christie slapped a hand across her mouth at the reckless thought. *No!* She screamed at herself internally. *None of those thoughts! Now's not the time! Not when you're alone in a room with him for work!*

"Please accept my apology in advance," he said as they settled onto the couch in his sitting area, "just in case you end up realizing that I'm too messed up for you to handle and you want to run for the hills to find a new partner."

Christie stared at him for a moment and eventually started giggling to herself.

"What's so funny, Detective?" he asked, wearing a grin himself.

"You are. I'm not going to run. I'm sure I'll be just fine sticking around."

"Of course you will be—until you aren't."

Christie arched her eyebrows. "Is that supposed to mean something?"

"Not at all," Jed answered quickly, mentally chiding himself for having spoken too much. "Just joking with you."

But Christie wouldn't let him get away, not that easily. "Wait a minute." She leaned forward, pinning him with those penetrating, intense eyes of hers. "Were you just flirting with me, Jed Gray?"

A discomfiting heat spreading into Jed's palms, and he swallowed, hoping his face didn't show what he was feeling. "You know, this is beginning to sound more and more like an interrogation session." He barked out a short laugh. "Now, can we begin this sharing session, please? I'm already nervous enough as it is."

A coy smile still spread across her lips, Christie leaned back. "Of course," she told him softly. "And you don't have to be nervous at all. I very much look forward to hearing whatever it is you're going to tell me about yourself."

Jed let the sentiment settle into his skin and calm him down a little.

He'd called his mom for moral support before he'd knocked on Christie's door, deciding that now was a good time to talk with her about how he had really been doing. His mother had been as understanding and supportive as she always was.

"You don't need to put any pressure on the evening. She asked you to open up a bit, and you're giving her the opportunity to get to know you better. That's a huge step. I know you prefer to be a bit closed off, so to see you concerned enough about how she feels to let her in is so sweet. Just decide what's off limits before you start the conversation and let everything else flow."

Wise words indeed. His mother was full of them. She always seemed to have the right advice, the right thing to say, the right word to describe a complicated feeling. It was where he'd inherited his communication skills before going on to hone them in undergrad and postgrad. It was what Ethan had always commented on. *"How do you always know what to say?"*

Jed leaned back into the brown leather and closed his eyes for a moment, letting his mind settle.

"Last chance to back out."

"Jed!"

He laughed. "As you wish, Detective. Ready?"

Christie followed his lead, arranging herself so she was facing him, leaned into the soft supportive back of the couch across from him.

"Ready," she affirmed.

Jed nodded before sighing a little. "I took what you said seriously. About you not knowing me—and about the imbalance in our relationship. I want to fix that, so, naturally, I invited you over to my room on a Saturday night.

"It's only natural," she chimed.

Jed didn't respond for a moment, deep in thought as he looked at her.

"Well, Detective," he said, his voice a low rasp that made her shiver even though she wasn't cold. "The interrogation begins. You can ask me anything. My aim is to give you honest answers and start some conversations that we can continue throughout our friendship."

"Nothing's off the table?"

Jed's eyes narrowed just a fraction. "I want to say yes, but the point of tonight is to stop holding back," he answered, eyes still level with hers. "Ask as you please."

Christie nodded.

"How's your heart, Jed?"

His hands paused midway through the air as he brought his glass of sparkling water to his lips. He had poured them both a glass before knocking, anticipating that he would need a drink to sustain him through the conversation ahead or have it ready as a distraction.

He wanted to do what he usually did when clients asked him how he was—give a casual response, divert the question back to them, and focus on getting them through their hardships. But he wasn't being a therapist right now. He was being an honest friend. He wanted to be an honest lover, but he would take what he could get.

"My heart is in multiple states at once," he began, still holding the glass. "It is whole, relaxed, and happy," he paused, raising his eyes to meet hers, "because I'm with you."

Her own heart trilled.

"At the same time, one half of it is shattered into a million fragments, and the other half is submerged below a wild ocean of grief."

Finally, he took a sip. Christie nodded, thinking through the response.

"Can you talk more about the whole, relaxed, and happy part?" she asked.

She was overcome with empathy for Jed and wanted nothing more than to pull him into her arms and hush him to sleep. He must be feeling terribly disoriented and confused with all those emotions in his heart at once. On the outside, it never showed. He went on working and analyzing and helping everyone else like all was well. Her eyes burned just a little.

Jed nodded. "When I'm with you, I always feel one of three things. Either whole, happy, or relaxed. Sometimes I feel two of those things at once, or all three."

"Do you know why that is?"

"I haven't fully figured it out yet. But the way I explain it to myself, is that for as much as I'm an introvert, when I'm around you, I don't feel like I'm using up my energy. I feel like I'm charging my batteries."

"Awww."

Jed smiled, a little sheepishly, at Christie's pouting face and teary eyes.

"I'm happy I can be that for you. I hope to always make you feel safe in that way so you can allow yourself to lower your guard and recharge." She took a deep breath. "Now, the other emotions. Why is half your heart shattered, and how can I pick up the pieces?"

Jed chuckled to himself at her optimism. "It's cute that you're so optimistic about this. My heart broke when I found out Ethan was one of the victims. It's not a pain I can describe very clearly, what with being a therapist well-acquainted with the human range of emotions."

"Try using non-emotions to describe it, like soggy bread or broken glass."

Jed toyed with the idea for a moment, his arms now folded across his chest, his eyes on the glass resting on the coffee table between them.

"That's a good idea, Detective. It feels like…" he paused, a shudder trying to run through his body. "It feels like you're a kid, young and innocent and bursting with life, a kid who goes to the beach and dips his hands into the warm, soft sand."

Jed closed his eyes, felt his uneven breathing, and continued in an equally uneven voice. "You play and play and play, letting that warm, silky sand cover your arms, legs and, entire body. You play for hours, watching the sun slowly slide toward the horizon. And just when dusk is about to fall, you find out."

Jed's eyes opened. They were rimmed with red.

"You find out that the sand you were playing with wasn't really sand at all, but glass—tiny, wickedly sharp shards of broken glass covering the beach, pretending to be sand. And you find your body is now covered with a million small cuts, each cut so small that you can't see it, yet still large enough to hurt and bleed." He paused, swallowed, and finished. "Imagine being covered with bruises, to the point where it seems like you're made entirely out of them. You can't tell anyone where it hurts because it hurts all over. And you can't tell anyone where to apply the bandage because the wound is everywhere. *Everywhere.*"

There was a long silence, where Christie simply sat and stared at him, her eyes watery. Finally, she managed to speak in a whispery voice, "That's a wonderful description. I can almost perfectly imagine how painful that is. Are the miniscule cuts all the memories?"

"Yeah."

That was all he said, and Christie was on high alert.

"Do you want to talk about something else?"

Jed shook his head. "No. I'm just trying not to get choked up."

"Oh."

Feet now on the soft rug, she stood up and padded over to Jed's side where she stood in front of him and stretched out her arms. Christie expected him to stand to accept the hug and was completely caught off guard when he slipped his hands around her waist and pulled her down next to him in a tight embrace.

His hold tightened even more when she wrapped her arms around his neck. She melted into his arms, her muscles untensing, her cheek coming to rest on his shoulder. Jed's heart hummed at the way she settled into his arms with ease.

"I'm so sorry you are in pain. I wish I could just put all the tiny pieces of your heart back together," Christie cooed into his ear.

Jed released Christie reluctantly, knowing that holding her the way he was, he would either fall asleep, or something else inside him would come awake at the wrong time. He sat back in the couch again the way he had before, only now, Christie was sitting on the couch with him, close enough for her to see the smoldering thoughts flickering in his eyes.

"It will heal on its own, with time. It's just part of the grieving process. Besides, I wouldn't want you getting your pretty little hands cut, Detective."

"Do you have a set grieving strategy or process?"

Jed nodded. "Fortunately, I do. I'd expected to already be out of this phase of grief. It's been weeks. This one was a particularly hard hit. He was so young, so promising, so kindhearted. And he's just …gone. No two losses are the same. They take as long as they take to work through."

Jed's eyes glazed over. "I remember the first time he walked into my office. He was skittish, looking around the room multiple times, trying to commit every detail to memory. He sat on the edge of the chair, and he was so hunched up the whole time that I began to worry his posture would hurt his back. But he never moved much, except for his leg bouncing all the time because he was so anxious. Then we got to talking. He shared his story. I learned his fears. We worked to diffuse his triggers, to see light in the situations that didn't make sense and push past the incorrect alliances he had. I thought we made great progress. The case was solved, and Ethan continued therapy to support his sobriety."

Christie barely breathed. She stayed as still as she could, hoping her lack of movement would create a less stressful environment. She knew when she was super stressed out that people walking around or talking made her freak out even more. Then Jed's eyes seemed to focus on her again instead of being spaced out and far away in the past. She finally let out her breath.

"When you called me at five in the morning, crying, I immediately got scared that something had happened to you. You said there was another murder. I jumped out of bed, got dressed, and ran all the way to the station so I could be there with you through that moment. I remember I rushed into the station, took the elevator when I should have taken the stairs, and finally made it to your office. Then I found out it was Ethan, and in that moment, I felt like I was being crushed from every direction. Breathing became very difficult. I didn't believe it. When we got the autopsy report, confirming that it was Fentanyl, it felt like the world was crumbling apart all around me."

Tears were filling Christie's eyes, and she tried as discreetly as possible to swipe them away. Jed's eyes had gone unfocused again. She thought she really had been discreet until Jed leaned forward and brushed away the tears that remained with his thumb, looking so deeply into her eyes that for a moment she wanted to pull away.

"That day is definitely on my list of my hardest days ever lived through." He leaned back to settle into his position, his eyes now softer, his gaze less intense, and once more focused on her.

"I'm not sure what to say."

Jed smiled, but it didn't reach his eyes. "Your being here is enough."

She nodded. "And why is the other half of your heart in a sea of grief? Is it the same situation about Ethan?"

Jed nodded. "It comes in waves. One moment everything is calm and serene, you can't imagine ever feeling any other way. Then the storm comes in, suddenly and out of nowhere—like it always does—and now you're covered in darkness and feeling the icy waves raging violently around you, threatening to drown you within their lightless, freezing depths." He shrugged. "That's the way it is with grief."

For a moment, all she could do was nod, and Jed smiled.

"Too heavy?"

"I can handle it."

His eyes darkened, but he swallowed his response. Christie noticed.

"Something tells me you're still holding things back from me."

"And what might that 'something' be, Detective?"

"That something is my intuition."

"Well, maybe you just aren't asking the right questions, Detective. You know how it is in suspect interviews." His eyes were fixed on her, and both amusement and an unknown intensity could be found in his gaze.

"Why do you do that?" her brows pulled together in the dim light.

He didn't speak for a moment, only looked at her. "You are so beautiful."

Christie's cheeks burned, and she wanted to scream into the pillow next to her, but she smiled instead.

"Thank you."

"Now, why do I do what?"

"The way you use that word. 'Detective'. It always feels so… intimate. And I can't shake the feeling, even when you tell me it's just for fun. Why?"

Jed never moved his eyes away from hers. Even though the room was already dim, she could see his pupils locked onto her with a burning focus, like coals glowing faintly at the bottom of a well. "I'm glad you noticed that it's intimate. That is my intention."

Christie wasn't sure what she had been expecting him to say, but it wasn't that. She was completely unprepared for his answer. She was out of words. Her brain was suddenly as empty as a brand-new fishbowl.

"Everything about the way I interact with you is intentional, Detective. The way I say your name, the way I look at you, the way I talk to you… none of it is by chance."

"I hope I don't sound ridiculous for asking this…"

His lips split into a grin that made the words die in her throat for a minute. His smile was so handsome, and whenever Jed graced her with that sort of spontaneous smile, it always stunned her into silence. It was the first time he'd really smiled since they'd started talking about the heavy stuff.

"I'm sure you won't sound ridiculous," he replied as she tried to remember her question.

"Are you saying that sometimes you're flirting with me when you say 'Detective'?" Christie batted her lashes at him playfully. "Last time I asked that question, you conveniently skirted around it. I hope you won't do the same this time."

Jed met her gaze and answered in a calm voice. "Yes, I am. *Detective.*"

Even though she was the one that had asked the question, she was once again unprepared to hear that response.

"You are so charming when you're flustered. I find it quite endearing. It makes you look… innocent."

Her eyes flashed to his. His expression was as serious as it had always been, except for the hint of amusement in his eyes. Jed looked down at his hands for a moment before returning his gaze to hers.

"You asked me to let you in, remember? If this gets too intense, or uncomfortable, tell me, and I'll stop immediately."

Usually, Christie would opt out, but tonight, her curiosity was winning out by a long shot.

"That sounds like something you'd say to someone before you tie them to your bedposts."

Jed snorted and ran a hand through his hair. "If you ask me what I actually say, I'd oblige."

His eyes seemed to convey skepticism, an air of 'I don't think you've got the guts to do it'. Naturally, she asked the question, if only to disprove his smug confidence that she would shy away was wrong.

"What do you say to someone before you tie them to your bedposts?"

"A risk-taker tonight, are we?" Jed mused, his eyes fixed on her features. "If this gets too intense, or uncomfortable, stop me. If you want me to stop… beg."

Christie's mouth turned into an 'O', and her cheeks burned. She hid her face behind her hands when Jed started laughing heartily. Her ears were pink, too. "Oh, *God*."

"No, but seriously," Jed said as his laughter faded. "If you want to return to the less intense version of me, don't hesitate to say so. Like I said at the beginning, I really don't want to make you uncomfortable. You already seem uncomfortable around me sometimes, and you refuse to tell me why that it is."

"It's nothing," she responded quickly.

"Oh, but it is. I just haven't figured it out yet or gotten you to confess."

"And you won't get me to confess."

Jed's head tilted comically to the side, "I thought you said there wasn't anything."

They both laughed.

"Do I make you uncomfortable, Detective?"

"No, you don't."

"Weirded out?"

"No."

"Annoyed?"

"No."

Jed's lips curled into a devilish smile that sent shivers down her spine.

"Do I make you happy?"

Christie hesitated for a second too long.

"I *do* make you happy. But you don't want to admit it?"

She was scrambling internally for an explanation.

"What else do I make you? Nervous? Excited?"

Christie sighed and smiled.

"The other kind of excited?"

Her eyes widened.

"Jed!"

He burst out laughing, and she covered her cheeks, embarrassed.

"What made you think saying my name right then was the best option, based on what I asked you, Detective?"

She fanned his hands away when he tried to pull her hands away from hiding her cheeks. She eventually gave into the laughter that was bubbling up from her chest.

After their laughter had subsided, Jed continued.

"Laughter aside, Detective, I appreciate the sentiment. I don't open up very easily, especially with women I think are as beautiful and as incredible as you are. I can be intense sometimes. So, I'm careful about how I engage with you."

"You don't seem intense right now, though."

That made Jed grin. "Thank you. That's because I'm still restraining myself. There's lots of invisible lines between us that can't be crossed—things I could say but shouldn't, and things you should admit but won't tell me until I pry them out of you."

He got to his feet, stretching his arms above his head for a few moments. Christie watched as he reached for her hand and pulled her to her feet and into a quick hug that left her reeling from his scent. She had been reveling in it all night and wondered which fragrance it was. He watched her think for a moment before she looked up at him and decided to ask.

"What fragrance are you wearing? Can I see it?"

"You can."

He took the other route, away from her and around the sofa, indicating she should follow his lead. As she approached his bed, she noticed the scent get stronger and wondered even more at its strength. He had likely sprayed it onto himself hours ago, yet both he and the room still smelled delicious. He stopped at the foot of the bed and pointed to a glass tray on the nightstand with a bottle of cologne resting on it. Christie picked up the bottle and uncapped it so she could smell its delicious scent.

"Ohhhhh. This is divine."

So are you, Jed thought to himself as he watched her put it down. She gasped.

"It's so… masculine. I adore it."

He watched her take a long whiff, look at the label again, before putting it back in its place. She turned to look at him and seemed surprised to see him still standing at the end of the bed.

"What?" she teased as she walked back to him. "Your bedroom is too small to hold us both at the same time?"

His only response was a glance over at the bed—the same bed she had asked about earlier. Her cheeks went bright pink again, and Jed grinned and shook his head.

"You are so cute when you blush like that. I don't believe it, but it's already almost ten. Ready for bed?"

She nodded.

"Alright, let's go."

They walked back to the connecting door. Christie turned to him. "I don't regret it."

"Hm?" he asked.

"I don't regret getting closer to your heart."

He felt that soothing warmth in his chest again, like her words were lighting a candle just beneath his heart.

"It wasn't too messy for you? Or too intense? Too inappropriate?" he queried, watching her expression for anything that would give away she hadn't liked something.

She shook her head. "No. I want to hear much, much more about the things that happen in your mind, and how your heart feels, and how it heals. And I want to talk more about other things about you, too."

"You do?"

"I do."

He looked at her for a long moment before nodding. "We can do that, over time."

"We can."

She walked over the threshold and turned back to look up at him. He was leaning against the doorway, hands in his pockets, eyes already on her.

"So..." she began.

"So?" he asked.

"There's two things I still have to say."

"What's on your mind?" Jed asked.

"You apologized in case I ran for the hills, right?"

"Yes, I did."

"Well, I didn't run for the hills. So, now what?"

Jed cocked his head to the side, a grin forming. "Now, I say thank you for being supportive and willing to listen tonight."

"You're welcome. Thank you for sharing with me. I know it wasn't easy."

Jed smiled again, and so did Christie. His energy already seemed lighter and more like his usual self.

"Just as long as you don't close up again."

"I would never give you something and take it back. Not even my heart." Jed winked over at her.

"Good. Because I want far more of your heart in any case."

Jed took a deep breath, letting the cool air sink into his brain and clear out all the heavy thoughts. *Good. Because I want far more of your heart.* He wanted to swoon.

"It's been a good evening, Detective. But before I give you a hug and send you off to bed, what was the other thing you said you had to say?"

"Whenever we do this again, when I get to see your heart a little more, I want you to tell me more about these lines you say are between us," Christie looked down at the space between them, then looked seriously back up at Jed, "because I don't see any."

His breath caught for a moment when she smiled up at him.

"And I wanna hear all the things you could say but shouldn't, in particular," she added.

"Only if you admit the things you should but won't," Jed countered.

She frowned, and Jed grinned. "Gotcha!"

Christie rolled her eyes as she laughed. "Let's make a deal?"

"I don't make deals with law enforcement, Detective."

"Oh, come on, Jed!"

He laughed. "Alright. You admit, I'll tell."

They shook hands, and Jed pulled Christie in for a long hug. "Goodnight, Detective."

Christie closed the door behind her as she walked back into her room. Jed waited to hear the 'click' as she locked the door from her side. The sound of the click never came.

Chapter 7

As she lay in bed, Christie found herself unable to stop thinking about her conversation with Jed. She could still smell his masculine scent.

They had begun their conversation at eight. Jed had seen her to her room at ten. And now, it was a few minutes past midnight. Yet sleep still continued to evade her like she was the plague. Her mind whirred and buzzed incessantly inside her head, fueled by an adrenaline that had turned her limbs jerky and energetic. She was as far away from sleeping as a person could be, and her lips were parted in a slight, dreamy smile.

Jed had opened up to her. Finally. That single thought was enough to make her content. Christie stared up at the darkened ceiling of her room and wondered if the next phase of their partnership and friendship had finally begun, the phase where their bond deepened even further, and they drew closer together, closer than mere acquaintances or professional colleagues.

Closer even that just friends?

Maybe.

Another fact which made her happy was that she also hadn't gotten the impression that he had felt coerced or pressured to open up. In fact, it felt like the opposite. He wanted to let her in that deeply. When she had noticed some unspoken thoughts in his eyes as looked at her and had mentioned it to him, his casual response had just been, *Maybe you're asking the wrong questions. You know how it is in suspect interviews, Detective.* So, there were things he was still not saying… well, there were things he was not volunteering. But if she asked the right questions, Jed didn't seem like he would hesitate to answer. He'd answered her question about flirting. It was a simple affirmation. She hadn't expected that, even though she'd some hunches.

What was Christie supposed to do with that information? In any other situation, that kind of confession would have made her feel a little bit put-off. She would have retreated into her shell right away and been a lot more cautious about how she engaged with him in the future. But this wasn't just any man saying that he was flirting with her. This was *Jed*. She had sensed it, noticed the intensity in his eyes at points in their partnership. She also knew that flirting with your work partner was not ideal for their working relationship. She also trusted his self-restraint. He had demonstrated that since the very moment they started working together.

Jed rarely touched her unless she had already reached for him, or unless he verbalized he was going to hug her. He never made her feel uncomfortable by staring at her lips or her body. He always walked on the outside of the curb, he always let her go through doors first, and he always opened those doors. Christie never felt like she was the subject of his inappropriate desires, even when he *was* flirting. It always felt clean—completely innocent and genuine.

Despite the lack of sexual intent and pressure in their inter-actions, she didn't think he was just flirting to mess with her mind, or as a joke. Christie couldn't be sure, though, because she hadn't asked that question. Still, she got the impression that his flirting was sincere. She also got the impression that he wanted to do more than flirt. Sometimes, his eyes betrayed the way he felt. She was sure, almost afraid, that her eyes also betrayed how she felt at times.

Then there was the matter of his grief and his heartbreak. She knew all too well the sting of death. The 'what -if' madness could consume a person. *What if I had done something differently? Should I have done something differently? What if I could have changed the outcome? Is this whole situation my fault?* She had asked herself all those questions as she tried to navigate her parents' passing. Every day, she had gone to work, done her job like normal, and then went home to cry herself to sleep. The question that she had asked herself throughout that time the most was, *What if I had been there? Could I have saved them? Maybe I could have gotten Mom out of the fire, and Dad could have gotten himself out? They needed me, and I wasn't there.* But on the heels of those thoughts, she knew that her father's death had been his own choice. He made the choice to go with the love of his life.

They had showed Christie what love really meant, especially when she was a child. She had never doubted whether her parents loved each other, supported each other, or supported her. In fact, they had reminded her every chance they got they loved her and were rooting for her always. And in a weird, sort of twisted way, she supposed that was why she had avoided relationships of her own for so long. She had only had one serious relationship, and it had ended right before her parents passed away. There had been no drama, or any cheating, or any toxic outbursts. They had just not been on the same page or path. He wanted to move to a state on the other side of the country to pursue a job opportunity, and she'd had no intentions of leaving home. They weren't ready to get married either, but deep down, Christie had known that he wasn't the one she wanted to spend the rest of her life with. There was nothing wrong with him, and her feelings had been no fault of his. He was very talented, extremely kind, and he treated her well.

She wasn't even sure how to explain it. He just… didn't make her soul quiver, not nearly the way Jed did. Christie grabbed a pillow and pulled it over her face. She hated that she felt that way—really, really hated it. For as much as Jed was always kind, gentle, chivalrous, and oh so masculine, she didn't like how she felt. She was uncomfortable not having full control of her feelings when he was near her. She had never experienced that before.

Christie figured he was just being playful. Maybe he had interest on the surface level but not much deeper than that. She wanted deeper than that. She wanted *him* deeper than that. At the same time, he had said that everything about the way he interacted with her was intentional, that none of it was accidental or lighthearted. She was torn between two realities.

On the one hand, after seeing what genuine love meant, from her parents' example, and seeing what real love had cost them, she did not want to end up romantically attached to someone who didn't want that level of commitment. For her, it was all or nothing. And she wanted all of it with Jed. Maybe she had just asked the wrong questions or asked the right question the wrong way. In their next deep conversation, where they both were going to have to expose pieces of their heart, maybe she could take the chance and ask him how he really felt about her.

For now, they were at a work retreat, and she would not let her focus be so far distracted that she did poorly on their team assignments. She was the only woman here, and she wanted to show the men that she was in charge. They had a couple of activities planned for the next day, and they would be tested on them at the end of the retreat, so she needed to put on her game face in the morning.

Christie didn't know when it happened, but she eventually drifted into a surprisingly restful sleep.

The next morning at 8:30, Jed knocked on the connecting door between their rooms.

"Come in," she called.

He had messaged her earlier that morning, letting her know that he would 'pick her up' so they could walk to the common area for breakfast. She watched the knob turn, and Jed stepped in. His hair was freshly washed, she noticed. The ends were still wet where he had brushed them back into his usual style. He had yet to look at her and was closing the door with one foot while fastening the buttons on his sleeve with his hand. Then, their eyes met.

"Good morning, Detective."

"Hi, Jed."

He walked over to where she was sitting on the end of her bed and stood before her as she buckled her watch around her wrist, he slipped his hands into his pockets. The previous night, she had struggled to fall asleep—both because she had been stuck in her mind, trying to figure out how to be a good support system for Jed as he navigated his grief, and because she was trying to stop the fantasies that were popping into her mind. They were in rooms that shared a connecting door. If she went over to his room, or he came over to hers, no one else in the building would know. The thought haunted her mind, sending chills racing down her spine every time she rolled over in bed. She hadn't locked her side of the door. And while she had been waiting to hear if Jed would lock his side, after they had closed the door between them last night, she had heard no sound of the locking mechanism. That meant that the door was still unlocked, and that he was sleeping just beyond it.

Now, as the sun was streaming in through the surrounding windows, Jed was watching her as she stood and reached for her necklace. He stepped forward to take it from her hands. She glanced up at him, and he smiled.

"May I help you with that?"

She nodded, turning to face the mirror next to her bed. Christie watched as he slipped the necklace over her head and down around her, then gently moved her hair out of the way so he could fasten the clasps at the back of her neck. When he was done, he looked at her in the mirror.

"All ready to go?"

Christie nodded. Jed's brows pulled together.

"Is everything alright, Detective? You're very quiet this morning."

Christie cleared her throat. "Oh, it's nothing. I just wake up feeling a little sore whenever I sleep in a bed that's not my own for the first time."

Jed's eyes softened, and he nodded. "I'm sorry to hear that. I hope it's not too bad."

She sighed and shrugged. His head did that familiar tilt to the side. "But what's the other part of the answer?"

Christie turned to head toward the door that would take them to the living room to join the others, and Jed wrapped an arm around her, spinning her back to face him and stepping around her so that he blocked the door.

"Penny for your thoughts, Christie?"

"So, you're using my name now?"

Jed's eyes narrowed just a fraction. "Yes, because I want you to know that I'm not being playful right now. Is everything alright with you?"

Christie nodded.

She watched the muscles in his jaw flex. "I sense that is not a truthful answer."

Christie folded her arms across her chest. "What gives you that impression?"

"You're not holding eye contact with me, and you've essentially gone mute."

She didn't respond.

"What happened between us in the space of a couple of hours that's made you go cold on me?"

"Nothing's happened."

Jed stepped toward her, and she swallowed. His eyes narrowed even more, spotting the movement immediately.

"This is the same nervous freeze you did at the station after we talked about Ethan, and I asked you whether I was doing something that made you uncomfortable."

Christie looked away from his eyes. That made him step forward again until they were brushing against each other. Jed put a thumb under her chin and tilted her face up to his.

"Detective, you know you can tell me what's going on, right?"

She nodded.

"Use your words."

She swallowed. "I know."

Jed searched her eyes for a moment. "Then why do you hesitate when you know what you want? I can see it in your eyes. We need to work on your avoidance of your emotions."

Christie huffed and rolled her eyes. "Does the NYPD pay you extra to psychoanalyze me?"

Jed didn't miss a beat. "For you, I would do it for free."

Before she could respond, the sound of yelling interrupted their exchange. She and Jed looked at each other for a split second before both rushed for the door and out into the hallway. They saw Derek sprinting down the corridor, his eyes wide-open and his arms flailing. When he saw them, he came to a stumbling, gasping halt, as if he had just run a marathon. Christie noticed that his skin had turned a terrible shade of white.

"Derek, what's going on?" Jed demanded, grabbing the man by his shaking shoulders. "Did something happen? Is everybody okay?"

Derek shook his head but did not speak. His eyes were scanning the walls and the empty corridor, as if there were invisible threats lurking everywhere that only he could see.

"Derek!" Jed shook him again, hard. It seemed to work. Derek stopped moving and looked up at Jed with confused eyes, as if he were just seeing him. Then he spoke.

"Someone just… I don't even… I…" Derek's voice was a thin rasp.

Jed watched Derek looking at him with grim, haunted eyes. His hands were slightly sweaty. Jed was starting to get a bad feeling.

"The chef, Joel," Derek began darkly, "he just fell down. There's a dart in his neck. I don't know…" He shook his head again, lips curling with the fresh horror of the memory. "We're checking for a pulse, but we don't think there is one. We're not sure what happened, but we think it came from outside." He looked up at them both then, eyes even wider than before, staring at their faces in a silent plea, almost an apology, as if he was responsible for the bad news he was delivering. "Aaron's calling the ambulance, but I don't think Joel will make it."

The world seemed to fall right out from underneath Jed's feet. He knew they all worked with scenes like this every day, but it could never prepare you for being part of the scene.

"What?" he blurted. "What do you mean, a dart?"

Derek seemed in no state to explain further, and Jed was in no mood to wait. He launched himself forward, running down the rest of the hallway and into the kitchen. Aaron was kneeling on the ground in the kitchen next to something that Jed could not see. He rushed around the island to find that the chef was lying on the ground, face down. Aaron was holding his phone to his ear, talking frantically to someone on the other end.

"Yes, he just fell down. No, we don't know what happened." Aaron's tone was a tightly strung wire dripping with grimness. His mouth was contorted into a pained grimace, like he was having trouble seeing what lay before him.

Jed turned to look at Christie, who was now at his side. They both stared at each other, fear, confusion, and sadness swirling in their eyes.

"There is a dart in his neck. No, we don't know where the dart came from," Aaron shared on the phone.

Christie looked back down at the chef's body. He was wearing his chef's uniform, apron, and hat, just as he had been at lunch and dinner last night.

"No, I have not touched him or the dart—except to check for a pulse. I can't find one. Yes, he's lying face down. He hasn't moved since he fell." Aaron's voice was now melding with Jed's own thoughts.

Jed stared at the scene unfolding before him. How did a dart get into the man's neck? That would require a dart gun. Did anyone here have a dart gun? That was unlikely. Jed looked around the room, eyes settling on the window across from the kitchen that led to the back of the house. It was open.

"I'm not sure if he's still alive. Yes, we will start CPR until you get here."

Jed stared at Aaron, then the chef, his eyes moving between the two men, back and forth. He wasn't sure what to do or what to make of the situation. How was he supposed to process this? What was going on? How did the chef fall? Darts? Where did they come from? Where were the rest of the officers?

Derek had come back into the room and now kneeled beside Joel's body. Christie joined him. Without any words spoken, they slowly and gently rolled Joel onto his back, and Derek began chest compressions.

Christie's voice was quick and firm as she directed, "He just fell, so he wouldn't have stopped breathing for long. I'll do the rescue breathing while you do the compressions. Let me know when you want to switch."

Jason walked into the room right then.

"Jason, we need gloves and evidence bags from the Chief's cars so we can remove the dart. EMS also wants us to give him Naloxone."

Jason nodded, turning quickly and heading back outside.

"Where's everyone else?" Jed asked.

Aaron looked up at him, strain all over his face. His brows were pulled together, his jaw was tense, and his lips were pressed into a thin line.

"Joseph and Graham are outside. I sent them to wait for the ambulance to arrive so that we didn't have more confusion than necessary in the room. And Carter hasn't come out of his room yet. I think he's still asleep. In the rush and the confusion, I don't think anyone went to get him."

Just then, as if on cue, Carter rounded the corner and turned to look at the people in the kitchen. He was about to speak when his eyes fell to the ground and noticed the body lying flat and still. His smile dropped, and his expression paled. He opened his mouth to speak, but a startled croak came out. Carter took a step forward, eyes fixed on the body lying on the floor.

"What's going on?" he asked, a shrill edge to his voice. "Did something happen?"

He rushed over to join everyone in the kitchen. Christie and Derek were switching positions, and Christie started doing compressions.

"Well," Jed began, "Aaron says that he and the other guys were all in the living room when they saw the chef suddenly fall. When they went over to see if he was alright, he was unresponsive, and there's a dart in his neck. No one knows where the dart came from."

"Holy shit."

Carter ran a hand through his hair, exhaling sharply. A muscle in his lower jaw shook with a spasm.

"But… that could have been any of us."

Jed didn't like to think about it, but Carter was right. It could have been any of them that had been hit by that dart. And if that dart had come from outside, which he was assuming it had, and contained something so deadly that it could take down a grown man immediately, he was sure that whoever did this probably had enough poison to take down the entire group. But he hadn't.

"Where's the rest of the guys?"

Jason returned with the Naloxone. All of them had been trained to administer Naloxone and carried it in their kits in their cars. He quickly opened the kit and administered the first dose. He waited a few moments, but there was no response from Joel. He administered a second dose with the same lack of response.

Jed looked back over at Carter, who was still staring at the body on the ground, his eyes wide.

"The guys are outside waiting for the ambulance to arrive," Aaron answered, finally finishing his call.

"Holy shit," Carter said again. "This is insane."

Jason opened the evidence kit he had brought in with him. He retrieved evidence bags and gloves. Sliding the gloves on, he prepared the bag, and without thinking, he chose to make it double-bagged. Then he slowly and gently removed the dart from Joel's neck and placed it in the bag. They didn't know what they were dealing with, so he knew to be extra cautious.

They could hear the ambulance siren as it pulled up outside. Carter turned to leave, making a beeline for the front door to help the paramedics.

It didn't take long for the paramedics to enter the kitchen and take over the CPR. They asked everyone to give them room to work, so the crew slowly left the kitchen and headed for the living room.

"Well, everyone," Aaron sighed as he entered the living room, "we've got a new case on our hands."

"Yes, we sure do," Jed murmured. Christie's only response was a nod, and Jed let his eyes rove across her features. She was deep in thought. He could see it from the distant look in her eyes, the way her lips were pursed slightly and by the thin line of wrinkles touching her forehead.

"We'll all have to stay out of the way so that the scene can be processed," Christie finally spoke, in an oddly flat tone. "And since we were all here when this happened, we'll all have to be processed as witnesses and suspects."

"Yes. Yes, we will," Aaron confirmed as he nodded.

Joseph and Graham entered the living room with two police officers. They had filled them in on the events. One of the uniformed officers announced, "I don't have to tell you all to stay here until the forensics and rest of the team arrive to take your statements and collect samples, and then you can leave."

The officer was visibly uncomfortable addressing everyone in the room, as they all outranked him. He avoided making eye contact with any of them. He then answered a call on his cell that no one could be sure was real as he walked out of the room with the other officer.

Christe nodded in return. "I'll be in my room."

Without waiting for a response, she turned to head back to her room. Jed watched her leave before sighing and turning back to Aaron. Aaron was already looking at him.

"I'm not sure what to make of this whole situation," Aaron spoke with a frown, his fingers drumming against his left leg. "Joel was such a kind-hearted person. I can't imagine why anyone would have done this."

The man sighed, shaking his head.

"But I guess that's the same with all murder cases. They all start out with no clues or hints or any reason to understand why someone would want that person killed. Then, you figure it out."

Jed shook his head and smiled bitterly. "You failed to mention all the weeks of unending stress and struggle and a million dead-ends. You went right from murder to case solved."

Aaron coughed awkwardly. "Yeah, I skipped over that, didn't I? But we have the murder investigation dream team here today—you guys got this!"

Jed nodded. "Do we have surveillance footage for inside this Airbnb? Or outside?"

"I thought of that," Aaron muttered, looking down at his phone. "There are surveillance cameras in all the common areas of the Airbnb, but I don't think there are any on the outside. I'll update the chief and ask him to double-check for possible surveillance on the property and to get in touch with the owner of the listing."

Jed nodded again. "That will be the place to start."

CHAPTER 8

IT WAS SUNDAY MORNING, the day after the mysterious dart had killed Joel. After the scene had been processed and they had all been interviewed, the tired team had separated for the evening to crawl back to their respective apartments. Jed was going through all the events of yesterday as he lay in his bed in his apartment. When he had almost been through packing, Aaron had come to knock and say that the EMTs and HAZMAT Team were finished. Unfortunately, Joel was pronounced dead at the scene. They could not revive him. Jed and Christie had both gone out to watch them remove the body, dressed in protective suits to avoid contamination with any of the poison that might remain in the dart or Joel. Thankfully, they had come prepared.

The dart was sent to the lab for testing. In the afternoon, after they had given their statements and the crime scene was processed, as they were preparing to leave, an argument had broken out. Jed rubbed his hand across his face to wipe away the remaining cobwebs of sleep as he focused on his memories of the event.

One minute, their group was fine, and the next minute, people were all pointing fingers at each other. Or rather, Jason was pointing fingers at people. He was the one that had started it. Jason had asked Derek what he had been doing by the kitchen island right before Joel had fallen to the ground. Everyone in the room had frozen. Aaron had sighed, Jed had rolled his eyes, and Christie had turned to look out the window. At the insinuation, Derek's response was shocked silence, and Jed couldn't blame him. It was a terrible look to blast a fellow officer in such a manner right after a murder had happened. It didn't even matter whether he was the one who had done it or not. What mattered was that Jason should have known better than to ask that question at that point in time. It simply was neither the time nor the place. They were officers of the law. There were procedures for investigations, and Jason had just broken all of them.

Derek hadn't bothered to respond, which, in Jed's opinion, was the best decision he could have made in that moment. It had told Jed more about his character than anything he could have said. He had simply glared at Jason so harshly that Jason had backed down without Derek even needing to say anything.

"I'm not implying anything," Jason had uttered defensively, feigning an innocent expression. "I was just asking if you saw anything… you know, worth mentioning."

"Just zip it, Jason," Graham had demanded, rolling his eyes. "You know very well that Derek wasn't facing Joel. His back was to him! Don't go creating conflict for no reason."

"Don't you talk to me in that tone!" Jason had shot back, nostrils flaring. "Who left and made you king? And since when were questions outlawed in this group?"

"Jason," Jed had chimed in gently, seeing Joseph run a frustrated hand through his hair and knowing they were soon approaching their point of explosion, "there's no need for asking questions outside of a formal investigative capacity. There's no benefit we can possibly attain from that. So, let's just remain silent and civil until things clear up further."

Jason, however, didn't seem to have any intention of stopping. Upon hearing Jed's voice, he had whirled on him, anger still smeared across his features like a garish mask. "Okay then, Mr. Know-It-All. Who made you lead detective?"

"Jason, you're being ridiculous. Just shut up," Joseph had angrily muttered. At that point, Christie had motioned to Jed that she was ready to leave, and she and Jed headed for the door. "Wait a minute, where the hell are you two going?" Jason asked.

Graham glared at him. "How many times are we gonna have to tell him to shut up?"

What a nightmare, Jed thought to himself as he sat up in bed. They had been on a team-building exercise, and that was all it took to break the group apart? Jed knew that there was no reason to throw around accusations or ask questions until they confirmed what they could access from the surveillance footage. That was the first line of attack. If there was no footage, then they would launch an investigation through questioning the witnesses. But even then, there were no true witnesses. At that precise moment, everyone seemed to have had their backs turned to Joel. It was a tragedy of great proportions.

Jed had driven Christie home yesterday evening since she had taken an Uber to the Airbnb, and after that tense conversation in the kitchen of the Airbnb among the officers, she had been mostly silent the whole ride home. Thinking it wise to give her some room to think, Jed hadn't bothered to breach the silence. Eventually, she had looked over at him while darkness crept across the land and the streetlights were coming on, and said, "Buckle up, Gray. We've got quite the doozy on our hands yet again."

Jed had agreed.

Then Christie had continued, "How the dart came out of nowhere is very concerning. There was one open window next to the kitchen, with the line of sight stretched all the way across and into the living room. One panel of that window was open when we all rushed into the kitchen. I think that may have been where the dart came from, which implies that the person who did this must have had a dart gun to shoot so accurately from such a distance. If everyone was in the living room, except Carter, who was sleeping, and you and I were in my room, that means that this was an outside job. But those are all preliminary observations. We still have no idea what was in the dart. Whatever it was, it's definitely extremely lethal. I've never seen any poison work that fast before. Where would someone even get that kind of thing? Surely, they're not selling those kinds of things on the street?"

Christie turned her head to look at Jed. "I don't mean to offend you," she'd said, "but I mean, you should know more about that than me." Jed had almost choked on his own saliva at that, and Christie had burst out laughing.

"Yeah, you're right," he had said after clearing his throat and letting a sheepish grin take over his face. "I've seen overdoses happen, and sometimes those range in times—seconds, minutes, or much slower and more gruesome. It all depends on what the drug is. The trouble is that the substance in the dart must have been in liquid form, unlike the usual solid and powder forms most drugs come in. That was definitely just an outright poison or toxin. We'll have to see what comes back from the lab."

Christie nodded. "There should be some trace left inside the dart that can identify the substance."

Jed had dropped Christie off at her apartment, and then they had parted ways for the night. He had thought the evening was finally over. When he got back to his own apartment, he had hopped into the shower and was getting ready for bed when he received a call from Christie.

"*Hi, Detective. Is everything alright?*"

"*Jed.*" Christie had just spoken that one word, and it was enough for Jed to guess that something was not right. No, something had gone terribly wrong.

"*Christie?*" Jed had asked, squeezing the phone against his ear. His heart had hammered dully in his chest.

"*Jed,*" Christie had repeated again in that same dread-infused voice, "*I just got word that one of the forensic analysts got infected while analyzing the poison in the dart. She's in the ER in critical condition. Her liver and kidneys are both threatening to give up, even though the doctors say they found very miniscule quantities of the poison present in her bloodstream.*"

"*What?*" Jed had nearly yelled, his mind caught in a whirlwind. He could not believe what he was hearing.

"*How is that possible?*" He had managed to get out through his dry, sandpapery mouth.

"*There was barely enough poison remaining inside the dart, but somehow, it was still enough to be lethal through absorption, and even though she was wearing protective gear, they suspect she may have spilled some of the liquid on her gloves, which came in contact with her skin when she removed them improperly, or via faulty equipment such as leak in her mask or piercing in her glove. They are trying to determine how it got into her system. Everyone at the lab is very shaken up.*" Christie had paused, and Jed could sense the enormous effort she was exerting to hold herself together.

This case had quickly changed from a murder investigation into some kind of apocalyptic horror film.

"Christie, I don't... I don't even know what to say." Jed had gritted his teeth and fought back the dread twisting his stomach into a barbed knot. *"How is this happening? How can something be so potent?"*

"That's what I said to the chief. We're dealing with some extremely dangerous stuff. We still have no idea what it is because, of course, they had to stop the analysis and get her to the hospital. She was almost gone by the time they hauled her into the ER. That also means that the results are going to be delayed, probably by a day. Hopefully, we'll be able to hear something by tomorrow morning or tomorrow evening. I'd like to get started while we're still all fresh from what happened, since we were witnesses to the crime."

Jed had nodded. *"Let's hope that they get something back to us soon. We should take a moment to thank the universe that none of us came into contact with this nasty substance. You and Derek were at the greatest risk while you were doing CPR."*

Now that it was Sunday morning, Jed wondered if they had discovered anything about this mystery poison yet. It was incredibly frightening that such a poison that existed—that just by touching it you could die, and die so quickly. In theory, in his distant knowledge of the world of poisonous substances, he knew that this was completely plausible. But to witness it firsthand, and to see it destroy two lives, drove fear into his heart.

It was a good thing that Aaron had relayed the 911 operator's instructions to remove the dart very carefully to Jason, or they could have all been exposed to the deadly substance. Joel was not the average man one saw walking around in New York City. He stood at 6 ft 4 inches tall and was a man of absolute muscle. He could have been a bodybuilder. And to see a dart that only had the capacity of about two or three milliliters of substance drop him like a hunter drops a deer with one shot was very frightening.

What if whoever had done this had made it their mission to attack everyone in the group? It was as simple as a couple more well-placed darts. As soon as Joel dropped and everyone rushed over to him, they were also in the window's sightline, which meant that the person with the darts could have dropped them one by one. What if it was a bait and switch? Was it possible that this killer had wanted to aim at Christie or someone else at the retreat?

Suddenly remembering the threat Christe had mentioned, Jed launched himself out of bed and over to his phone. He found Christie in his contacts and pressed dial.

"Christie?"

Still groggy, she murmured a response.

"I hate to wake you up this early, but this is urgent. Do you remember how you told me you had been threatened?

The suspect you apprehended in the hit and run? Who said he could get your head on a plate if he wanted it? You and all the officers?"

In her room, Christy sat upright right away.

"Yes, I remember. What are you getting at?"

"Well," Jed said, "I've been contemplating how powerful this poison is that we're dealing with. They shot Joel with the dart when he was in the kitchen cooking."

"Right."

"What if this person wasn't really after Joel, and I hate to say this or suggest this, but what if they were after you? I just thought that the fact that Joel dropped and then all the other officers rushed over to him, that put them in the window's sightline as well, which meant that if the killer had intentions to kill all of us, he could have."

Christie's heart was pounding. "Right, but he didn't. So, what are you saying?"

"Well, I considered the possibility that since you were threatened, but you weren't present in the room when Joel was shot with the dart, you could have been the target. Perhaps the kitchen was the best line for the shot, and he was trying to draw all of us there so he could then find his actual target... You."

"So, since I wasn't there, and I didn't rush to his aid, the killer might have refrained from shooting? When I did enter the kitchen, I knelt down beside Joel to help with CPR, so I was out of sight."

"That's what crossed my mind," Jed said. "I don't like this theory, so I'm hoping it's all not true, but it crossed my mind, and there is some level of plausibility, so I thought I should bring it up to you."

"You're right," Christie eventually responded after thinking for a while. "There is a level of plausibility, so it's a good thing you shared it with me." She sighed, and Jed discerned the storm of thoughts she was likely choosing to withhold. "I'll be at the station all day. You can pop in if you want to."

Jed shook his head, a grin on his face. "We're going to work on your avoidance of your emotions, Detective. But, yes. I'd like to join you."

Jed ran into Derek on his way to Christie's office. The tall, tawny-haired fellow was walking briskly with a thick folder held in his hands. His brows were scrunched together, and there was a look of absent worry on his face.

"Hello, Derek," Jed greeted him, watching his words pull the man out of whatever dark train of thoughts he had been traveling in.

"Jed, hey." Derek answered in a hollow voice, coming to a stop. "Are you looking for Christie? She's in t—"

"I know where she is," Jed interrupted gently. "I just saw you and thought of saying hello because you looked quite zonked out. Is everything okay?"

A shadow passed over Derek's face. "No, not really," he muttered in a thick voice. "This whole business with the cook has me pretty shaken, you know. That tiny dart... it could've hit any one of us." He looked at Jed, his face teeming with dread, and Jed knew what was bothering the man even before he spoke it.

"I've got a family, man!" Derek whispered harshly. "A beautiful wife and an angelic little baby boy who's just learned how to walk! If that dart had hit me..." His voice trailed off, and he shook his head, bowing his chin down slightly.

"But it didn't hit you, Derek. You're alive and perfectly okay." Jed reached out with one hand a bit hesitantly, then clasped Derek's shoulder. "Besides, this is part of what you all signed up for when you joined the police force. Protecting civilians from all sorts of threats. Your profession wouldn't nearly be so noble if it didn't require you to put your life on the line now, would it?"

Jed's words seemed to calm Derek down a bit. He nodded softly, lifting his gaze back up to Jed.

"Yeah, I guess you're right," Derek mused. "It is different when we are out on the street, on duty, instead of horsing around at a retreat." A faint smile tugged at the corners of his lips. "You're really good at this therapy stuff, aren't you? I can see why she likes you so much."

"What?" Jed asked, his heart skipping a beat.

But Derek just shook his head, the smile widening on his face. "Nothing. I have to go. Someone's waiting for me to give them this file. Catch you later, Mr. Therapist." And with that, he was off, clapping Jed on the back once before heading down the hallway. Jed watched him leave, his mind swirling with unspoken and unanswered questions.

As he walked up to Christie's door and knocked, Jed noticed Jason coming down the hallway. He wondered whether the man had any theories about what had happened. At the Airbnb, he certainly had. He had seemed to want to jump into the investigations right away. As it stood, Jed had no reason to distrust the man. Some behaviors that he'd displayed at the retreat came across as someone who was insecure, but there weren't any major red flags that Jed could identify—not yet, at least. To his surprise, but also unsurprisingly, Jason walked by without acknowledging him.

Jed shook his head as he opened the when Christie called, "Come in."

"Good morning, Detective," Jed greeted her as he pushed the door closed with his foot. Freshly cooked hot dogs from Jamie's stand lathered with all sorts of delectable sauces and cushioned between two toasted buns rested in a paper bag he held in one hand. Jed handed one of the hot dogs to Christie, who was just now looking up from her papers.

"Thank you, Jed." Christie sniffed the hot dog's tantalizing scent and licked her lips hungrily. "This is very thoughtful of you. How did you know I didn't eat breakfast this morning?"

Jed's movements paused as he was about to sit down, and he stopped midway to the seat.

"You didn't eat?"

Christie paused in the middle of biting her hot dog, a smile forming on her lips. She watched Jed slowly sit, his eyes never leaving her. She chewed through the yummy hot dog slowly. Jed still hadn't bitten into his. When she had finished swallowing, Jed's eyes narrowed.

"What's so funny, Detective?"

That made her smile widen. "Oh, nothing. Just watching you turn into an overprotective friend is adorable."

Jed nodded slowly.

"I skipped breakfast this morning. I was in a hurry."

Jed nodded again. "Then it's a good thing I stopped to get you something. I should do that more often. Just in case."

"If you bring me these delicious hot dogs too often, I won't be able to resist, and we will both be taken down by heart attacks," she chuckled.

Satisfied, Jed looked down at the open folder in front of her, in which a single page was filled with her handwriting. He let the silence stretch for a while.

"What do we have so far?" Jed inquired.

"Well," Christie started, "we have exactly what you already know. On Saturday morning at around 8:45, our team of four police officers and the deputy chief of the NYPD were in the living room at the Airbnb, when our chef, Joel, suddenly fell down. Our team rushed over to check on him, and he was immediately found to be unresponsive, not breathing, and a dart was in the right side of his neck."

Christie glanced up at Jed, who was taking a bite out of his hotdog.

"Other notes I have are about the location of the window and that no one was facing him when this happened, which means that no one could see or identify where the dart came from. I've also got Joel's physical stats—height, weight, build, that kind of thing."

She'd rested the hotdog on the table next to her folder as she scanned her notes.

"I also added in the notes that I called you last night to report. One of the forensic analysts, Lisa, passed away after inadvertently touching a remnant of the poison from the dart as it was being processed. They found that she absorbed it on her wrist, most likely as she was removing her gloves. And finally," she said, still tapping her pen, "I have the theory that you called to tell me this morning—that Joel may have not been the target. I'm still mulling over that one and trying to identify any angles I could look into. Like you said on the phone, I would rather it not be related, but there's definitely a level of plausibility to it."

Jed nodded along. "Do you have anything on surveillance or any info from the poison sample yet?"

Christie sat upright, swiveling her chair backwards as she pulled the drawer to her left open.

"That's one thing I wanted to talk to you about before starting. The chief called, and he let me know that they were able to get the surveillance footage of inside the house, but there are no cameras on the outside. So, we'll at least be able to see what happened to Joel and how the dart came into the picture, but we won't be able to see outside, so we have no basis for who the perpetrator is."

Christie's eyes darted up to Jed. "Another team has already reviewed the tape and cleared us to have access to it." She paused. "Otherwise, we wouldn't have this. The outside investigative team did me a solid and made me a copy of the original tape."

Jed sighed. "Lots of red tape when you're both investigator and suspect."

"We'll also be able to verify everyone's position in the room at the time of the dart attack and rule out any involvement or discrepancies from our end. That also clears everyone on the team."

Rising, she walked around the desk and toward the door, Jed on her heels. They both headed to the investigative room, and once they sat down, Christie pointed a remote at the screen and loaded it up. Then, they could see the inside of the Airbnb on the screen.

The video showed that Derek, Joseph, Graham, Aaron, and Jason were all sitting in the living room together. The men appeared to be talking, and nothing happened for a while until Derek got to his feet and headed toward the kitchen island where he took up a position sitting on one stool, facing the rest of the group. His back was turned to Joel, and so were the backs of everyone else. Jason was the only one sitting in a position that allowed him to face toward the kitchen, but right through the footage, he was concentrating on his cell phone. Then, they watched as Joel seemed to crumple and fall out of nowhere.

Christie paused the video.

"I watched this video a few times before you got here, and I spent most of the playtime trying to spot the dart. I couldn't, until I slowed the video down drastically, and even then, the dart enters the scene as a blur, right before Joel falls. The reaction time between his collapse and the dart hitting him is a few seconds. That's definitely a testament to just how powerful that poison is. He dropped so fast he didn't even get the chance to make a sound. One minute he was here, and the next he was gone."

A shudder ran through Jed's body. Christie was arranging the settings of the video playback as she spoke, and when she pressed play once more, they watched the scene again. Everyone's movements slowed down until they looked silly. They watched Derek take up position at the kitchen island, then Jed focused his eyes on the space between the open window and Joel. A few moments dragged by before Jed finally spotted the moving blur.

114

"Wow. It's moving incredibly fast. And it definitely came from outside the window."

Christie nodded. "And here you can see the reaction time of everyone else. Nobody was paying attention until Joel hit the floor, and then everyone got up and rushed toward him all at once."

Jed watched the video in silence, completely focusing on the dart, then Joel falling.

"You were right," Christie said. "Now I see what you mean about the window of time in which the perpetrator could have taken down the entire group. Everyone rushed toward him. They were all in full view of the window, and at that point, they still hadn't noticed that there was a dart sticking out of Joel's neck. Those seconds could have been their last if the perpetrator had really wanted to do harm to the entire group."

"The other thing," Jed said, "is that if you watch the video back, someone was always paying attention to what was going on in the kitchen. At the start of the video, Jason was watching Joel cook, then when he looked away, that's when Derek got up and walked towards the island. It's when Derek is facing away and Jason is occupied with his phone, and no one else is noticing what's going on—that's when the dart comes flying."

"What are you saying?" Christie asked.

Jed shook his head, that uneasy feeling within him increasing. "The timing is perfect. *Too* perfect. Whoever shot the dart must have been waiting there for a long time."

Christie was silent for a moment. "You're right," she finally admitted, sounding just as unsettled as Jed felt. Her face was troubled. She was chewing on her lower lip absently. "This was a… perfectly planned murder. Every detail was planned beforehand." A shadow crossed across her eyes, and Christie wrapped her arms across her chest, as if struck by an unseen wind. "We need to be on our toes now, moving forward. We can't afford to be lazy."

Jed stared at the frozen screen, thoughtful. "Can we get some specs on the dart that was used? I think that would be helpful in figuring out what the options are for dart guns in that category. That could give us an idea of the range of the gun so we can see how close or far away this person was standing. Would they have needed to be in the yard? Because if they were, how did no one notice that?"

"Those are all excellent questions." Christie jotted down what they were saying. "Any other bright ideas while you're in the zone?"

Jed grinned. "I think we should check out leads on Joel and do an investigation into the person who threatened you. Does that kid have the capacity to hire someone to get their dirty work done for them? Since he's already in custody and is going be called to court soon, it wouldn't have been him who showed up in person. But it could have been someone connected to him."

"I still don't understand how that would work, though," Christie muttered. "Why would they run the risk of killing someone else on accident when they weren't sure if I was going to show up? How would they have known I was going to be there in the first place? It's not like the retreat was public information. And no one has access to my location."

"That's a good point," Jed conceded as he thought about it and factored those questions into the picture. "It's possible that this person tracked you while you were on your way to the Airbnb and laid low while waiting for an opportunity. Any chance that kid overheard someone at the station mention something about the retreat while he was in custody?" Jed asked.

"It's possible," Christie spoke, "but I arrived alone. If he had been targeting me, that would have been the perfect time to attack—not after the fact. Especially since I wasn't even in the room to begin with. But it could be that the killer followed me there and waited around to see if other people arrived. Depending on how many others there were, they would have to adjust their plans. If they could see Joel and the rest of the guys in order to execute the perfect shot, wouldn't they also have been able to see that you and I weren't present?"

"Maybe he couldn't see the entire room from his vantage point? That could be why he targeted Joel, hoping we would all go to the kitchen to his aid, where the perpetrator had a clear shot at all of us. It could be that they weren't after you but after one of our other officers." Jed paused as he thought for a moment. "We need to go walk around the grounds outside to see what the killer could actually see."

Christie agreed with a quick nod. "I'll have some of our officers do a walk-around of the Airbnb to check for footprints and any potential leads there." She reached for her phone. "We should be able to get confirmation on that relatively quickly."

After a curt conversation with someone on the other end of the phone, Christie returned to her note taking. She and Jed sat in silence for some time, letting their conversation simmer in their minds. The seconds passed by, turning into minutes, which almost turned into half-an-hour before Christie's cell lit up with an incoming call. Jed listened to her conversation, not able to hear the caller on the other end of the line.

"Good call, Jed. We've found footprints around the perimeter of the property, beginning at the back wall furthest from the front door. That leads us to believe that this person launched themselves over the wall to gain access to the property; then, their tracks show they made their way around the house until they were in the kitchen's sightline. There were no footprints near any of the windows, so that clears Carter from being a suspect. Since he was unaccounted for at the time of the incident, this clears up whether he might have slipped out of the house unnoticed through a window."

Christie was back to jotting down notes from their dis-
cussion, and Jed watched her as she wrote. When Christie
finished, she looked over at Jed and noticed that he seemed
like he was a world away in his thoughts.

"Penny for your thoughts, Gray?"

Jed continued sitting in a pensive silence. When he finally
spoke, it was in a reluctant, concerned voice. "I don't want
anything to happen to you,"

Christie stared at him.

"We need to figure this out, and fast." Now, he was agitat-
ed, like somewhere a clock was counting down, and he had
to solve this riddle before the timer struck zero—or something
awful would happen.

Christie sighed. "I agree. It's unnerving to realize that I
could have been or still am the target of this person's attack.
Or that this attack was meant to draw me into the open so that
they could attack me. Off the cuff, I know that the suspect
who threatened me does, in fact, have the means to hire out a
murder if he chose to. He comes from a very wealthy family
and has access to resources that would make killing someone
easy for him."

Christie looked lost in thoughts.

"At the same time, I don't know that his threat was sincere.
He's still a kid, and it's probable that he was just blowing
smoke to try to intimidate me. He definitely has very little
experience with not getting his own way. Still, a threat is a

threat and should never be taken lightly, especially when a wealthy white man promises you death."

Jed's jaws tightened, and Christie watched as a multitude of thoughts and feelings raced across his face. "Yeah," he said. "We need to figure this out."

"And we will," Christie assured him.

Already deciding to sit down sooner rather than later and work through the kinks in this case, Jed nodded firmly. "Yeah, we will."

CHAPTER 9

ON MONDAY MORNING, AS Jed prepared to go into the office for his first day of work since the murder, the possibility that the threat to Christie was connected to this new murder lingered in his mind. He was coming up short so far, but that didn't mean there was no answer. All it meant was he didn't know what the answer was yet.

He had already called her when he'd woken up, just to make sure that nothing had happened to her overnight. Jed didn't let her know that was why he'd called, though, and had just casually checked in with her, asking how she was feeling and how she had slept. As usual, she had reported not sleeping very well. That was something else he needed to spend some time thinking through. He had some theories, but needed to work on how he would discuss them with her. Jed buttoned his sleeves, took one last look in the mirror, then headed out the door.

Today, he was scheduled to meet with two clients: one who was fresh out of rehab and one he had been seeing for a good amount of time already. This client, in particular, he had been seeing for around four months. Her name was June, and she had initially come to him because she was being pressured by her parents to commit to therapy. They were the ones paying for her sessions. Her parents loved her dearly and wanted what was best for her, and so they had set a firm boundary. Either she started therapy, or they would disown her, and she would be on her own. That was how against therapy she had been at the start of their time together.

Now, though, she was leaning more and more into it, and she liked their visits so much that at the end of their sessions, she often found herself a little upset when they needed to wrap up. Though Jed had pinpointed exactly why she experienced that anger and fear at the end of their session, which often drove her to shut down, he hadn't yet been able to break through her resistance to expressing those emotions. It was simple, wasn't it? If you were feeling sad that the session was ending, all you had to do was to accept that—'I'm feeling sad that the session is ending'. But of course, nothing was truly that simple. After all, Jed *was* a therapist. He was used to helping people who were afraid to voice their feelings for fear of being seen as weak, or feeling small, or because they thought those feelings could be used against them. Regardless of what the reason was, he was determined to break those barriers with June.

For June, Jed had recognized that her resistance to expressing her emotions was part of the reason she had turned to substance abuse in the first place. Even though she grew up in a home with parents who loved her and who showed their support in all the ways they knew how, she had often felt unseen and hardly heard. Because of this, June had allowed herself to be led astray by her peers who were into drugs. Jed knew that 'led astray' was a very specific way to express what she had experienced. She had admitted that she'd known better than to take those first pills and smoke that weed. In fact, she'd shared that for a long time, she had resisted their efforts at convincing her to join their group smoking sessions. At some point, the longer she'd spent feeling unheard and unseen at home, she had given in. Not that she had given in reluctantly either. She had made a conscious decision to engage in using drugs to soothe the pain she was feeling at home. All of this was by her own confession. When Jed had asked whether she had tried to speak with her parents about how she was feeling at home or what her experience at home was like, she had shrugged and just said 'no'. June hadn't bothered to express how she was feeling to her parents because her experience was that she would not be heard anyway.

Jed could understand the thought process behind that, even if on the surface, it seemed counterproductive. As a teenager, he had done the same thing. He hadn't confided in his own mother about how he had been feeling and what his experiences had been like visiting his father's home, and as a result it had driven him to the point of trying to take his own life. Now, though, he knew better. Of course he did. It was always better to keep trying to reach out to those around you, even if you had already experienced what felt like rejection from those people. Why? Well, because it wasn't about the people and their reactions. It wasn't those people you were doing a favor by trying to communicate how you were feeling; it was yourself. You were the one who was at risk the longer you went without reaching out.

He wasn't yet sure what he was going to use to bring that point across to her. She was young—still in high school—and deathly afraid that her friends would find out she was in therapy. June considered it so uncool to ask for help.

"Hmm," Jed mused. "Maybe that's exactly what I'll need to use."

Jed let the cold air slam into him as he walked out of the building and onto the street. He was grateful that his coat kept the chill from sinking into his bones. The last thing he needed was to get sick at a time like this, when both his case and his clients needed him. On his way to the office, he walked by three homeless people—two men and one woman. It was early fall in New York, and the chill was seeping into the city. Jed knew that the colder it got, the harder it was for homeless people all around the city to keep up their resilience. But Jed knew just what would do the trick and help them feel seen and better in this chilly weather, if only for a little while. There was a coffee shop at the end of the block, and he walked in, making an order for three steaming black coffees. Then, from their breakfast menu, he ordered one double-smoked bacon, cheddar, and egg sandwich, one chicken, maple butter, and egg sandwich, and one bacon, gouda, and egg sandwich.

As he exited back out into the brisk air, Jed walked down the block toward the three people he had passed. He handed out a sandwich and coffee to the first person, who immediately teared up, then walked further down to hand out the next one to the woman he had passed, who was trembling from the cold and thanked him over and over, and the next one to the second man, who was sleeping. Jed left the sandwich and coffee next to him.

Pushing his hands into his pockets, he turned around and walked back up the block the rest of the way to work. It was going to be a good day.

"Hi, Mom."

"Hi, Jed! How are you? Calling me first thing on Monday morning isn't really your style. Is everything alright?"

Jed chuckled a little, sitting in his chair at his desk before clearing his throat. "Well, Mom, I'm just calling you to let you know that I'm in the middle of another case. This one's a murder, again, and we have absolutely no idea what's going on or how things are going to play out. We have no leads, we haven't heard from forensics, and it's just... a bit of a mess.

But I wanted to let you know before things got too crazy. I don't want you to think I'm holding out on you again."

Laurie's hand tightened on her armrest as she listened to Jed talk about another murder. She wasn't quite sure what to say. Her son's previous case had taken a bit of a toll on her, though she had never let on. She was always confident that he could handle himself well and that he was capable enough to lead those around him. Even so, the thought of him being involved in a murder case was unnerving. On the other side of things, she had used it as motivation to start writing her own mystery book. She still wasn't done. Actually, she still hadn't hit the halfway point. But there were a lot of plot points in the novel based on how she envisioned Jed would handle certain situations that he might face.

"Well, darling, how are you feeling about this fresh case?"

"It's very unsettling mom. It feels like it's all getting worse, actually. The first case, we didn't really see the solution until we got way deep into it, and it required a lot of thinking on my part. In this case, there's a substance involved that none of us have interacted with before, and that's really scary. It feels like time is already ticking, like we don't have the luxury to be sitting around and not solving the issue as fast as we can. I feel a bit like we're sitting ducks."

"Oh, dear," Laurie murmured to herself.

Jed continued. "We don't have that kind of grace period this time. Time really is not on our side. It never is, in a murder case. The longer it takes to solve, the more you risk losing potential evidence and leads."

"Oh, dear," was all Laurie could say again.

Jed laughed a little. "Am I overwhelming you, Mom?"

"Well, it's not quite that I'm overwhelmed. I'm worried for you. I just don't want anything to happen to you. But I'm confident that you will be careful and that you have what it takes to solve this case. Besides, you and Christie make a great team. I know you both will figure this out in no time."

After he hung up and had stored his phone away into his top drawer to focus on the papers in front of him, Jed couldn't help but feel a small seed of doubt creep into his heart. It had been there since Christie had called to let him know that one of the forensic analysts had died from absorbing the poison.

That single detail was the most illuminating one in this entire case. The others probably hadn't even realized it yet, but the nature of the poison used was their single biggest key to getting an insight into the nature of the killer.

And that insight wasn't a good one.

Jed leaned back in his chair, reexamining the conclusion he had reached a while ago and trying, fruitlessly, to stop that same dreadful premonition of doom from gripping him again. They were dealing with a poison so lethal that simply coming into the barest of contact with it resulted in almost-certain death.

What kind of a person used such a poison?

If the risk really was this high, then it was not just them who had been exposed to it, *but also the killer*. In fact, the killer had a much greater risk because he had actually unpacked the poison, filled the dart with it, and then loaded the gun with the dart before firing his killing shot.

What kind of person did something like this? Risked their life for a murder?

Someone obsessed with revenge?

A madman?

Or both?

Sighing deeply, knowing no answer would come, Jed pulled the stack of papers lying on his desk toward him and began to fill out the form of the new client he would now be seeing.

"Hi, Braxton. How are you doing?"

Jed was now sitting across from his newest client. Braxton was in his late forties, around 5 feet 8 inches tall, medium build with tanned skin, and his arms were covered with tattoos. He even had a couple on his face. And after spending years in gangs, running the city, and taking on anyone who opposed him, he certainly looked the part. His hair was cut into a low crop, and he wore a washed-out band t-shirt and baggy jeans that had rips at the knees.

"I'm good, man," Braxton mumbled in a slightly gravelly voice.

Jed nodded, looking down at his papers for a moment.

"Well, welcome to the start of your recovery, and congratulations on choosing to change the trajectory of your life."

Braxton didn't reply, and Jed saw no smile gracing his lips.

Unfazed, Jed continued. "Is there anything that you would like to let me know before we begin? Your forms and your officer told me you wanted to say something before we started?"

Braxton wrung his hands together, a crack forming in his nonchalant facade. "Yeah, man. I just wanted to say that... you know... don't like, let my image and how I look... affect how you see me, you know?" He paused.

"Why do you think it would have any bearing on how I see you?" Jed asked.

"Well, as soon as everybody looks at me, they think I'm a thug, and they think I got this hard mindset and this really tough perspective on things. They don't really give me a chance or try to get to know me for real. I just didn't want you to turn into one of those therapists that... I don't know, man... just bash their client."

Braxton sounded a bit unsure of himself, like he had already spent a lot of time worrying about how therapy was going to work, or not going to work, for him. His hands were crossed over his chest, and the pointer of his left finger was tapping against his side.

"Well, you have nothing to fear here," Jed assured him. "I do not judge my clients on their appearances, on their experiences, or anything else, actually. Nothing you say is going to throw me off. Nothing you've done is going to change my mind about the fact that I want to help you, and none of your beliefs or ingrained mindsets will make me think twice about helping you."

Braxton stared at Jed for a long moment without speaking. "Yeah, man, they told me you're different from the rest of them. I'm not sure I believe that entirely, but I'm willing to find out."

"That's fair," Jed remarked. "I think that we both have some work to do to show each other our true selves."

"What do you mean?"

"This is therapy." Jed replied, "which is going to require you to open up about a lot of your experiences—things that might still hurt, things you don't even think are relevant to the conversation or the process of healing. Getting out of addiction is more than just talking about what drugs you took and how much you want to stop taking them. It's about exploring all our triggers, our traumas, understanding where the turning point was for us so that we can move forward into a life that no longer includes those substances."

Braxton nodded.

"Any questions?" Jed asked gently.

Braxton was looking at Jed kind of weirdly, and Jed figured that the man had something on his mind that he wasn't saying.

It was quiet in the room for a while, and Jed let the silence stretch. He wasn't one for filling up silences, because if he did, he ended up giving his clients something else to think about instead of allowing them to face their thoughts and have their internal monologue.

"You talk like a book," Braxton finally spoke.

Jed felt his heart splinter, and his eyes began to burn. He smiled. "So I've been told."

Braxton nodded, more to himself than to Jed. "Okay, I'm going to give it a shot."

"That's good. We can get started. What do you want to know?" Jed leaned back a bit, deciding to allow Braxton to lead this session. It would be very helpful because it would give the man confidence to open up further and say what was truly on his mind and, perhaps, also what was lurking in the hidden recesses of his heart.

Braxton shrugged, looking mildly uncomfortable. "I mean, did you do drugs?"

"I did. I have done a multitude of substances, starting from around the time that I was 15 years old."

"Which ones?" Now there was a gleam on interest in Braxton's eyes.

Jed held his gaze. "Marijuana, heroin, cocaine, fentanyl, dirty fentanyl, opioids, basically whatever I could get my hands on."

Braxton's eyes narrowed even further. "Man, what? You did all those?"

Jed smiled. "I did. I was a lost cause. But here I am, clean and sober."

"How long have you been clean, man?"

"Sixteen years."

Braxton was quiet for a long time.

"I've never met someone who's truly recovered before." And there it was, the crux of the problem laid out bare before him. It was the same problem countless other addicts faced, which kept pushing them back into their self-destructive patterns. It was a complete lack of hope, a complete lack of belief that things actually could get better.

Jed's heart was cracking even more, and the barrier between his grief and his facial expressions was weakening. Braxton reminded him a lot of Ethan, and they were only 10 minutes into the one-hour session. Jed sighed.

"Many people are successful in recovery and never talk about their experiences again. They carry a lot of shame related to their addiction. I think it's because drugs make you so helpless, and you're also so volatile. The realization that you were completely out of control, and that you were a danger to the people around you, is a heavy one to carry. Few people want to be known for that. Not many people want their story to even include that. So, once they recover, they just move on and pretend it never happened and never talk about it. On the other hand, people who have not dealt with addictions don't fully understand. For most, the unknown and not understanding turns into fear. As a result, I think people who are in current addiction have few examples of what it could look like to really be free of addiction. So, they think that the people around them who are also actively struggling with drugs are the only depictions of what life is like once you come in contact with drugs."

Braxton's attention was completely focused on Jed.

"If you don't know anyone who's recovered from a disease, you automatically think that the disease is going to kill you. It's a matter of hope, which is why I do what I do."

Braxton nodded and cleared his throat. "Well, what made you really recover for good?"

Jed smiled, memories flooding back into his mind. "My mom. She stood with me throughout the whole ordeal, and I was getting worse and worse, flunking out of rehab after rehab, detox clinic after detox clinic. Eventually, I hit rock bottom, and that really woke me up. It made me realize I was so close to the edge, and if I didn't do something right away, I was going to die. And I didn't want to die. I just didn't want to continue living the way I was living and running away from my feelings."

Jed was looking down at his desk, his arms crossed over his chest. "I was young. I felt like I had so much to live for, but I was actively throwing it away just to get a couple minutes of a high. So, I let my mom take me to a detox clinic after I came down from my last high, and that day, I decided to change for the better."

Braxton seemed awe-struck. "Wow. I mean, I've mainly been addicted to alcohol. It's kind of why I ended up in prison in the first place."

The man shuffled, and Jed could see that he felt a bit embarrassed by this.

"But I've also tried a couple of other things. I've tried weed, I've tried cocaine, but the first time I tried cocaine, I swear it almost killed me. And I was so scared of it I never tried it again. Weed was an on and off thing for me. In the early years before I really lost control, the job I had meant I really couldn't be smoking too much because I would have to deal with patients and stuff like that, and they… they would notice, you know? If I was smelling like weed all day at work."

"What kind of work did you do?" Jed asked.

"Man, I worked at a doctor's office, like as a receptionist, for a little while. And then I went back to school and got my certification as a dental hygienist. So, I couldn't really be smoking, you know? I was in people's mouths all day. I can't be smoking and smelling like weed all the time. Plus, I couldn't be drunk either, but I used to still sneak and drink at work, you know? I couldn't help it. I would drink here and there between patients, but I never let myself get tipsy."

Jed nodded as he took some notes.

"But as soon as the workday ended, man, I was blackout drunk at home on my couch. I was just… I don't even know. I was in love with the feeling of just not being in control of myself. But that was before things really got bad. In any case,

134

I left my career behind and made some very poor decisions to support my drinking."

Jed paused and looked at the man for a moment. "What about being in control of yourself scares you?"

Braxton froze for a second. He blinked a couple times before shaking his head, as though trying to shake off some kind of brain fog.

"I mean... I don't even know. What kind of question even is that? Nobody's ever asked me that before." He was quiet for a while, and Jed could see that he was thinking about the question more. "At the same time, though, I think it's a great question. When I drink, I feel like I lose the part of myself that's constantly stressed out and working toward things I feel like I can't even get. "

"And what is it you're working toward that you think won't ever happen?"

Braxton considered the question. "I'm not sure how to answer."

Jed nodded. "And that's perfectly fine. Thank you for letting me know that you're not clear on what I'm asking so that I can rephrase and hold better space for you."

Braxton's brows pulled together.

"What I'm asking," Jed continued, "is what is your highest goal in life? What's the thing that you really, really want?"

Then, after being quiet for a moment, the man across from him on the sofa sighed.

"Well," he said, leaning back and putting his feet up on the coffee table, "what I really want is to have my own family. I grew up without my dad, and I vowed to myself when I was young that I would not repeat that pattern. You know? I don't want my kids to go through unnecessary hardship just because I decided I wanted to be free."

His 'free' was in air quotes. Jed made a note of what he was saying.

"Have you been working toward building that family in any practical ways that you can identify for me?"

Braxton shook his head. "I've never really been good with the ladies, you know? I feel like they don't really see me. I'm not the best-looking guy in the world. Hell, I don't even think I'm average, man. Sometimes, I think I'm kinda ugly. And so when I see a beautiful woman I feel like I would be interested in, I don't really make a move. I just kind of fall back."

Jed could see his embarrassment made clear through his body language. "You don't think women find you attractive?"

He shook his head.

"Do *you* think you're attractive?"

His brows pulled together again.

"What's the difference?" Braxton asked.

Jed smiled. "Well, I like to think that there's two levels of attractiveness. There's how we think we're perceived by other people, and then there's how we feel about ourselves. One can influence the other. If we're very confident about how we look and how attractive we are, it can actually help us be perceived in a better way by people around us. But if we think people think we're not attractive, it can take a toll on our personal confidence, and then we can end up hating the way we look because we think other people find us ugly."

Braxton nodded thoughtfully. "Well, in that case, I guess I don't really think I'm attractive. I don't think I'm terrible-looking… I think maybe that I'm on like the bottom end of average."

"And is there anything you think you could do to make yourself feel more confident?" Jed pressed him gently.

"I mean, I think I could do that… wait a minute." Braxton's eyes narrowed even more. "How come you said 'make myself feel more confident' instead of 'make myself look more attractive'?"

Jed smiled. "I asked in that way because I don't think there's anything wrong with you. I don't think you're unattractive. I just think that you could do with spending some time working on building your confidence and self-esteem, increasing the level of respect with which you view yourself."

It was silent in the room for a few heartbeats.

"Do they teach you how to talk like books while you're in college?"

Jed let himself laugh, even though what he wanted to do was cry.

conspicuous than they realized, and their target would be thrown off by the tension or awkwardness of their presence.

New York was the perfect place to practice being an investigator. There were so many opportunities to people watch. Now, as he let himself be carried in the direction of home by the crowd around him, Jed started to think about Christie. Usually, when he was in the middle of breaking down and his defense systems were failing him despite his best efforts, the last thing he wanted to do was draw attention to himself. The furthest thing from his mind in those hard moments was the task of spending time trying to communicate the horrors of his mind to someone else, all in the name of inviting someone in. If he truly needed it, his mom was his last resort.

But in this moment, he didn't feel like ringing his mom. He didn't want to bother her. She was an early sleeper, preferring to rest early in the evenings and wake very early in the mornings. Jed knew she wrote and worked on her book in the mornings, and he didn't want to interrupt that cycle for her. He wasn't that far gone to interrupt her unnecessarily. Christie was the only other person he felt comfortable enough to call. But he also didn't think it would be a good idea to offload on her, especially when she could be the target of the case they were both trying to understand. He would have to work through his feelings himself.

When he arrived home, Jed forced himself to prepare a light dinner and sat on the couch in his living room to slowly make his way through his meal. He wasn't sure whether he should head straight to bed to drown out his thoughts or stay up and spend some time journaling. After thinking about it and going back and forth between the two options for a few more minutes, he decided that journaling would be his best bet. After picking up the leather-bound book and his pen from the nightstand where he kept them, Jed sat on the edge of his bed and looked out the window at the New York City streets for a long minute.

As he took up his pen to begin his entry for the day, his cell phone rang. It was Christie. Jed stared at it for a moment, letting the realization that she was calling him sink in. Was the universe conspiring against him again? Or was she just calling with an update on the case? Had he not *just* decided against calling her? Now here she was, calling him. If she asked how he was doing, he wasn't sure he would be able to hold the tidal wave of emotion back.

"Detective?" he answered, trying his best to sound normal.

"Hey, Jed. Are you alright?" Christie inquired, skipping her usual greeting.

Jed let out a long, weary sigh. On the other line, Christie was already on alert. "Detective, are you a mind reader?"

Christie laughed a little, her concern growing. "No, I'm not. But I did have this tiny feeling telling me to check on you tonight. Are you alright, Jed?"

Jed's eyes began to burn again, with a mixture of both grief and exhaustion. He felt angry tears prickling and fought them back.

"No," he admitted heavily, "I'm not fine. Actually, I'm the furthest from fine I've been in an incredibly long time."

On the other end of the line was the clear sound of Christie getting to her feet. "What's wrong? Did something happen at work?"

Jed sighed again. Christie's alarm was increasing by the moment, despite her best attempts to remain calm.

"I spent the day working with my newest client," Jed answered. "And all was well, except that he started to remind me very much of Ethan."

Christie took a sharp breath. Now, she was beginning to understand the strain in Jed's voice that seemed to be holding back so many things he wanted to say but probably felt as though he shouldn't.

"What was it about him that reminded you of Ethan?" Christie asked, as noninvasively as she could.

Jed ran a hand across his face. "It was a little bit of everything," he confessed, "which is the worst kind of pain. It was the way he spoke; it was the questions he asked; it was even some of his mannerisms. But I think what really sliced my heart open was the question he kept asking over and over. Even in normal circumstances outside of therapy, a lot of people ask me that question. They think I talk like a book. And I kind of do. But that was a question Ethan asked me constantly. He was always staring at me with this confused, kind of intimidated look in his eyes, asking me where I had learned to 'talk like a book'. Hearing someone else ask the same question in the same capacity was a pain I did not realize would slice so deep."

"Oh, Jed," Christie whispered. The phone was clenched in her hands. She didn't know what else to say.

Jed drew a deep, shaky breath. "Yes, Detective, it hurts. It hurts deep."

An idea came suddenly to Christie, and she squirmed where she sat, battling with whether or not to say it. Would Jed think she was being too forward? Or would he appreciate the gesture?

There was only one way to find out,

"Jed." She braced herself and then rushed on before her courage deserted her. "Would it be weird if I asked you if I could come over and spend some time with you since you're going through a hard thing right now?"

Jed chuckled. "Detective," he replied, "you're always welcome wherever I am. Should I come and pick you up?"

Christie shook her head, already grabbing her keys and a few other important items she never left home without.

"No, no," she said. "I don't wanna put you out of your way. If you come pick me up, then it'll feel like you're doing me the favor instead of me showing up for you."

In his room, Jed 's head did that tilt that made him look like a predator surveying his prey. "That's an interesting way to say that, Detective. In any case, I'll let you do that if that's what you prefer."

In her room, Christie's movements paused. How did he keep doing that? How did he manage to see through everything she said and did even when he was in the throes of his own pain? It didn't make sense. It was so intimidating and, simultaneously, so arousing to be in the presence of a man who could truly see you. She shivered.

"I'll be over soon," she replied.

In his own room, Jed nodded. "Yes, you will. Because if you aren't, I'll come hunting for you."

Christie laughed. "Why would you come hunting for me? It's not like I'm a five-year-old, bound to get lost. I know where you live, remember?"

"I have no doubts that you can make it here without getting lost, Detective. You've proven yourself a capable, independent woman. But in case you've forgotten, we're in the middle of an active case with theories that concern you being the point of attack. It's my job to ensure that nothing happens to you. I'll restrain myself from overriding your independence and coming to get you despite what you say, but if you're not here soon, I'll be on my way to get you."

Christie swallowed as she walked through her living room, stopping in the kitchen to grab a bottle of water.

"If I'm not there in half an hour, you can sound the alarm," she answered.

"That's far too much time," Jed replied, a smile pulling on his lips. "You'd better be here in 15 minutes, or I'm gonna get in my car and be on my way over to you."

Christie sighed dramatically. "Fifteen minutes it is. Let's pray that I can get an Uber fast."

By the time she was knocking on his door, Jed had changed into more company-appropriate nightwear. He never slept in anything except his bare torso and sweatpants, under which he often wore no boxers. With Christie coming over, he couldn't nearly be so relaxed. He opened the door. She was looking up at him, the way she usually did, except now, there was no trace of the usual playfulness she normally exuded. Instead, there was only solemn sadness. Jed wanted to sigh but refrained, instead letting her into the apartment. As she made her way to the couch, Jed let his eyes rove across her body from behind.

"I take it you had no trouble on your way here?" he asked.

Christie shook her head, holding his gaze. "No trouble to report, Captain."

Jed nodded in turn. "Good. That means I don't need to start a manhunt."

They sat together on the sofa, the silence stretching for a moment as Christie toyed with her hands in her lap. Jed watched her, letting the sound of her breathing soothe the part of him that was already wanting to cry.

"Something on your mind, Detective?" he asked, trying to get her to say something… anything.

Christie just looked at him with those penetrating eyes. "Well, you are."

Jed fought off the nervous tingle which arced down his spine. "What about me?"

Christie continued looking at him with her piercing eyes. "Well," she began, "I find it so interesting how well you just seem to bear all the heavy things that burden you. It shows a striking resilience." She looked down at her hands. "And that resilience is hard to crack." Her eyes softened as she looked at him. "So, for you to be cracking right now… I'm worried."

Jed shook his head in a manner that was almost apologetic, his face resigned. "I'm sorry to worry you."

Christie gave him a faint, sad smile. "Don't be sorry," she murmured. "You're worth worrying about."

Jed didn't know what to say to that immediately. He let the words wash over him.

"Am I?" he finally asked.

Christie nodded with vigor. "You are. I worry about you quite a lot." She broke eye-contact again to look down at her hands. "And it's not because I think you're incapable of handling yourself or handling your emotions. It's because I know you're *good* at handling your emotions. That's what worries me. It might not make any sense, and it's kind of hard to explain, but the better you are handling your emotions, the more I worry. Because since you're relying on only yourself to handle everything, I never know when to step in. I kinda just feel like I'm trespassing, or like I'm gonna wait too long to intervene, and then you would already have been breaking down without me noticing."

Jed blinked in surprise. That was a lot to take in all at once, and yet, surprisingly, he knew exactly what she was trying to say.

"I had no idea you worried about me like that, Detective."

Christie wrung her hands in agitation. "Well, I do. Do you remember when you decided it was a good idea to scout around the city at midnight, hoping to draw out the murderer on our last case?"

Jed nodded.

"When I got the ping, and after I called you, I could do nothing the whole rest of the night. I was so scared. That was the first time I realized just how far into your own head you can get—to the point where you didn't even think to tell me what your plans were. It scared the shit out of me, but it also made me realize just how much more intentional I need to be with asking you how you're doing and checking in with you. That's one of the reasons I really pushed for our friendship to go to the next level, so we could actually have conversations about how you're doing before it gets to the breaking point."

Jed swallowed hard, past the sudden lump in his throat.

"I didn't realize that would be a concern for you," he mumbled as he watched the concern take over her beautiful features.

"Yes, I've realized that, too. I know you don't usually have anyone else around you to consider when you're regulating how you operate and handle your emotions, and for as much as you're so good at regulating other people, I think that it makes you overconfident sometimes." Christie's brows pulled together. She hummed. "I don't think overconfidence is the right word."

Jed smiled, though the gesture did not reach his eyes. Christie noticed the sadness that filled them.

"Makes me self-sufficient?" Jed guessed.

"Yes, that's exactly it," Christie agreed. "And to your own detriment because you don't ask for help." She wagged her finger at him. "You think that because you're a therapist you can analyze all your own emotions and handle it all on your own. It drives me nuts sometimes, watching you keep all those thoughts in that mind of yours and never letting them out except when they manage to slip through your eyes."

Jed's throat was now dry. His mouth felt like it was clogged with wet sand. He hadn't realized that this was going to be a psychoanalysis session. But somehow, he didn't mind. Actually, it was making him feel very... seen. He smiled suddenly. He wasn't used to being at this end of the conversation.

"Is the NYPD paying you extra to psychoanalyze me?"

Christie gave him another one of her rueful smiles. "For you, I would do it for free."

Jed sighed. Looking over Christie's head to the kitchen in the far corner of the wide space, he let her words and concern settle into his mind.

"You're right," he admitted, after exhausting all the other possible responses he could offer. "There's no point in trying to explain why I do it or how I ended up being so committed to this practice of mine. You're right." He looked back down at her. "It tickles me that you've been paying so much attention to me, though, Detective. Whenever I point out the subtle things that you do, you make it seem like I'm being weird for noticing your patterns and habits."

Christie shifted uncomfortably under Jed's intense gaze. "Well," she began, "it's just that no one else has ever really…"

Jed picked up the sentence where she had left off, "… *seen* me the way you do."

If the surprise in her eyes was anything to go by, she hadn't anticipated that he would pick up on what she was going to say. Jed smiled at her.

"It's interesting that we both feel the same way. I'm happy that I make you feel seen."

Christie swallowed, watching the way his eyes darkened as they studied her face. "I'm happy I make you feel seen, too," she added, "but I'm not gonna let you change the subject, Jed. How is your heart?"

Reaching forward, Christie took Jed's hand in hers and squeezed. Jed groaned.

"I'm feeling very unwell. I don't even know what to do with myself. I've journaled, kept up my routines, but nothing seems to ease the burning in my heart. And by natural progression, I know that since my routines are solid and my journaling habit is sound, the only thing I can do is feel the feelings and let them pass. This is grief we're talking about. Of course it hasn't disappeared in three weeks. I don't know why I'm expecting it to go away so fast. I know the stages, I know the symptoms, I know how to process pain, and I'm still struggling so hard."

Absentmindedly, Christie let her fingers slip between Jed's. He looked down at their connected hands, willing himself not to pull her into his chest and hold her captive there. "It's hard. And I know it's supposed to be hard. But it's still hard that it's hard."

Christie was nodding along. Everything Jed was saying made perfect sense.

"Do you think that because you're a therapist, and you know all the stages and all the timelines, that you put additional pressure on yourself to get through them quickly?" Christie asked. "Or at least to get through them perfectly?"

Jed's thoughts paused for a moment, and he rolled the question around in his mind. Eventually, he laughed a little.

"Yeah, Detective, you're spot on. Intellectualizing your emotions is a sure away to find yourself in a loop of misunderstanding. Even though you know that emotions do not follow logical protocol 99% of the time, you still expect them to. We all do it. We intellectually know what we should do, what the right thing to do is… but we often fall into our comfort zones and continue doing what we have always done—to our detriment, even when we know better."

"And," Christie added, "you still beat yourself up when they don't work, even though you know what the failure rate is." Her eyes softened. "Do you think you're still doing it because somewhere in your mind, you're still holding yourself responsible for not noticing that Ethan was slipping back into addiction?"

Jed winced. "Fuck, you're really going in tonight, huh?" He chuckled dryly. "Really going for the throat, Detective."

Christie flushed. Jed ran his free hand through his hair, keeping his eyes on their intertwined hands. The urge to pull her into his arms so she was lying flat on his chest on top of him had not disappeared. In fact, the longer he sat across from her, watching her eyes alight with concern and worry for him, the more he wanted to comfort her until she was back to her happy self.

"It probably is, Detective," Jed sighed. "At this stage…" he hesitated, biting down on his lip. "At this stage, it might seem stupid to say, but something about the way the case wrapped up still rubs me the wrong way. There are still things about it I haven't been able to reconcile. And I guess that part of me is holding me responsible for not seeing the signs because it can see something I can't."

"Oh, Jed," Christie offered. "Are you okay with the realization that you may never be able to truly reconcile those things?"

"No," Jed replied firmly. "Sooner or later, when I have enough mental space to breathe, I'm going to revisit the case, just to walk through the events that took place. It may seem like desperately clutching at straws to you, but there's something there I need to revisit—something I haven't been able to shake, a weird premonition of sorts. Everything has logical reasoning, as well as a host of emotional components—every murder, every glass of alcohol a man drinks, every inch of hair a woman cuts off each night in the bathroom when she's trying to change her appearance. And the only thing that's different with murder cases is the added element of the perpetrator because we can't be sure what they were thinking. With Ethan's death, neither the logical progression nor the emotional components make sense to me. And that lets me know that there's more to it than we can see."

Christie squeezed Jed's hand again. "I get that," she said, "and I partly agree."

Jed raised a brow. "Only partly?"

Christie smiled. "Yes, partly. I just mean that I don't have the full context of who Ethan was. I don't know his story, or where he had been in in his journey when he was killed. So, I can't see all the elements you're seeing. But I trust that you're seeing clearly."

"I appreciate that, Detective."

Christie's warm smile spread across her face. "I brought you a gift," she said, reaching for her purse on the table and letting go of Jed's hand.

Jed watched her dig through her purse. "Oh? You did? What kind of gift might that be?"

"Oh, it's nothing that special," Christie's voice was nonchalant.

Jed watched her pull out a large bar of chocolate. He hummed, satisfaction settling into his heart.

"I remember you saying at some point in our conversations that this was your favorite chocolate," Christie stated, her eyes beaming with excitement. "So, I got you a bar on my way over."

She handed it to him. Jed took it in his left hand, then stretched his right hand out to her. Confusion filtered into her features, and Jed watched her face as she tried to figure out what he wanted. After a moment, she looked up at him, her brows scrunched cutely together.

"What's the matter? I only brought one."

Jed let his eyes drop to her hands. "Your hand, Detective. Our hands were intertwined. I want your hand back where it was. In mine."

Christie flushed again before placing her hand in his. He slipped his fingers between hers and settled their hands in the same position that they had been in. With his other hand, he deftly opened the wrapper of the chocolate and popped a piece into his mouth. Then, Jed broke off another piece and stretched his hand out to Christie, toward her lips. Her ears burned as she parted her lips and let Jed slip the chocolate between them. He leaned back, seemingly unaffected, as he chewed through his own piece.

She chided herself. *You need to get your mind out of the gutter.* Jed tilted his head, surveying her.

"What's the matter, Detective? Not used to being fed?"

She sighed, resigning herself to the fact that her ears were going to be burning for at least the next five minutes and chuckled. "No, I'm afraid I'm not. I am quite proficient at feeding myself. I've been doing it for many years now."

Jed nodded, watching her through dark eyes.

"I think it's wonderful that you were so touched by Ethan's life that you want to look deeper into his case. I don't think you're crazy for wanting to find answers. I don't think it makes you avoidant or deluded. If anything, I think it makes you brave and far more in touch with your core and your values than you let on. We all have certain cases that affect us deeply, and we carry them with us. The unsolved ones can really haunt you."

Jed's movement paused, and he looked over at Christie. "Thank you," he said. "That means a lot."

Suddenly leaning forward, Christie pulled her hand out of his before stretching both her arms out to offer Jed a hug. Grinning, Jed put the chocolate down on the coffee table and reached forward, slipping his arms around Christie's waist, pulled her forward so that she was resting completely on his chest. *Oh no,* she thought. *My cheeks are absolutely flaming. I'll never live this down.* Jed didn't seem to notice Christie's dilemma, and if he did, he certainly didn't mind.

"I've been wanting to do this since you first got here," he admitted under his breath, "but I didn't want to be the one to initiate it because I didn't want you to think my intentions are skewed."

"And what would I think those intentions were?" Christie dared to ask.

Jed laughed, the sound making her heart race as she felt his chest move beneath hers. "Your curiosity is admirable, Detective."

That was all he said. Christie fell silent for a while, until she had a thought she felt was worth saying. In truth, a million things had been racing through her mind in the small space of time since they had settled into their new position, but she hadn't trusted that anything that came out of her mouth while she was still so nervous would have made sense.

"Jed," she ventured as she melted even further into his arms, "what's your love language? Have I ever asked you that before?"

Jed smiled, leaning his cheek down against the side of her head. "No, Detective, you haven't. My primary love languages are physical touch and quality time."

Christie blinked. "That makes... so much sense."

Jed looked down at her.

She nodded. "It does. I've noticed that even though you like physical contact, you don't tend to initiate it. And I've noticed that, of course, you enjoy spending time with me... and people in general. I imagine it's the same with all the people in your life?"

Jed was quiet for a while as he let his mind think through all the relationships in his life. "It is. I haven't seen my friends in a while, and I haven't visited my mom in a while either. But of course, I do try to make the quality time aspect of things work through talking to my friends—random texts here and there, a quick call once in a while."

"Is that what you meant when you said that you spending time with me charges your batteries? Or is that different?"

Jed thought for a moment. "It's different, but it's the same. It's different in the way that being with you is...easier on my energy than being with my friends. A lot of the time... hell, all the time, when I'm with my friends, I fall into the role of being the fixer. It's so natural. But spending time with you doesn't pull on my energy reserves in the same way. Most of the time, I would be content to just fall asleep with you in the same space. I don't feel pressured to talk. I don't feel like I have to solve all your problems in one session. It doesn't feel... like I'm at work. And I'm not saying that my friends are bad people or that they're using me. That's not it at all. It's just that being the helper and the fixer is my default as a friend."

Jed paused for a moment, thinking through the words he wanted to say next.

"But when I say filling my tank," he said, trailing his hand up to tangle their fingers together, "physical touch is more like filling up your gas tank at the gas station, while quality time feels more like taking a rest day from the gym so that you don't cause yourself more pain. One actively fills up the tank, while the other mostly just doesn't detract anything from what is there. Is that confusing?" Jed asked, realizing that he had probably butchered that explanation.

"No, I understand you perfectly," Christie quickly said.

Jed took a deep breath in and then sighed. "Good. That's good. I'm glad that you understand."

"Is that why you never initiate physical contact?" Christie asked suddenly, as though the dots had just connected in her mind. "The way you sometimes demand quality time?"

Jed laughed. "Yes and no. Physical touch feels like I'm taking from you, so I don't necessarily want to constantly be doing it. Quality time is easier for both of us."

"But physical touch is better at filling up your tank," Christie finished for him. "Even when your tanks are empty, you're busy worrying about other people. It really is admirable. Most people I've worked with in this industry are only ever concerned about how the situations and people around them benefit them. It's rare to find someone who's actively concerned about the way their presence and their needs impact other people."

Pressing her hands into the soft material of the sofa beneath Jed, Christie pushed until she had raised herself up enough to look him straight in the eye.

"But I don't want you to feel so concerned about the way your needs impact me," she continued. She tilted her head at him the way he always did. "I'm not as fragile as you may think."

The space between them was small enough for Jed to feel her breath on his lips, and his heart quivered at the thought that ran through him—the thought that almost slipped out of his lips. *I want to kiss you so badly.*

"If you need a hug," Christie said, "you should just tell me instead of keeping it all to yourself and trying to supplement that with quality time. If you're hungry, you can't keep drinking water and expect to feel full."

Jed smiled. "Yeah, the NYPD must be giving you a hefty bonus this month. You are working overtime."

Christie laughed before lowering herself again to settle into his hold. She tightened her arms around Jed, hoping the silent gesture would reassure him that she had meant everything she had said. His hands were stroking through her hair, and exhaustion seeped into her bones. She would only rest in his arms for a few more minutes, and then she would head home.

CHAPTER 11

THE NEXT MORNING, AS Christie's eyes opened and she stretched, raising her arms above her head and yawning, a startling realization froze her midway.

She didn't feel tired. After a long, long time, it seemed like her night's sleep had actually fulfilled its purpose: it had fully recharged her batteries. Just a few hours ago, her mind had been a dusty, dirt-riddled window which now felt squeaky clean. And as she rolled over lazily in bed, enjoying this new restful energy coursing through her, last night's memories came trickling back. Christie remembered how she had dozed off in Jed's arms, lulled into a deep sleep by the warm, protective comfort of his embrace. She also recalled coming slightly awake a while later, only to find herself in Jed's car as he drove her home. Beyond that, the last thing she could recall was Jed tucking her into her own bed, pulling the covers up to her chin like her mother used to do when she was young.

A dreamy smile broke its way onto Christie's face. She squeezed her eyes shut and relished those warm, happy memories, basking in their glow. She was only able to enjoy it for a few moments, though, before her phone pinged with a message.

Good morning, Detective. I hope you slept well.

Before she could respond in the affirmative, her ringtone blared, and Chief Lucas' caller ID popped up. *Uh oh.* That could only mean one thing.

"Morning, Detective," Chief Lucas said. His voice was gruff, and there was no sign of sleepiness in it. "We've got a murder on our hands to start the morning off—a drive by shooting on 57th St. at the hot dog stand near the coffee shop at the four-way intersection."

"Hot dog stand?" Christie repeated, launching herself out of bed and rushing into her bathroom to start getting ready so she could get to the station as soon as possible.

"Yes," the chief affirmed. "One of the customers was gunned down while he was in the middle of his order. There weren't very many people at the stall at that time. The owner's busy time is lunch and supper. In the mornings, he offers coffee and breakfast wraps. Only a handful people were around, but the owner of the stall and the other customers that were present are all understandably shaken up by this whole ordeal."

Christie nodded as she rummaged through the drawers on her bathroom vanity, pulling out her brush and hair scrunchy. She walked to her bedroom and grabbed a pair of pants and shirt from the closet.

"Right. I will stop by the scene on my way to the office. Are you able to request access to the CCTV footage of the incident? I'll take a look at it and start a breakdown of events as soon as I'm at the station."

In his own office, the chief sighed and nodded. "Yeah, keep me updated as always. I know you and Jed will get to the bottom of this one, too."

She splashed her face with some water, pulled her hair into a quick ponytail, then she brushed her teeth. As she was getting dressed, she was replaying the chief's conversation. 57th St—that was the street Jed's office was on. She shuddered at the thought of him walking by while the shooting was happening and was very relieved that the owner of the stall hadn't been shot. Christie hurried through the rest of her routine before calling Jed.

In his office, Jed picked up the call on the first ring.

"Detective?"

"Gray. Where are you?" Christie demanded.

"I'm in my office, just getting started on the day's papers. Good morning to you, too. Is everything alright?"

"Far from it, I'm afraid. There's been a murder on your street this morning, at the hot dog stand you love so much. I've had word that officers are processing the scene and that we've requested the CCTV footage. I can get to the office soon. I'd like you to pop in so we can review. Do you have any clients this morning?"

"I have a client call later in the afternoon at around four." Jed's voice had turned brisk and businesslike. There was also an undertone of dismay in it he was trying to conceal. "Otherwise, today is paperwork day. I'm all yours."

In her room, Christie nodded. "Great. I'm going down to the scene, and then I'll see you at the station in an hour."

"I'll be there," Jed answered swiftly, before hanging up.

Jed finished up the application he had been working on and read it over for any errors before emailing it off. He looked at his watch; it had been thirty minutes since Christie's call. He would wrap up things now and head down to the station.

Outside his office building, Jed peered down the street, trying to get a good sightline of Jamie's stall. It was a good distance away, far enough that he doubted he would have heard any gunshots ring out, if a gun was what had been used to execute the murder. Christie hadn't mentioned any details about the murder itself, or the victim. His stomach twisted into a nauseous knot as that foreboding thought entered his mind yet again. Jed pushed it away. He couldn't stand here worrying about who had gotten shot. If it was Jamie, the owner of the stall, Jed didn't have a very good feeling about that. Jamie's death suggested a pattern, one way or the other. Either the two strange deaths were unconnected, or the killer was purposefully targeting people from the culinary industry.

Or people that Jed knew.

That was also possible.

As he was making his way past the crime scene, the police officers he had seen when he peered down the road were still present. There were five officers that he could see, two of them still speaking to people who must have witnessed the incident. Three other officers were taking photos as evidence that would be used in the investigations. Now that he was closer, he recognized them as Carter, Graham, Jason, Derek, and Joseph.

Jed stopped for a quick chat with them, and they gave him a debrief of their initial findings. He could still see the dried, red stain on the sidewalk. The body had already been removed. Jed knew he would see those photos later on.

When he arrived at the station and had made his way to Christie's office, Jed found her chewing on a croissant, and drinking coffee. Jed was surprised to see Joseph was standing by her side; he must have driven from the scene to the station in a hurry. The young, boyish looking fellow's hair was plastered to his forehead in wet clumps, and his eyes were ringed with weariness. Clearly, this new murder was adding to the already stressful workload the police force was dealing with.

"Hey, guys," Jed greeted them as he walked over. His eyes drifted to Joseph, and he saw that the poor guy looked even more disheveled from up close. A wild patch of bronze stubble coated his face, thicker in some places than in others. There were dark circles as big as craters hovering just beneath his eyes, resembling purplish-blue bruises.

Jed was a therapist. Helping people out was his profession. Before he could even realize what he was doing, the words were already out of his mouth.

"Seems like you're going through a bit of a rough patch, Joseph."

Joseph looked slightly startled at Jed's observation, as if he hadn't been expecting him to say that. But then his shoulders sagged, and he just nodded.

"Joseph's little brother often passes by the hotdog stand on his way to school," Christie explained to Jed. "His name's Henry, and he's the cutest eleven-year-old boy you'll ever meet. Joseph was just worried that if the shooting had taken place at any other time…"

Jed sucked in a sharp breath, not needing any more explanation. He took in Joseph's stricken face and marveled at the ripple effect one murder could have—how it affected dozens, if not hundreds and thousands of people, even if they had no relation to the victim.

"I just spent the whole weekend playing Tekken 5 with him," Joseph murmured, trying for a smile but managing only a grimace. "We stayed up late, till four in the morning, hell-bent on kicking each other's asses. And then I receive this news about the drive-by shooting. God, I can't even imagine what I would have done if Henry had been passing by t—"

"You don't need to imagine, Joseph," Christie interrupted him softly. "Henry is perfectly fine, and you've been working too hard. Go, take the day off. Get the sleep you need and come back tomorrow refreshed. Then we, can work together to find the sons of bitches who did this."

Joseph nodded before muttering a quiet farewell to both Jed and Christie and trudging out of the office. Jed watched him go, feeling a sudden prick of sympathy for the young man.

"Right." Christie cleared her throat and stood up. She scooped up a pair of files from her desk and gestured for Jed to follow her. "Come. We'll talk in the investigation room."

Frowning, Jed wordlessly obeyed. He was having flash-backs to the first murder they had worked on together. As they settled into the chairs in the room, Christie cleared her throat.

"I know what you're probably thinking," she began, "but no, you're not a suspect in this case." Then, she sighed.

"This current murder takes precedence over Joel's case, since it could possibly be related to gang violence, and those are always priority cases for the police." She brushed a stray lock of hair out of her eyes and continued, "Joel's case has been assigned to a subsidiary unit in the meantime. They'll be continuing their investigations, trying to trace the source of the poison or the gun from which it could have been fired. If and when they find anything, they'll contact us immediately.

In the meantime," she leaned forward and locked eyes with Jed, "I need your undivided attention for this newest murder."

"Got it, Detective," Jed answered softly.

Satisfied with his answer, Christie nodded once, then opened the file to its newest page and read from the single paragraph printed on it.

"Blake Gerald, 27 years old, 5 foot 11 inches tall, a construction worker by trade, was gunned down in a drive-by shooting this morning on 57th Street at Jamie's hot dog stand at around 8:15."

Christie paused and looked up at Jed, who was in the throes of sweet relief. It wasn't Jamie that had gotten shot. By the time he had passed the stall on his way to the station, he hadn't seen Jamie. He nodded, and Christie continued.

"His injuries include three gunshot wounds to the chest and abdomen, and he succumbed to those injuries before he made it to the hospital. The assailants drove down the street and opened fire from inside their vehicle. We have eyewitness reports and CCTV footage showing that they were driving in a blacked-out Honda Civic."

Jed suddenly twitched, as if attacked with a seizure. A muscle in his lower jaw clenched, and his hands squirmed uneasily on his lap. Christie did not fail to notice.

"What's up? Is everything alright, Gray?"

Jed nodded, not wanting to distract her from the matter at hand. Christie looked skeptical but continued.

"Initial background checks have turned up with results that lead us to the understanding that Blake has been having a number of previous run-ins with the dominant gang around these parts. I did some looking into our records about this gang and found out that they had a run-in with our officers a couple of months ago. The round up of that altercation was that both gangsters were shot and injured, then arrested in connection to the murders that took place."

Jed said nothing. He already knew how the story ended. He had quite literally watched it all play out. He listened to her explain the rest of her findings and deductions, until she had gone through everything on her list. At the end of it, Christie looked up again.

"You look like you've got something to say." Christie's voice was wary. "What's up?"

"The gang you're mentioning and their run-in with the officers... I worked on that case."

Surprise flowered across her face, wrinkling her forehead.

"You did?" Christie looked down at her notes again, reading through them. "That seems like a big detail to miss in a situation like this." She looked up at Jed again. "How did I overlook that?" she asked, more to herself than to Jed.

Jed swallowed, trying to regain his voice. He could sense a numbness leaking into his body, spreading quickly to his hands and legs.

"That case is how I met Ethan," he finally croaked.

Christie's head snapped up, and her eyes were dismayed.

"He witnessed a murder by that same gang, and our plot to corner them led to the shooting match that left both of them injured and arrested… and one of our detectives also injured."

Shock warred with the dismay and sadness on Christie's face, turning her expressions into a battlefield of heated emotions. She scowled. "Since that arrest, they have been laying almost completely low, with only two reports coming in since then of two victims who were robbed in separate incidents."

Jed nodded. "What made them come out of the woodwork the last time was that someone witnessed one of their heinous attacks. It's probable that Blake had also witnessed something."

Christie nodded as she wrote. "That is a good angle to look at it from. I'll have to do some digging and see if we can interview some of the people closest to him about whether he had mentioned anything of this sort."

"It could be a number of things," Jed added. "It could be that he witnessed something, it could be that he owed them money, or a favor, or it could be that he had stolen from them. All of those things are big enough threats to the gang's operation and the sovereignty they're trying to establish to make them come out of hiding and shoot someone in broad daylight. That's what happened with Ethan's case."

Christie waited, her eyes resting on Jed, as he continued the story. "They pulled up to shoot the drug dealer Ethan and his friend, Ryan, had just bought drugs from not even a minute before. And of course, they shot him, and he died. No one can run faster than bullets discharged from a gun, after all. But because Ethan and Ryan had found themselves in the age-old predicament of being in the wrong place at the wrong time, the gang started a manhunt for them both. Ryan was gunned down in his apartment before Ethan could even let him know he had heard that they were looking for them, and because Ethan was my client at the time, recommended to me by the NYPD, he and I got to talking about the case. In the end, the arrest for the murders the gang committed in that timeframe was settled because Ethan gave his witness testimony."

Christie stared at Jed, watching him relay the heavy story and critical information without flinching or any hint of sadness. She would have to check in with him later about it. For now, they needed to get as much information about the events that had been unfolding as fast as was feasible.

"So, they attack in the open when you make them feel threatened. It sends a clear message to anyone else that may be thinking of challenging the gang. Word spreads quickly with witnesses," Jed finished.

"That makes sense. The family and friends we'll interview should give us a good footing to figure out their motive for the attack." Christie leaned back in her seat. "Regardless of their motives, we do have CCTV footage that shows the vehicle used in the attack, as well as, of course, the surroundings right before and during the shooting."

Christie the remote at the screen and pulled up the video for them to watch. Sighing heavily as she readied herself to watch the tragedy unfold, she glanced over at Jed.

"Ready?" she asked.

Jed met her eyes, and his only response was another nod. She clicked 'play'.

For 30 seconds, they watched in silence as the screen showed the milling about of the morning crowds on 57th St. At 37 seconds into the video, Blake walked into the frame from the right-hand side, heading up the street. He approached Jamie's stall, and for another 15 seconds, he stood in front of the stall, waiting for whatever he had ordered to be prepared. Jed could see Jamie's hands shuffling, choosing toppings and squirting cheese and mayo. If he closed his eyes and tried to see the scene in his mind, he could smell the delicious aroma of the breakfast wrap Jamie was preparing.

Then, right before Blake raised his hand to accept his breakfast, a blacked-out Honda Civic drove into the frame from the right side, the same direction from which Blake had appeared. That meant they had been trailing him, waiting for the perfect moment to strike. At one minute and five seconds into the footage, the car's tinted black window slid down. The sleek barrel of a gun poked through it, pointing at its target who was entirely unaware that his life had reached its end. A moment later, the gun fired, its muzzle drowned in a white flash as the bullet tore its way through the black throat of its prison. There was no sound in the footage. All they saw was

Blake convulse comically to one side, as if he had suddenly decided to burst out into an eccentric dance. He went flying to the left, but his feet never left the ground. Instead, they crumpled beneath him, and soon he was lying on the sidewalk in a twisted heap, his face staring up at nothing.

In the fray, Jamie and all the other patrons, as well as the people who had been passing by, scrambled in every direction, and the black Civic sped off up the street, leaving a trail of destruction behind it. When the video had ended, Jed looked down at the table for a long moment without speaking. Christy interjected, breaking the silence.

"Do you recognize the vehicle?"

Jed nodded, raising his head to look at her. "It looks exactly the same as the one that was following Ethan and me. It might just be that the gang has multiple other cars of the exact make model and style. Maybe that's their version of a uniform."

Christie was nodding along and taking notes, and Jed paused for a while.

"What I can say, though, is this: these guys are very good at tracking down their targets, and have excellent aim."

Christie looked up at him, confusion clear in her expression. Jed shrugged.

"In the initial case, where I first had the displeasure of interacting with the damage they are capable of, they had tracked down the drug dealer, shot him dead, and tracked down Ryan, who, even though he was a witness, hadn't even actually seen the murder in the first place. Ethan was the one who saw what happened. They killed another drug dealer and a little girl between murdering Ryan and trying to find Ethan. But they got to Ryan in just a matter of a day or so, shot him dead, and by the time Ethan realized he needed to give his statement—after he had abandoned his apartment and moved somewhere safer—they were tracking him down, too. They showed up outside my office as we were in the process of entering the police car to go to the station for his witness statement."

Christie was writing briskly, not stopping to look up at Jed or respond.

"The run-in we had was because they were tailing us in their car, probably hoping we wouldn't recognize them and that we would get out of the car at the police station where they could open fire in a drive-by attack. Luckily, Ethan recognized them as we got into the police cruiser, so the police could come up with a plan to save us."

Christie was listening intently, pausing every now and then to make more notes about what Jed was saying.

"This is all very valuable information," she murmured as she wrote. "I'm so glad to have you on my team, Gray."

For the first time since he'd arrived, Jed cracked a smile. "You have Ethan to thank for that. He's the reason the NYPD decided to forge our collaboration."

Christie looked up at him, sadness returning to her eyes. "I am far more indebted to Ethan than I could have ever realized."

The two looked at each other for a long while, neither of them speaking as they let the words spoken between them settle into the air.

"Well," Jed breathed in a shudder, deciding to share what he had been thinking during the past few moments of silence, "one thing is interesting. When you told me initially that there had been a murder at Jamie's stall, my first thought was that this murder would be connected to Joel's murder. But so far, the two are on opposite ends of the spectrum. The only thing that connects them is the fact that Joel had been in the middle of cooking and Blake was ordering food, right about to collect it. The common thread between the two is food and a good shot."

Christie tapped a pen against the table. "So, do you think we should look into these same gang members being potentially involved with Joel's murder? And speaking of Joel, we've had the reports finally come in this morning when I arrived." Christie sighed heavily, and Jed watched her run a hand through her hair to push the strands out of her face. "The poison inside the dart is called VX. It's a very potent nerve agent. It can be fatal via inhalation or by absorption through the skin. And of course, in Joel's case, if it gets directly into your bloodstream, you're dead instantly."

Jed's eyes narrowed, a thought that he'd had in the initial aftermath of Joel's murder coming back to mind.

'That's the thing," he grunted, crossing his arms over his chest. "Whoever the person is that shot that dart must have also loaded the dart with the poison. It's not as though there are prepackaged VX darts already available on the market for anyone to buy. They would have had to acquire the poison, acquire the dart gun, *and* fill the dart up with the poison themselves. I think that shows just how manically determined this killer is. Who would risk their own life to kill someone else? They had to accept that danger at an early stage. Before they even figured out where the Airbnb was, who was in attendance, or who their target was, they would have had to interact with that nerve agent themselves."

Christie's lips pressed in a thin line as she took in Jed's deductions.

"This person is completely unhinged," he added. "That does not rule out the gang, though. They have murdered people in broad daylight, in public places, and in front of witnesses. I wonder if they commit murders-for-hire. Maybe rich, little Mr. Brooks hired them."

"Based on what you're seeing here, I agree," Christie mused. "This person is completely reckless and clearly has no regard for their own life in the pursuit of taking the life of another. The time is ticking for us. With this kind of poison in their hands, they could be anywhere—staked out, with more darts ready to go, waiting for the perfect opportunity to strike."

Jed's eyes narrowed at Christie, and she frowned. "The longer I think about you walking around alone at night, the more I feel the urgency of solving this case, Detective. We cannot afford to give this killer the chance to aim at you… or at anyone else."

Christie nodded solemnly. "Okay. The first thing we need to focus on is getting these interviews done. I'll have Graham and Joseph contact Blake's family and friends, and we can go from there. Next, we need to look into trying to make out the license plate number of this blacked-out Honda from what footage we have. That will help us find out the registered owner of the vehicle much more easily than just walking around New York, hoping to run into the car. I'll ask Joseph to get on that when he comes back in."

Jed was watching Christie make a short note and shuffle her papers around.

"I would suggest that we orchestrate a stake out, but that would be too dangerous. Those guys aren't at all the type to let someone walk away from an interaction after someone's rubbed them the wrong way. I'm surprised at how long Blake lasted, if he really had been having run-ins with them in the past," Jed said.

Christie agreed, noting all the points Jed was making. "We'll have to go the route of the license plate, and if that turns up nothing, I'll have Jason, Carter, and Derek do some scouting in plain clothes around the areas we know are teeming with gang activity—thanks to our initial case with Ethan. I will reach out to the gang unit to see if they have any insights as well."

Jed chimed in, "After that, I want two things in motion. I want us to focus on the logistics of Joel's murder. I'm gonna do some research on my own time and find out as much about the VX as I can. You…" Jed said firmly, pointing at Christie as he spoke, "your instructions are simple, Detective. You cannot leave this police station unless you are in the company of an armed police officer in a police vehicle or unless you are with me. That includes going to and from work and going anywhere else. I will not let you walk around freely until we bring this person down."

Christie swallowed. She wanted to resist the restriction that Jed was placing on her, but she knew he was right. There was no wisdom in fighting the issue, since she could very well be in grave danger at any moment. Poison like that, which had already claimed two lives, could not be taken lightly—especially when they weren't sure whether the two murders were connected or if there was a more sinister, larger looming over them as they tried to figure it all out.

CHAPTER 12

"You know, Mom," Jed said, using the hands-free speaker on his cellphone as he made his way to his sofa and sat down after closing the door behind him. "I think I'm finding myself getting more and more frustrated about this case." He set the phone down on the cushion next to him as he made himself comfortable.

"Why is that?" Laurie asked, setting her writing aside as she listened to her son continue.

"I'm not even sure," Jed breathed, sighing as he let the frustration of the day settle into his mind. "There was another murder today. So, for starters, we're already at two murders in two days. But outside of that, things just aren't making sense to me. I'm starting to get a very subtle, unsettled feeling that I'm missing something. It's the same feeling I had when Christie and I were working on Ethan's case. Nothing seems to be adding up yet. I feel like, if I could only get a bird's-eye view, I would finally understand what's actually going on. But right now, I feel like I'm stuck inside of a maze—one of left turns and right turns and circles and loops that land me right back where I started out. The walls are too high for

179

me to climb up to see anything even resembling a bird's-eye view. Overall, it's really annoying. And my worry for Christie is increasing."

Laurie had inclined her head in thoughtful acknowledgement. What Jed was saying made sense. The only reason she was able to write her story about the small-town murder that had taken place and the detective's journey to figuring out who had done the deed was because of her bird's-eye view as the author. She knew who had done it. Even if she hadn't worked out all the mechanics of how it would happen or what the motives were, or how best to portray the detectives' journey to figuring it out, the important thing was that she knew who did it. Jed didn't know. And that was what was frustrating about the situation.

"I suppose I understand," Laurie finally agreed after a few moments. "I guess it's sometimes that the bird's-eye view comes at the end, when we already have all the pieces and can see how everything fits together."

Sprawled on the sofa of the living room, Jed hummed in agreement. "Yeah, and sometimes that happens too late. By the time all the elements come together, multiple lives have been lost that could have been saved, and a lot of time has been wasted that could have also been saved." His voice was knotted with worry. "Sometimes, I just wish I could fly. Maybe I'd get to the top of this maze easier and be able to see my way out."

Laurie laughed along with her son as they settled into the rest of the conversation.

"And what about Christie?" she asked, suddenly remembering that Jed had mentioned her.

"She was working on a case that wrapped up right before this one started." Jed responded. "The suspect threatened her, and then the murder occurred at the Airbnb where we were staying. I'm not sure if it's connected to his threat, but I'm keeping my eyes open. I don't want to minimize the potential link between the threat and the events that have been happening, then risk her being injured... or worse. We have some theories we're working with but nothing concrete so far. I can't help feeling like there are still things missing. We need to sort through the evidence, and we need to come up with some solutions. It feels like the answers are just in my periphery. But when I turn to look, they disappear."

Laurie chewed her bottom lip thoughtfully. "So, I guess we're at the point in the story where things are heating up but we're not sure how they're gonna all work out?"

Jed muttered a yes, realizing his mom was likening his real-life experiences to the book she was writing. She had messaged him earlier that day to tell him that she had finally made a breakthrough in how the case in her story would be solved.

"The stakes are rising," Jed said. "This time, I don't even feel like I have enough time or room to escape to the lake and try to figure things out. I feel like I have to keep my feet on the ground at all times and try to work through this while everything is still happening all around me."

"How have you been managing with Ethan's passing?" Laurie asked.

Jed groaned in response. "Not great, Mom. Not great at all. Christie and I actually had a conversation about that recently, and I've been trying to be more open with letting people know I'm not necessarily doing 'well'."

Laurie grinned. "Well, that's good to hear. I'm glad you were able to share with Christie and are sharing it with me. You know, I think I quite like that young lady. She's getting through to you in all the right ways."

In the darkness of his room, Jed flushed. His ears burned. "Yeah, whatever, Mom."

Laurie laughed. "I hope you find a way to clear your mind enough to focus on the things that are in front of you, or beside you, as you said. Even if you can't see overhead, you can try the elimination tactic you did at the lake—logical progression and all that. That's been helping me with my story. One of the leads you have must take you somewhere. And if the one you have leads nowhere, it means that there are others you haven't seen yet. You just have to keep searching and find the one that takes you out of that maze you're stuck in."

"Uh-huh," Jed murmured. "Yeah, you're right. I'm gonna stay up tonight and do some thinking. I need to work through what's happened and lay it all out. I can't let anything happen to Christie."

After hanging up the call, Jed found himself alone with his own thoughts once more. Like most of the days he'd had recently, today had been long. After making Christie promise that she wouldn't leave the station unless she was accompanied by an officer, Jed had walked himself home.

Of course, thoughts of Christie being alone with another man kept him from fully relaxing. It was completely unnecessary, the worry and jealousy that gripped his heart. He knew it was unfounded. But even then, though he tried to talk himself down off the cliff he seemed to be on, he hadn't truly relaxed until Christie had messaged him saying that she had gotten home safely. He had made her promise to do that, too.

After making himself some dinner—it was just him plating a pizza he had ordered instead of eating from the box—Jed settled into his evening. He started with journaling. That turned into a strangely prolonged writing session where Jed's fingers clutched the pen, simply refused to stop moving. The words continued to materialize in front of him, his own worried thoughts taking the form of dull blue ink. And with every stroke Jed made with the pen's nib, he found himself brimming with even more to say. So many emotions and unspoken feelings were crying out for release, pleading to escape into the white freedom of the paper.

By the time he was done, a good hour later, Jed's wrist was sore, and his fingers ached. He rose up with a tired grunt and made his way over to the shower, which was his second-biggest tool for unwinding. As the scalding water pelted his skin and flattened his hair, Jed stood in the wide cubicle and stared at the wispy curls of steam rising all around him. He was suddenly very grateful that he had persevered in his early days when he had been apartment hunting before deciding on this place. The shower in this apartment was a godsend. It was wide enough to comfortably hold around six people, should he ever feel frisky enough to host a shower party.

As soon as thoughts of a shower party came to mind, he went back to Christie and the case. As Jed washed his hair, trying not to let the shampoo run straight into his eyes, he thought of all the links and angles and how they played into each other with the murders of both Blake and Joel.

Joel's murder was where this case started. A nerve agent as powerful as VX was an uncommon weapon in murder cases, even in the most gruesome. In their conversation at the station earlier that day, they had done some checks into that. As far as the NYPD's records extended, in the City of New York, poisoning accounted for about 31% of murders, but even then, nerve agents like VX, or military grade poisons, were very low on the list—slim to nil. As Jed had anticipated, most poisonings that took place were concocted or procured from household agents. Rat bait was by far the most common. That had not been a surprise to him nor Christie. It was accessible, it was easy to mix into various meals, and it was very effective.

Then, they had launched a search into the "how" of obtaining such a powerful substance. It had been almost impossible to find out where to purchase the substance, and it wasn't nearly as easily obtainable as something one could more easily use to poison someone. It was not like it could be ordered online from a retailer, or as though one could walk into a pharmacy and find it on the shelf. So, where had Joel's killer sourced VX from? Was the person who went to this extent to take Joel down in the military? Were they a hired killer who had high-level contacts? In the government even? Those kinds of connections weren't totally farfetched, since to be clear, VX was a substance used by the most powerful militaries worldwide in chemical warfare. That was the extent of what they were dealing with. But it was not so realistic for a common citizen to get their hands on it.

Many things were uncertain about the nature of the poison that had been chosen to kill Joel. One thing was certain about his killer—they were no ordinary person. As he and Christie had done more and more reading in an attempt to learn about the nature of sourcing the poison, Jed had found himself both impressed and very frightened. The person who had chosen to use this substance was clearly either a psychopath or had a massive vendetta—enough to cloud their own judgment about the realistic nature of risking one's own life—against Joel.

After they had spent some time digging into the nature of VX, their focus had switched to the murder that had taken place that day. Like Jed had mentioned to Christie earlier in the conversation, a connection was present. Both victims held some degree of connection to food. While Joel's connection was undoubtedly stronger, the other murder had taken place at a food stall, which was just as clearly a link to food. They were both violent and open. The killer wanted witnesses. Was the killer sending a message? Conversation had led them to explore a possible connection between the gang and Joel's murder. In theory, Jed knew that anything was possible with gangsters. They were, by nature, criminals, and they were privy to a number of ways by which to execute their plans. They would have connections to all kinds of people and different weapons. Drive-by shootings, breaking and entering, luring their victims into traps, poisonings even, were all feasible. It was plausible that they had a connection to Joel, somehow, and that they would have chosen to kill him via poisoning.

The difficulty in accessing the VX nerve agent was throwing Jed's idea off. Could they have used it? It wasn't impossible that they could have. But how would they have had access to it? As it stood, they had already made plans to try to find out what kind of interactions Blake had been having with the gang, and Jed was hopeful they would find some important information. Was anyone in the gang connected enough to get VX? Were they smart enough to use VX without killing themselves in the process?

Had Blake's offence been so low on their priority list that he had only warranted a drive-by surprise shooting versus Joel's offense being something bigger and more serious that warranted the gang going out of their way to source a rare nerve agent and risk their own lives?

Blake's death was definitely a message. It was public, with witnesses during the day. They wanted people to see it and talk about it. That is how gangs perpetuated their control over communities—using fear. Joel's death, on the other hand, was quiet and private, but witnesses were still present. Two very different messages. Hence, two different modes of operandi.

Jed would have to run that by Christie before the thought slipped out of his mind. He dialed her number. Her phone rang once, twice, three times, and then it went to voicemail. Jed's heartbeat picked up. He called again. It rang, once, twice, three times, then voicemail again. Jed launched himself across his bed, grabbing his keys before having to rush back across the room to grab his phone. Flinging a jacket over his shoulders, he headed toward his apartment door. His phone rang. It was Christie.

"Hi, Jed," Christie said a little breathlessly. "Sorry about that. I was in the kitchen and away from my phone."

"Are you alone?" Jed blurted out without thinking and then immediately hated the inquisitive tone of his voice.

Christie hesitated. "Yes, I am... unless someone has snuck in without me realizing." She looked around her living room to make sure that she was, in fact, alone.

Jed's sigh of relief surprised her.

"Everything alright, Gray?" she asked cautiously.

"No, Detective. You almost gave me a heart attack. I called you twice, and you didn't pick up. I immediately thought that something must have gone wrong, and I was about to be on my way over to your apartment."

Christie's mouth made a small 'o' of surprise. "Right. I'll keep my phone tied to my hip from now on, just in case you call."

Jed balked at the dismissive response. He stepped back inside his apartment and closed the door behind him.

"Well, what can I help you with?" Christie asked, making her way back to her room.

Jed's eyes narrowed. "I was thinking about the connection between the gang we've established as primary suspects in Blake's case. I was thinking through some angles and wondered if they could have had a hand in the first murder as well. We looked at sourcing procedures for VX, and it isn't easy to get. Gangs have many connections to bad people and even worse weapons. Everyone and everything has a price. I wonder if the gang was hired for the murder. It's a lead, and we need as many of those to look into as possible. I did also start to think about the possibility of it being the person who threatened you originally, and I'm not liking just how possible it's turning out to be in my mind. With all the red tape and lack of information publicly available about the sourcing of VX, and the connections it requires, the suspect you interviewed… that threatened you…" Jed paused as he tried to remember the boy's name, "Brooks. His family could very well know someone or themselves be holders of the required connections to access and handle a poison like that."

Having gone back into her kitchen after noticing how heavily her stomach was rumbling, Christie quickly slapped together two loaves of bread slathered with mayonnaise and a thick slice of ham. She listened as Jed continued, nodding at the mention of the 16-year-old's family potentially being connected in that way.

"Thanks, Gray," she replied when Jed had finished. "I'll add that to my list of things to look into in the morning when I get into work."

Jed nodded. "I'll let you enjoy the rest of your evening undisturbed."

Christie's eyes narrowed at the comment, but before she could reply, Jed had hung up.

It was yet again another Friday evening, and Jed's energy was spent from another week of saving the world—at least, that was what it felt like. He hadn't really been flying around the city preventing nuclear wars or thwarting alien invasions. But he had been shouldering the brunt of his clients' hard pasts and helping them walk through immensely difficult things. In his mind, it equaled out to be about the same amount of effort.

He had spoken little to Christie since their call earlier that week on Tuesday evening, and when they had spoken, it was strictly about the case. They had set up interview dates, case updates, and discussed follow-up information and new records that had come up that would influence the way they moved forward with investigations. It was all pretty clinical.

Jed had let it continue that way, despite how his heart burned. He missed their usual dynamic. He was furious with himself for letting the pattern continue. It had started after his father left. His self-preservation turned into sabotage whenever he was in a particularly emotionally charged moment in his relationships—pull away before you get too deep so you don't get hurt.

He tried to convince himself that Christie probably hadn't noticed the emotional distance as he sat at his desk, waiting for Max to call in for their weekly chat. Was it just because their working relationship was a little strained? Was that why Jed was feeling the intense ache of longing in his chest every time he thought of her? Of course. After all, that was all they were—colleagues.

He ran a hand through his hair, kicking his feet up onto his desk, reclining in the chair and crossing his arms over his chest. Jed looked at his shoes. Actually, he was a little embarrassed that Christie's casual statement had hurt him so much. It wasn't even what she'd said that had made him feel small; it was more so the tone she had used. *"I'll keep my phone tied to my hip next time, just in case you call."* Ouch. It was as though he had been interrupting her night with his incessant calling. He rolled his eyes and sighed aloud. Maybe she thought his worry for her safety was overbearing?

It wasn't as though she had made any genuine effort to repair the silence they had fallen into these past days. Maybe she hadn't even noticed—she was so caught up with work and her own life. Or maybe she simply preferred it that way. Or… maybe he was a coward. Either way, their friendship was off-kilter, and it seemed to be up to him to mend it. Jed was the only one who seemed bothered by the difference, an ever-present reminder that he was more invested in their relationship than she was. She only saw them as work partners. Of course, she wasn't having her entire week thrown off by a change in their communication levels and patterns. He huffed.

The phone rang.

"Hi, Max. How are you doing?"

"Mr. G, what's up with you on this fine Friday afternoon?"

"I'm doing well, Maxwell. How are you?"

Max chuckled as though he knew something Jed didn't.

"I'm alright, man. Y'know, Mr. G, we've got some pretty nervous agents on the ground these days. Opps. You catch my drift, Mr. G?"

After his previous case had been cracked because of Max's deductive skills, Jed took everything Max said seriously. The combination of nerve and agent in the same sentence had definitely captured his attention.

"Remind me what 'opps' are. I fear I've grown too old for the street lingo of the day."

Jed could hear Max's smile as he responded. "Opps be the people that are out to get you, trying to get your body into that there morgue on your block."

Jed's voice was casual but strained. "And there are opps on your end?"

In his usual fashion, Max laughed. "Nah, man. On your end. I know who my opps are."

Jed hummed in response. His brows scrunched at the vague references, but he made a note of what Max was saying. He would have to revisit this and chew on it long enough to figure out what the boy was trying to tell him.

"On another note, though, them boys sure love them blacked-out Hondas, huh?"

Jed had caught that throw clear as day. He needed to revisit that one with Christie, but for now, as Max was talking, he needed to put most of his attention on what else Max might say. In true form, Max changed the subject.

"But I wanted to ask you something."

"What's on your mind?" Jed asked as he settled into a comfortable position, pen poised to take more notes.

"How do you…" Max hesitated. "Y'know… fix conflicts in your friendships and relationships?"

Jed's mind blanked for a split second. The question was so off-topic, so strangely distant from all the murders and lethal poisons that filled his thoughts daily. He ran his tongue across his dry lips. Was the universe conspiring against him again?

"The best way to work through conflict in any relationship is to communicate about what's happened," Jed answered when he had recovered.

In his usual spot high in the oak tree, Max made a noise of agreement, lips splitting into a grin.

"You think it's easier or harder when it's a romantic relationship over a friendship? B'cuz talking to a friend is a one, two, three, BAP! And we're good, y'know? With women, it's like… all our wires get crossed, and suddenly we don't know how to talk no more, y'know?"

Oh, I know. I know very well.

Jed sighed. He wished he *didn't* know it so well.

"That's often the case, yes, even though that's not what we want deep down," Jed agreed.

"So, what do you think makes us give up so easy instead of just talking it out?" Max asked.

Jed tried not to sigh again and, instead, focused on stepping deeper into his role as a therapist—hear with therapist's ears, and respond with therapist's advice instead of taking everything the client was saying personally and extrapolating it to your own life.

"There are several elements that all seem to come out to play in these situations. First, there's pride. We might not want to be the ones to start the conversation because we may feel as though we were wronged, or we were right, or we were the ones who tried/initiated the resolution last time."

"Yeah," Max chimed in, his voice no longer so chipper. "That sucks when it seems like you're the only one who seems bothered by the whole thing."

In his office, Jed nodded slowly, noticing both the change in Max's tone and the way his own heart ached the longer the conversation continued.

"Yes, it does suck. It sucks tremendously," Jed affirmed. "But I suppose that, in the same way we're hiding what we're feeling and hesitating to make a move toward reconciliation, the other person is doing the same thing. Neither of the parties involved wants to make the first move because that involves us being vulnerable first. We risk being rejected, ridiculed, misunderstood, and a host of other things that would make anyone frightened. It usually boils down to fear. We don't want to admit we are scared and vulnerable."

Max's voice was even smaller and sadder when he asked his next question. "So, what do I do?"

Jed closed his eyes, realizing the words he was about to say to Max also applied perfectly to his own situation. "You have to decide. There are only two options when we really look at the situation. We can choose to ignore the conflict altogether and continue to suffer the pain of missing the person and of prolonged misunderstandings, or we can do the brave thing and reach out first by admitting we are scared, which allows us to face our fears."

Max sighed a deep sigh that Jed felt sink into him as well.

"I don't know, man. I just... I don't know. This is the first big fight we've had, y'know? And things just went quiet. I'm not used to the silence, man. I don't know what she's thinking. I don't know if she thinks I don't love her anymore or if she's already moved on or if she just... doesn't care whether we work it out or not."

Jed nodded. "Well, Maxwell, my advice would be to get down from your little spot in the tree, go see her, and talk to her. She's probably thinking the same things about you—that you probably don't even care that she's hurting or that you don't love her anymore."

"But I do!" Max insisted, frustration clear in his voice. "But it just... hurts, man. It's hard to work up the nerve."

Jed hummed. "I know the feeling."

Max perked up at that. "Do you? Have you ever been in a situation like that?"

Jed sighed thoughtfully. "Indeed. I have and I am. It's a tricky place to be in. I'm the one that has to make the move—not even just because the other person won't say anything. But more so because I'm the one that's taking the hit."

"Yeah, man. I know how that feels for sure."

"Try not to think too much about it," Jed answered. "Just do it. Breach the silence and try to make a connection. In the end, it is conversations like these where you are willing to be vulnerable that solidify your relationship and make it stronger."

Shuffling, Max started to make his way down the tree, realizing that Jed was right. He couldn't afford to let his relationship fade away because he was scared to make a move. "Yeah, man. You're right."

Now that Max had ended their call, only spending five minutes talking through the matter of conflicts and how to solve them with communication, Jed was staring at his shoes once more. Max's decision to prioritize his relationship over his therapy session wasn't lost on Jed. It was a big call for the boy to make, and Jed realized that now that his workday had ended unexpectedly early, Max had unknowingly presented him with the opportunity to do the same thing.

He stood, shutting down his systems and locking away the case file for Max that had been open on his desk. Jed pulled out his phone as he stepped into the elevator and pressed the button for the ground floor, then messaged Christie. He had mulled over whether to text or call to initiate the contact between them and had decided that the text was easiest. It gave him time to figure out what he wanted to say.

Detective, can I take you out to dinner tonight? (Please say yes.)

It was a risky text to send, and as he walked home, waving a hello to a still-shaken-up Jamie and turning down the street that led to his building, his heart was thumping harder than usual in his chest. What if she didn't want to go to dinner with him? Was it too last-minute of an invitation? What if she had plans with someone else already in place?

When he'd stepped into the elevator in his apartment complex, he forced himself to look down at his phone for a response to his message.

Sure :)

A heavy sigh of relief escaped him. The doors opened, and he walked down the hallway to his apartment and opened the door to head inside. That was a good sign—a great sign even. She said yes. That was the first step for their reconnection.

I'll pick you up at 6:00.

After showering, dressing, and grabbing his keys, Jed headed out the door once more into the early evening. Now, inside his Jeep, pulling out into the crisp, cool evening and heading to Christie's apartment, Jed felt his nerves jangling with anxiety.

It was like he was a teenage boy seeing his crush for the first time. That familiar, sweaty ache filled the center of his palms, and his heart seemed about to trip over itself with its rapid, thudding beats. Jed swallowed once, wishing he had brought a water bottle with him. His mouth was parched, his throat a dried-up well itching roughly. It would be just his luck that she didn't even realize why he was offering to connect with her outside their usual routine at the station or at the odd restaurant after discussing a case. This… this had come out of nowhere. He'd even gone to get flowers.

He pulled into a space in the parking garage, cut the engine off, and hopped out of the Jeep with his flowers in tow. Running a hand through his hair as he waited for the elevator to stop at her floor, Jed tapped his foot against the carpet.

At the door, he knocked. Now, his heart was pounding inside him louder than a trapped bull, threatening to explode out of his chest. But then she opened the door, and all his anxiety faded into a hot mix of desire and relief. She was here, in front of him, dressed and ready to go. She looked from his eyes, down to the flowers he was holding, and back to his eyes.

He reached forward, slipped his hands around her and pulled her into his chest into the tightest hug he'd given someone in a long time. Christie melted into his hold as easily as if she had been butter in a hot pan. Her arms reached up around his neck and held there, his nose pressed into her neck.

"Fuck," he whispered. "I'm sorry I went cold on you, Christie."

Christie's throat had already closed up from the sheer emotion in Jed's hug, but now she was sure that her eyes were growing moist, too. She wasn't sure what to say.

"It was terrible of me to shut down without communicating about it, especially since it was something so trivial."

They separated, and a single tear rolled down Christie's cheek. Jed wiped it away with his thumb immediately.

"I don't know how we ended up here," Jed admitted as his heart ached at the sadness he could see in Christie's features. He sighed. "Actually, I do know what happened. Something you said that hurt my feelings that I should have brought up right away. I am such an idiot."

Christie's expression shifted into one of confusion. "What did I say?"

Jed paused and closed his eyes for a moment. When he looked at her again, his head cocked to the side. "The way you asked me 'what can I do for you', and your comment about keeping your phone tied to your hip." He watched her expression for any reactions that would tell him whether she had meant to hurt him. "It made it seem like I was bothering you—like you wanted to get me off the phone."

His heart was racing again, and he felt tears prickle at the back of his eyes. Jed felt silly. That shouldn't have hurt him the way it did to begin with, but it had. It had, and now he was having to own up to it. What was the matter with him? Christie's expression softened, and she shook her head.

"You weren't bothering me. I was flattered that you called. I was just… I got into an argument with Jason before he left earlier in the evening, and the frustration might have bled into our call a little. I'm sorry."

Jed's whole body stiffened. He didn't even seem to hear the apology. "Jason?"

Christie nodded, not noticing the way Jed's eyes had darkened. "He dropped me home. You know," she said, looking up at him with a sly smile, "you said I wasn't allowed to leave the office without you or an armed officer, remember?"

Jed nodded. "I remember, alright. What was the confrontation about? Between you and him?"

"I'm not even sure how it started," Christie admitted, chewing on the inside of her cheek. "He asked to come in with me, and I said no. That's simple enough. I didn't want to blur the lines with a colleague, especially one that I outrank."

"And he didn't take kindly to you saying no?" Jed was getting angrier by the minute. Pushing back on a woman's rejection was unacceptable.

"He seemed fine about it, laughed it off. And when we got to my door, and I guess he realized I was serious, he got an attitude." Christie shrugged. "I asked him what the issue was, and he made a snarky remark about not being allowed in."

She was noticing Jed's eyes were dark, and his attention hadn't moved away from her face since she mentioned Jason.

"And you closed the door in his face and ignored him, right?"

Christie smiled sheepishly. "Yes. I told him goodnight and then came inside."

"That's my girl," Jed answered without really thinking through the connotations.

Christie's cheeks went red immediately.

"It seems like Jason needs a stern talking-to about pushing boundaries." Jed's jaws tightened. "So, you weren't annoyed that I was calling you multiple times? And you didn't think I was being a pain in the ass?"

Christie shook her head.

"And you're not... tired of me?"

She narrowed her eyes at that. "As if that could ever happen, Jed."

Jed's smile was small and tight. "Good to hear, Detective."

Reaching forward, he pulled her into another long hug, his heart finally no longer burning.

"I promise not to go cold on you again. And if you ever speak to me in a tone like that again, instead of shutting down, I'm going to assume you want me to show up on your doorstep so we can work it out."

Christie's thighs were warm, and she tried to force herself to stop blushing so furiously.

"Are we clear, Detective?" Jed pressed.

Christie nodded.

"Good." Jed looked down at the flowers in his hand. "We should put these is some water and get going. Our reservation is at seven, Detective."

When they got to the restaurant, Jed and Christie tried to keep the evening light. They did their best not to talk about work or the case, just focusing on enjoying each other's company. Jed had picked his favorite Italian restaurant, a small, family gem in the heart of the city called Gino's. The restaurant was small and family-run, using secret recipes passed through generations. Everything was made freshly every day, and the smells of their herbs and spices were delicious. There were only nine small tables in the entire place, with one tea light candle illuminating an ornate holder on each table. It was quiet, intimate.

Jed couldn't help the upticks in his heart rate every time the candlelight flickered across Christie's brown eyes and at the way it highlighted her lips. The golden light was picking up the highlights in her hair, too, where the curls fell over her shoulders. He knew she could feel his attention on her, constantly. She never looked away from his dark eyes, and it felt like their eyes were communicating things neither of their lips were saying.

Christie enjoyed the way he looked at her over the rim of his glass of water. His dark eyes seemed to pierce deep into her soul and caress it as she spoke. She never wanted the night to end. The food was amazing, and they sampled each other's dishes. Jed had the lobster-stuffed ravioli in a rich sauce, and Christie went with the pasta carbonara.

They had planned to walk down to the ice cream parlor they always went to for dessert after dinner, but once they finished eating, they were both too stuffed for anything more.

They drove back to Christie's apartment, taking a longer, more scenic route, neither of them wanting the night to end. The New York nightlife buzzed around them, yet somehow, they only had eyes for each other.

CHAPTER 13

THE SATURDAY MORNING SUN was weak, but it still shone through the lone window in the room.

"Good morning, Mr. Jones," Christie said, looking across the table at the man opposite her. "Do you mind if I record our conversation?

"No, go ahead. I just want to help," he responded.

Christie turned the recorder on and said, "Detective Christie Jamieson interviewing. Please state you name for the recording…"

"Jackson Jones," he responded evenly.

"I'm sorry for your loss. Let's start with you telling me how you know the victim, Blake Gerald."

Jackson Jones was a tall, reedy man sporting rimless glasses and a waxy complexion. His dirty blonde hair hung over his forehead in messy clumps. He wore faded denim jeans and a plain black t-shirt. The man's response was a heavy sigh—one that lasted so long that if Jed had been superstitious, he might have thought the man was releasing some kind of spell into the surrounding atmosphere. Christie was leading the interview with one of Blake's closest friends, and once again, Jed was viewing the interview from behind the one-way glass that shielded him from the interviewee's view. After his sigh, the man shrugged in a noncommittal way.

"I can't believe someone murdered my best friend," Jackson muttered in a tight voice, staring at the floor.

"Is there anything you can share with us to help us understand why this happened to your friend?" Christie asked as delicately as she could.

She saw the man roll his eyes.

"I should have been with him!" The dismay was gone now. In its place, the actual emotion Jackson had been concealing flickered to life, beginning to rage behind his eyes. It was guilt—a raw, smoldering guilt that was slowly burning him up from the inside. "But because of this stupid work trip, I missed the whole thing! Maybe if I had been there, I could have convinced him not to go to that hot dog stand when he knew good and well that bunch of idiots was trying to find him!" he blurted out, as if he was holding it in for days.

Jed perked up immediately. This was exactly what they were looking for.

"What idiots were looking for him?" Christie questioned casually, as though it was her first time coming across any information that could have implied that Blake was having run-ins with people who might want him dead.

"That gang." Jackson waved his hand dismissively. "I don't even remember what they're called. I told him not to get involved with them, but of course, he didn't listen. He con-

vinced himself that they would never have turned on him."
There was a pause, before he whispered under his breath,
"Idiot."

Jackson lowered his head, and Christie saw his hands clench
into fists as he held back the tidal wave of emotions welling
up inside him.

"Gangsters aren't loyal to anyone," he muttered harshly
under his breath. "They're only loyal to themselves and their
own causes."

Christie nodded along. "What exactly was it they were
trying to find him for? Did he owe them money?"

Jackson shook his head. "Oh, he owed them all right, but
it wasn't money. It was a favor. They had done something
or another for him in the past—I think he said he had been
in trouble with some other gang or something like that and
they had come to his aid. And as much as I warned him about
this whole thing, it still played out exactly the way I told him
it would."

Christie's lips twisted with confusion. She leaned forward,
homing in on the man with her entire focus.

"So, if he said they rescued him from another gang, what
made them turn on him?" she asked.

Jackson sighed deeply again, a sigh that seemed to emanate
from the depths of his guts. "They were supposed to protect
him from the other gang that's operating further down state
as long as he upheld his end of the agreement, and his end
was to supply them with drugs. Of course, he wasn't a dealer,

but he had his connections with the suppliers from the gang downstate and could get larger quantities for them."

Christie nodded. From his side of the glass, Jed grimaced and shook his head. It was a never-ending slippery slope with drugs. It didn't matter how drugs managed to seep into your life, it always led to trouble.

"And I take it he stopped providing?" she prompted.

Jackson nodded. "Yep. He got greedy and arrogant. He thought he was important to them. Irreplaceable. There's one thing I learned from having a run-in with a gang when I was a teenager, my first and last run-in, mind you, and it's that no one is indispensable to them. They'll toss you out just as fast as they toss out trash. Hell, they would toss their own mothers!" He let out a short, sour laugh brimming with bitterness.

Christie hummed to herself. "And I guess Blake found this out the hard way."

He nodded.

"Was your best friend in any way connected to the food industry?"

Jackson's smile was sad. "Only as a customer. He loved to try new foods, but he couldn't boil an egg to save his life."

"Well," she continued, "this is certainly valuable information, Mr. Jones. Thank you for your cooperation and coming down here today to help with the investigation. Any chance that you can remember the name of the gang? Having a direct lead, specific names, descriptions… it all helps us move faster to apprehend criminals and get justice for Blake." He turned his head away to break eye contact. "Do you know any of the members of the gang by name? Or any possible descriptions of them that could help us find them?"

Jackson nodded, understanding right away. "I don't remember any of their names. They don't throw their names around either. I try to keep a low profile, staying in the shadows and such. I avoid eye contact and mind my business. I try not to make myself a loose end they need to snuff out." He paused, looking to where the sun beam was coming in the window. "Blake wanted to tell me their names because he felt like knowing their names was a sign that he was in the core group." He smiled sadly. "I do know that they always travel around in blacked-out Honda Civics. The old ones, too—the ones from the early 2000s. They buy them used, they black them out with heavy tint, and they drive them around the city, kind of like an army."

Christie nodded. "Do you know anything about their means of operations?"

Jackson thought for a moment, his brows pulled together. "They frequent Manhattan at large, but they seem to particularly love hanging around parks. It's easy for buyers to walk up to them discretely instead of if they were on the street corner just hanging around in a gang." Jackson huffed. "I know they hang around further up—between 120th and 180th street. Not sure what the rhyme or reason for that is. But they don't tend to camp out or set up shop as much in the busiest parts of the city."

Christie was relieved. What Jackson was sharing added up with some of the bare bones information they already managed to gather. But by the wrinkle in his brow, she knew he wasn't quite finished.

"They're, of course, famous for eliminating people via drive-by shootings. That's their signature move. They come screeching down the street, open fire, and drive fear into everyone who knows of them and has dealings with them. It keeps everyone in line." He nodded to himself. "I don't know if that'll be much use to you, detective, but that's all I can tell you."

Christie smiled politely at the man. "Not to worry. We appreciate all the information you've provided so far. I'll run some checks, and of course, if we need you to come back in for any other interviews, we will be in touch. And again, I'm sorry for your loss."

Jackson's face was weary, as he rose to his feet. "Yeah. Me, too."

Back in her office, Christie sank into her chair with an exhausted groan and contemplated the information she had just received, her face marked with an inscrutable expression. Jed watched her carefully, letting the silence hang over them. Time passed by, each second seeming to trickle slowly.

"Is it weird that it feels strange that the answer came so easily?" Christie finally asked, looking at Jed. Her nose was wrinkled, as if she had just been exposed to something particularly distasteful. "This case is coming together too easily. It all feels too easy. But at the same time, there is still the unknown element of who killed Joel. Blake came back inconclusive for the connection to the food industry, so the initial link we had with him being at the food stand falls through." Christie sighed. "We have no leads for who could potentially have accessed VX on purpose just for this single killing. Let's hope it stays at just one. I had Graham run some background checks on the Brooks family and their potential connections to politics and the military. The initial report that I got back showed connections to local politicians in New York. But even though that little brat threatened me, and of course I take it seriously," she added while she raised her hand when Jed's eyes narrowed, "I don't think he has the balls to pull that off. I doubt he has enough respect built with his Daddy's contacts to make that move on his own, and his father is a smart man. He wouldn't risk everything just to deal with me."

She paused, staring at her desk. "I instructed my team to conduct a double-check into the military aspect of things and to investigate the politician the family is connected to for any independent military connections he might have. But I don't know. It still doesn't quite feel right." Christie's chair made a series of squeaking sounds as she swiveled around on it. "Is this how you feel about Ethan?" she asked suddenly, looking up from her desk and over to Jed. "Like there's just… I don't even know how to explain it…" she hesitated. "I keep thinking about how suddenly we lost both Joel and a member of our forensics team to this ominous poison."

Jed gave voice to her unspoken thoughts. "It feels like there's something we just can't see."

A shadow seemed to slide over Christie's expressions, a dark cloud signifying the arrival of an impending storm. "Yes, that's exactly how it feels—like there's just something we can't see. Something's happening behind the scenes, and we don't have the slightest clue as to what it is. I can't even put my finger on a direction or a motive or anything!" She grabbed the armrests of her chair in frustration and leaned back, fixing her brooding eyes on the ceiling.

Jed watched her and felt a similar darkness unfurling its wings inside him. He couldn't quite understand what it was, but it made him uneasy—deeply uneasy. "I feel the same. But what I have been doing, at least so we're not caught too much unawares, is trying to keep track of all the small things that just don't fit right. Like Ethan's wounds and his broken arm. Like the lack of DNA and the missing knife at the scene. Like the sourcing of the VX and the motive for killing Joel."

"Hmmm," Christie muttered. "Initial reports for Joel's connections to potential gangs came back as inconclusive. I went ahead and investigated the connection you had suggested between the gang and his murder. We have another interview this afternoon with his girlfriend. She was also out of state, which is why it took us a little while to find her and then arrange for her to come in. Joel seemed like a clean-cut, educated guy. Would he have connections to the gangs in some way? Hard to say. I have learned to never say never. People continue to surprise me every day—and not always in a good way. We need to follow the leads and where the evidence takes us."

"Do you remember the client that I had in our last case who gave me the clue to Hugh being the murderer?" Jed ventured.

Christie grinned. "How could I forget? We owe him, big time."

Jed leaned back in his chair, remembering their recent conversation that had pushed him to reconnect with Christie. "He mentioned something gang-related today. I caught on to what he was saying pretty much right away. He said something about the blacked-out Hondas. That is the type of car that chased us in Ethan's case."

Before Christie could say anything, Jed's eyes widened. His mouth dropped open in a look of sudden realization, and he slapped his palm on his forehead.

"Wait, of course!" Jed exclaimed. "It's so obvious! Why didn't I think of that before?" His eyes squeezed shut as he groaned. "God, how could I be so thick?"

Christie sat upright, anticipating that Jed was about to drop some kind of bombshell. His eyes were still wide and his lips parted in disbelief.

"What if Ethan's murder was connected to Joel's? As payback?" Jed's thoughts were racing so fast they had outrun his mouth, and for a moment, he couldn't speak further.

"Wait. No way!" he almost shouted, running a hand through his hair. "Is that what's happening?" He seemed to be talking to himself now.

Christie waited patiently as Jed tried to sort through his own thoughts. She was at the ready with her pen.

"Okay. Let me slow down and start over," he said more evenly, trying to catch his breath. "In the initial case, what happened was that Ethan and Ryan witnessed the murder of a drug dealer. Right?"

Christie nodded. "Right."

"Ryan was gunned down pretty much immediately—before Ethan could even warn him that the gang was looking for them."

Christie nodded again. "Right."

"Ethan's girlfriend at the time was the one who called to warn him because she was friends with one of the gang members' sisters."

"Uh-huh," Christie said.

"So, when they were looking for Ethan, he was locked in his apartment. They murdered Ryan, took his phone, and had been working on cracking his phone to figure out where Ethan lived. They found Ryan because he had left home, so they trailed him to his apartment that way."

Christie was scribbling furiously as Jed spoke, noting every-thing he said in case it might come in handy later.

"So, by the time Ethan found Ryan dead in his apartment, the gang was hacking Ryan's phone and figuring out how to find and attack Ethan. Ethan knew instantly that he was in danger, and he went into hiding. He didn't go back to his apartment. He stayed hidden in plain sight at a motel for a couple of days, then he came to see me."

Jed spoke with such clear confidence it seemed as if he were seeing the events unfolding before him rather than recalling them from memory.

"Ethan came to see me, and we did our session where he decided he was ready to give his witness statement. He told me he was ready to talk to the police because he felt responsible, as though it was his fault that Ryan had died. He told me that if he had just said something up front, this could have all been avoided. By the time I contacted the police, and they were downstairs waiting for us, the gang had figured out who Ethan was, where he lived, and where he was at that moment in time. So, when we went downstairs to get into the police car, they were waiting for Ethan to come out of the building."

Jed paused, thinking over the events. "As soon as Ethan recognized their car, the police were able to organize and set up a trap to stop their attempt on Ethan's life. Ethan got off free, even though he gave his witness testimony and put two of their members in jail. That gives them the perfect motive to try to catch up with Ethan again and kill him!"

His head sank into his hands as he groaned aloud. Christie's cheeks tinged pink at the sound coming out of his mouth. She chided herself internally, ashamed at the way his groans made her feel. They were in the middle of an investigation for crying out loud. It was not the time to be aroused, no matter how guttural and masculine his groans sounded.

"How didn't I see this before?" Jed asked with his head still in his hands.

Christie caught the pattern of his question before it could go any further.

"It's not your fault, Jed. We were caught up in the turmoil of trying to figure out who was murdering homeless people. That gang had no connection to the case, and by the time we apprehended Hugh and he had confessed to only three murders, we weren't thinking about the gang potentially being involved at all. It's not your fault that you didn't make the connection any sooner than you did. We are investigating them now. We will figure this out."

Christie could see that her consolation hadn't sunk into his mind. Jed was still trying to figure out how he hadn't noticed the connection from his expression and his gaze off into nowhere. She let him process for a few moments longer, and eventually, he sat upright. His sigh was heavy.

"What would I do without you, Detective?" he asked, sending a lopsided grin her away. "You're right. There's no point in me beating myself up when we weren't even focused in that direction at all. That case had us all over the place, to where we were even missing the actual lead we should have been following." Jed grinned. "I really do owe my client big time."

Christie laughed. "Maybe you could get him a gift one day."

He nodded. "I'm working on something. I've got a couple ideas up my sleeve."

They both leaned back in their chairs, and it was quiet for a while.

"When is Joel's girlfriend coming in for an interview?"

"This afternoon, actually," Christie answered, looking up from where she was writing her notes. "You up for another interview?"

Jed smiled, shaking his head. "I'm up for anything with you, Detective."

There was a knock on the door to her office, and after he had called 'come in', Graham entered the room with a stack of papers in his hand. He was the most intimidating-looking man out of Christie's whole unit, Jed thought, and yet his intuition told him that Graham had a soft interior.

"Hello, Graham," Jed spoke dryly, nodding his head at the man in greeting.

"Mr. Gray." Graham's voice was a deep-set echo that seemed to reverberate through the entire room. "How is everything going?"

"It's going," Jed answered mysteriously, and then added, "We're going to interview Joel's girlfriend. Any tips you might have for me?"

Graham's expression went blank for a moment, as if he hadn't been expecting the hotshot therapist to ask him for advice. But then he turned his attention to Jed, looking pleased. "Just remember the two key rules of a successful interrogation, and you'll be fine."

Jed leaned forward. "What two rules?"

Graham held up a single stubby finger. "The person who speaks the most in an interrogation has the least power." He paused, waiting for Jed to absorb the information, and then held up a second, equally stubby finger alongside the first. "And the angrier someone gets, the guiltier they are. The more confused they get, the more innocent they are."

"Hmmm." Jed leaned back, chewing on the wisdom of those words. "Thanks for the advice, Graham. I'll keep that in mind."

"No problem at all, Mr. Gray. And if you need any more help regarding anything, you can drop by my desk whenever you please." Looking positively pleased with himself, Graham deposited his load of files onto Christie's desk and left the room.

"Well," Christie breathed, getting to her feet, "it's show-time, Gray."

"Hi, Jaelyn. How are you? I'm so sorry for your loss."

Much like the man Christie had interviewed earlier, Jaelyn's sigh was long and heavy.

"I'm not doing great, Detective." She spoke like she was recovering from a long bout of illness. "I am not sure how I can be of assistance, but I'll be damned if I don't play my part in helping you guys track the bastard who took Joel from me."

Her appearance was as haggard as her voice, and Jed could read the pain in her body language. She was dark-skinned like Joel, with long braided hair and tattoos running down her right arm to the wrist. She was wearing a floral sun dress which stood in stark contrast to her dark mood and the almost ice-cold weather in New York. It was obvious that she had just flown in from somewhere much warmer—and much calmer.

"Well, Jaelyn, as you know, your partner, Joel, was murdered, so we wanted to get some background information from you to aid us in our investigations."

The young woman gave an almost imperceptible nod.

"My questions today are focused on the relationships that Joel might have had—with, per se," Christie paused for dramatic effect, "any gangs?"

Confusion ballooned across the despair-streaked expanse of Jaelyn's face, clouding her eyes. Christie could tell immediately that this was news to her. Clearly, Joel had not been that kind of a man.

She shook her head. "I have no idea if he was connected to any such thing, but he wasn't the type to be involved with crime. He was very strict about who he worked for, the kinds of things he engaged in, and his moral code. He never left home without his moral code. He was always trying to help people and give back to the community. Before I met him, when he was first starting out as a chef, he volunteered at a soup kitchen. He still helped out, every now and then, if he could, when they were in a bind."

"And do you know if Joel, perhaps, owed anyone any money, had done any favors for anyone, or had failed to uphold any agreements he had gotten himself into?" Christie inquired.

Jaelyn thought for a minute but shook her head again, the frown remaining on her face.

"No," she finally answered. "He was very proud—not the type to borrow money at all. Favors?" She hesitated. "He was always the type to try to help people, no matter how far out of his way it drove him, but they were favors that would never get you into trouble. More like catering for someone's birthday party even though they weren't able to pay the full price or making a cake for a homeless man when he knew that he wasn't going to be able to make rent that month because of it. That kind of thing."

Christie listened quietly.

"He wasn't the type for gambling or making big bets. He was a quiet guy who kept his routine to just going to work, going home, and doing what he could for people. He didn't even like to use his credit card. He wanted us to use cash instead of credit, even if it took us a bit longer."

Tears pricked the corners of Jaelyn's eyes, and she blinked twice to stop them from falling down her face.

"What about any of his friends?" Christie pressed. "Can you say if any of his friends had any kind of connections to gangs, people they might have owed money to, or anything like that?"

Jaelyn shook her head. "He didn't have very many friends—only a few trusted associates. And even with them, he kept his connections in a strict line. When he moved to America from the Caribbean, he had anticipated a lot of issues because of his skin color. So, he tried his best to stay out of trouble. But," she sighed, "I guess it wasn't enough."

CHAPTER 14

"MORNING, GRAY. ARE YOU up?"

"I'm up now, Detective," Jed laughed as he rolled in his bed so he could sit upright.

"Sorry to wake you up so early, but I just got some exciting news from our undercover team that we put into play to connect with the gang." A smile was clear in Christie's voice.

"They took the bait?" Jed asked, his voice hopeful.

"They took the bait," Christie affirmed. "We've got our boys. The next step is to apprehend them. Since you had an interaction with them before in the exact same context, I wanted to touch base with you before I finalize any plans. I wanted to hear what you thought about it, see if you had any suggestions about what I've come up with."

"I'm flattered, Detective," Jed replied. "So, what's the big plan?"

"Well," Christie began, "there's nothing super complicated or sophisticated. One of our guys, Joseph, managed to order something from one of the dealers that's connected to their core operations. We had him make a reasonably large personal order from their group and pay in cash right away to establish a good deal of trust with the gang quickly. Then, we had him make a large order—enough that he could potentially sell to someone else, or use at a large gathering, and request it for the time and date of our operation. This way, because the order is so large and the amount to be collected in payment is substantial, some of the higher-ups in the gang will likely be present. The plan is to get him to go back to the same location today to pay for and collect this large order. It's pretty simple, but it's enough of a bait that the dealers will definitely show up, and because we know from their patterns that they never travel alone, other members of the gang will show up as well. I guess the detail I wanted to find out from you was how many men do you think we need to have going into this operation."

Jed stared down at the rug below his feet, listening as carefully as he could to the details Christie was sharing. He flopped back onto his back.

Christie continued, "They've got firepower, and you know as well as I do that they're not afraid to use it. We need to be careful. We can't afford for the whole operation to be a bust, though, because if it were to fail without us being able to arrest the men that show up, a second attempt at luring them out would not nearly be so easy. This is our one shot. We have to get them this time and get them to flip on their boss."

He was still lying in his bed, staring at the ceiling. It was hardly 6:30 on a Sunday morning, but Christie had probably been up all-night thinking through the case and coming up with the plan.

"I get that, Detective. In my run-in with them, we had four or five patrol cars with officers flanking our own vehicle and blocking them in while we were driving to the station. So, that's around 10 or 11 officers, altogether, that took on two of the men. I think that was a good number and a good ratio for that situation. At the end of the altercation, we only sustained one injury to one of our officers, and they sustained two injuries. We had also noticed them in time so that there were police officers on rooftops nearby. It was a full-on operation."

Jed paused, thinking about the whole situation from a bird's-eye view as best as he could. "I think the more officers you can round up for this particular task, the better. It's also best if most of them are in plain clothes and just happen to be walking by when this interaction between the dealer and the gang and our officers is taking place. At the slightest sight of police cars or any sign of the presence of uniformed officers, they'll flip out right away and will be far more prepared to be on the offense with their weapons. That will increase the difficulty and the danger, along with decreasing our chances of apprehending them."

Jed looked out the window into the dreary Sunday morning outside.

"We want it all to seem like it's normal, natural Sunday happenings in New York," he continued, "until the literal last minute, when our officers are able to pull weapons and take them down. We don't want to give them a reason to be on guard at all. I think that's our best bet for making this operation successful. If we go into it in uniform, we've already failed."

On the other end of the line, Christie was smiling. "What would I do without you, Gray? You're spot on. I had been thinking of doing half plain-clothed, half uniform, but you're right. We're better off at least 90% playing citizen. I gotta call you back. I'll give the boys a call, and I'll give you an update before we move out."

"Wait a second," Jed demanded, "what do you mean we?"

Christie laughed. "We meaning the NYPD, Gray."

"If you're going, I'm going, Detective."

Christy sighed knowingly. "I'm currently home. I'm not even at the station yet. There's no need to worry your pretty little head about anything going wrong with me there. I won't be in the heart of the action."

Jed's jaw had tensed. "I'm not going to repeat myself."

Rising to his feet, he headed for the bathroom, the phone still pressed to his ear. Christie hummed.

"You've been very protective lately, Gray. Not that I'm complaining. But it's definitely interesting."

Jed only half smiled. "I'll see you at the station in twenty, Detective."

He made it to the station after a brief shower, wearing a plain white tee, jeans, black and white running shoes, and with his hair still wet at the ends from his shower. The atmosphere in the station was tense—heavy, like the air in New York right before a violent rainstorm was unleashed over the city, drenching its citizens and flooding its streets. Jed muttered a quick prayer under his breath as he made his way over to the elevator.

Jason, still in his uniform, came strolling down the hallway. He saw Jed but pretended that he hadn't and continued walking at his brisk pace. Jed was no stranger to such indirect challenges. He continued taking long strides forward, and soon, the two men's shoulders collided with each other. Unfortunately, it was Jason who took the brunt of the momentum, as Jed had been walking far faster than him. He whirled sideways, and the stack of papers held in his hand fluttered to the floor in a scattered mess. As Jed stepped into the elevator and turned around, the last thing he saw before the steel doors closed before him was Jason's scowling face while he kneeled on the floor, picking up his papers.

That ought to teach him some manners.

"Good job, Gray. Sometimes that arse needs to be taught a lesson."

Surprised, Jed turned back and found Carter standing behind him, grinning wolfishly.

Jed bit down the smile that was rising to his own face and stated in a slightly amused voice, "He keeps picking fights he can't win. It's not my fault."

Carter guffawed hard at that, his bushy brows bobbing up and down on his face. Jed liked him. He could tell that Carter was one of those carefree, jolly fellows who always lit up the room when they entered it.

"You seem like a good guy, Gray." Carter clapped him playfully on the shoulders as the elevator doors opened. "You should come golfing with us sometime. Just the precinct boys, no one else—get it? Not even your pretty detective." He winked knowingly at Jed, running a hand through his hair before turning around and leaving the elevator. Jed watched him go, and he could only shake his head in amusement.

When Jed made it to his partner's office, he knocked loudly. The door opened, and Christie's brows shot up.

"Morning, Gray."

When he closed the door behind himself, Jed sank into a chair. "Interesting."

Christie paused in the middle of fitting herself with a bullet-proof vest. "What's on your mind, Gray?"

You are. The response in his mind was immediate, but he did not let it turn into words. There was a knock on the door behind them, and Jed's eyes narrowed. Christie pulled the door open, and Jason's voice filtered into the room.

"The paperwork you requested is ready, Detective. The chief has signed off on all the documents."

Christie nodded, walking back to her desk as Jed chimed in.

"Warrants?"

Christie shook her head. "Fourth amendment in the nature of probable causes covers our activities today. I had the chief sign off on some things we'll discuss later on. If our operations were any larger today, they'd fall into SRG territory."

Jed nodded easily, remembering the term from his own research, as well as his master's program. The Strategic Response Group was an arm of the NYPD that got involved in responses to citywide mobilizations, civil disorders, major events, disorder responses, crime suppression, crowd control, parades, protests, mass shootings, bank robberies, missing persons, demonstrations, and other major incidents. Jed took a deep breath. Mobilizing this many officers of the law was a huge undertaking. He let his eyes search Christie for signs of stress. She stuffed her hands into her pockets and looked at the papers on the desk. Her shoulders were tensed, her usual relaxed posture disappearing under the pressure of their current situation. He saw her eyes had acquired that typical hard sheen they did when she was completely focused on something. Her index finger tapped against her desk. It had taken him some time, but he had come to recognize the tell-tale signs of her anxiousness. And right now, she was displaying many of those signs.

Jason, still in the room and standing behind Jed, seemed to await instructions. When she'd finished reading, Christie seemed to return to the present moment and looked around the room before her eyes settled on them once more—first on Jed, then on Jason. She blinked at him.

"Everyone has their instructions, and some of our groups should have already begun their journeys, correct?"

Jason nodded. "Correct."

Christie looked him up and down. "And you are still in your uniform because…?"

Jason suddenly looked confused. "I was asked by the chief to stay with you throughout the operation."

Christie nodded, turning back to the papers that she had rearranged on the table and gathered them together.

"I see. Hurry up and get in your street clothes, or we will be late."

And that was all she said without looking in his direction.

When Jason returned out of uniform, they all walked out of the station together.

150th street was where the dealer had decided to operate from today, and since they had no patrol cars to aid them, the officers all opted to walk, arranged in small groups or singly, trying to blend in as well as they could by stopping to window-shop every now and then, ordering something from a passing coffee shop or simply making sure that the path they took was a meandering one and did not make it seem like they were purposefully headed somewhere.

Everyone knew what the mission was. Everyone was focused and ready to fulfill their roles, just like they were taught in their training. It was like second nature now. They wanted to take those guys down. All their weapons were loaded, and all their vests were fitted underneath their clothing, remarkably undetectable at a glance—and even at a stare.

Jed's subgroup was small: just him, Christie, and Jason. The three walked in silence, following the pattern that the group had established as they moved up each new street. On 65th, they slowed down outside an old bookstore, following Christie inside as she marveled at a particular set of limited-edition Jane Austen novels. Their next stop was an ice cream parlor, where the trio savored a small carton of chocolate ice cream shared among them.

Outside the glass of each of their stops, Jed recognized other groups of officers pass them by. Each group stopped on every other street, a steady rotation and climb as they made their way up the busy streets. The cold weather was also playing into their plans. Because of the chill and slight wind, most of the officers had donned vests and jackets, which further concealed any potential outlines of their weapons and vests.

It was clear from Jason's body language and overall attitude that he was holding a silent grudge about something, and if Jed hadn't already known what the matter likely was, he would have thought the man had just suddenly begun to dislike his team leader out of nowhere.

He tried to focus on the events at hand. They were nearing the right street now. Once they'd left the station, also walking out of its wide gates in waves and groups, they had no real way of communicating with each other outside of their earpieces. Walking around with radios and leaning down to speak into them as you were casually strolling would not be conducive to their goal of remaining as discrete as possible until the very last minute.

As Christie had said in their last moments as a group of forty before they had dispersed to begin their journey, she was counting on everyone to follow the instructions they had been given, in the sequence they had been issued. Phase One consisted solely of getting to their destination without arousing any suspicion. As the fates would have it, that was the hardest part, and the part the entire plan depended on.

Their approach was slow and steady. Many of the officers joined and walked alongside small groups of civilians who were headed in the same direction, even falling into natural conversations with them.

Jed, Jason, and Christie walked mostly in silence, stopping randomly every few moments to point to some important landmark or monument and have a pointless conversation to give them a semblance of normalcy. It all seemed simple enough. In a matter of an hour, after a slow, and at times, excruciating, descent to 150th, Phase Two began to unfold before Jed's eyes. This was the phase of positions. Each group would need to position themselves naturally along the street, up and down. This was the second-hardest part. There were only so many places on the street for multiple small groups of people to gather without arousing suspicions immediately.

By the time Jed's group hit the top of the street, the last group to arrive, the street seemed almost empty. Jed was surprised but continued to walk with Christie and Jason until they came to their particular stake out point. On their way down the street to the small Chinese restaurant they would be watching the unfolding events from, they passed the dealer. Jed knew who he was without even needing a description. The man's movements seemed to scream suspicion. He was like an animal standing on-edge, ready to dart off at the slightest sound of an approaching predator. He was young, probably around twenty-five, with his arms covered with indiscernible patterns of dark ink. Jed stealthily observed him as he shifted and stirred in his place, exchanging concealed packages for cash from people who were approaching him. His movements were smooth, almost unnoticed, but his crack-addict alert eyes were enough to give him away.

They passed by him. But that wasn't the only thing they passed. Next to him, and lining the left side of the street where he stood, were four blacked-out Honda Civics.

When they had made their way into the restaurant and chosen a table that was thankfully near the windows that looked out onto the street, Jed and Christie looked across the table at each other, immediately understanding what the other was thinking.

"I was worried about this," Christie whispered.

"We can take 'em," Jed replied.

Jason looked between them. "What? You two have telepathy?"

Christie's lips pulled into a smirk. "Yes, we do. Keep up."

Jason's nod was curt, and Jed didn't miss the way his lips pressed into a thin line after that.

"There's more of them than we anticipated," she finally said out loud. "Four cars." She ripped her eyes away from the world outside the window to look across the table at Jed. "Part of me is wondering whether I underestimated this assignment. Maybe I should have called in the SRG instead of relying on just our strength."

"The SRG would have come storming in with uniforms and sirens blaring. That's not what we want."

Christie pursed her lips. "But they would have come storming in with their numbers, too."

Jed nodded. "Joseph is waiting on your cue. You can decide what to do. It's your call, Detective. Whatever your decision, I'll stand by it."

Christie's eyes blazed with a multitude of different plans of action. She swallowed. Focusing her attention back outside the glass to where the dealer was standing, she stared at the four cars hard enough to see that there were two people inside each one. Christie didn't know if they had only just arrived on the scene or were waiting for something in particular before they got out of their vehicles.

Whatever her decision was, Phase Three depended on it. Among the group of 40 officers, Joseph and Christie were the only ones with radios. The cues were established. Christie would give Joseph the cue when they arrived, after the situation was evaluated. If Joseph walked down to the dealer, made the exchange, then turned and walked back to the store he had been in, the gig was off. If he walked down to the dealer, then continued straight down the street and turned left, out of sight, the operation was on. And it was only when he had disappeared down the secondary street that the troops could move out.

Time was ticking. Her blood roared in her ears. One hand was tight around the radio that was now in her lap underneath the table; the other was tight around the glass of water in front of her. She looked over at Jed, who was wearing a goofy smile despite the severity of the situation.

The back of her eyes burned at his simple display of relaxed confidence in whatever her decision was. She took a deep breath in, then slowly exhaled. Bringing the radio up to her lips, she gave the signal that defined her decision, a smile taking over her lips that matched Jed's.

"Come on, boys. We need the goods for the office party, remember?"

A minute later, Joseph waltzed out of the restaurant opposite them, his steps taking him back up the street toward the dealer. Turning to meet him, the tattooed dealer gave him a grin before dapping him up in a quick handshake. Their conversation seemed to go well, and Jed wished he could hear what they were saying. Of course, Joseph was wired, but the recordings his tap was capturing wouldn't be available until after the whole operation went down.

As Joseph handed over the bag of money to the dealer and collected his bag of product in return, Jed's body tensed. The officer's role was almost complete. The men talked for a few moments longer before Joseph turned to head further up the street. All the nerves and muscles in Jed's body were wound tight like a spring. Joseph made it to the corner and disappeared, and that was when all hell broke loose.

Officers swarmed the street from every nook and cranny, pouring out of alleyways and buildings like bees that had just discovered a utopia of honey. The dealer had no time to react. Jed saw his face freeze with shock, and then a moment later, he was surrounded from all sides by the undercover police forces. One of the men whipped out a pair of handcuffs and tackled the stupefied target to the ground, yanking his arms behind his back and immobilizing him.

The rest of the swarm converged immediately on the cars, throwing doors open and pulling out the men hiding inside into pairs of waiting handcuffs. A slew of grunts and curses filled up the far end of the street, interspersed with the horrified gasps of civilians who were witnessing what was happening and backing away from the whole scene. Jed was still tense as the struggle continued, and though he waited for the sound of gunshots to ring out, it never came.

When the scuffle died down, nine men lay flat on the ground, their hands cuffed behind their backs. Jed breathed a sigh of relief as the wail of police sirens filtered into the air, patrol cars that had been ready and waiting on alternative streets screeching to a halt as the men were processed and put into the backs of those cars to be taken to the station. The sharp beeping of a reversing tow truck was also heard as it backed into position to load two of the four Hondas onto its carrying bed.

Jed looked away from the window and over to Christie, who was watching the actions unfold, one after the other outside the window, like a well-oiled machine. It was a thing of beauty. A smile was pulling at her lips. Jed noticed that her shoulders were now as relaxed as they had been before this operation was initiated that morning.

"What do you reckon, Detective?" Jed asked, a smile on his lips as well. "You think we'll have a good office party tonight?

Christie's smile split into a wide grin. "We sure will."

CHAPTER 15

"GRUESOME, ISN'T IT?" CHRISTIE asked, watching Jed sigh and sink into his chair across from her.

It was a Monday morning, and they were in the midst of conducting interviews with the members of the gang that had been apprehended in the NYPD's bust operation the day prior. The problem was that the men refused to talk. Each one came in more tight-lipped than the other, and no matter what tactic or strategy Christie tried, they never cracked. Some of them had even laughed at her, making her feel small and partially silly.

Was the whole operation a fluke then? If no one wanted to talk? She knew she couldn't think about it that way, but the thought still weaseled its way into her mind.

"You're doing a wonderful job. Stop beating yourself up."

Christie looked across the table at Jed, whose arms were now folded over his chest. There was always something intimate about sitting across a table from him. Even though they must have done it dozens of times by now, she was surprised at how she'd grown so accustomed to it that whenever anyone else sat in that seat, she felt a bit awkward.

She nodded, acknowledging his statement. Jed's eyes narrowed.

"You didn't hear what I said."

"Of course I did," she answered.

Jed shook his head. "You heard my voice and the words I said, but you didn't receive it. Which means you didn't *hear* me."

Christie waited for him to continue, and after watching her for a long moment, Jed obliged. "I'm very impressed by you, Detective. I've never seen someone else that can throw down quite like you. You work really hard at your job. Everyone respects you, values your opinions, and takes orders from you in operations like sheep to the slaughter. You've really made a name for yourself here in a matter of mere months."

She stared at him.

"You've solved one murder case with multiple homicides, are on the verge of cracking another, have interviewed more suspects and run more reports than I can keep track of, have been on-site at murder scene cleanups, have consoled grieving families and loved ones, and so much more than I could summon to memory right now. You've never cracked under pressure, even though I know you're struggling not to, and you always show up with a smile."

Christie wasn't sure what to say, or what to do with her hands. She was too stunned to blush either. Where had this onslaught of compliments and acknowledgement come from,

she wondered? At the same time, she hoped it would continue.

"You have no idea how incredible you are to work with either. You're kind, bubbly, cheerful, professional, and unimag-
inably good at persevering through the hard things."

Her throat was starting to burn just a little.

"And even though you sometimes shut down and retreat
behind those sad eyes, and you refuse to confide in me even
though you know I would carry your burdens gladly, you're
the only detective I want to work with. I wouldn't have our
partnership any other way."

Jed leaned forward, grabbed his bottle of water, and put
it to his lips. He let the final part of the previous thought
filter through his mind unsaid. *And God, you make me hot and
desperate like I've never been before.*

"Somehow, despite all of those things and endlessly more,
you're still sitting across from me right now, beating yourself
up because these hardened criminals didn't fess up to the
killing in their first interviews."

Christie's cheeks warmed from embarrassment.

"No one else is surprised or thrown off by the fact that the
men refuse to talk. But your demand of perfectionism from
yourself is keeping you from accepting that it'll likely take
multiple rounds of interrogations to wear them down."

"Do you get a bonus from NYPD for psychoanalyzing
me?" Christie asked playfully, though there was no wind in
her sails.

"For you? No charge, remember?" Jed replied, eyes steady on her.

The silence stretched between them as Christie tried and failed to find something witty to say. Instead of witty responses, she only came up with a sigh. She let one slip out, and Jed's gaze softened.

"Stop beating yourself up. If you set yourself up to bat with a 100% or nothing rate, you'll fail—always. And it'll be your own fault."

Christie sighed again, but she nodded eventually. Her expression was shifting into amusement.

"I don't think I've ever heard you express your opinion of me to that extent before," she remarked, watching Jed squirm only slightly before he slipped back into his 'in control' energy.

"There's lots more that I could say," he finally replied. "But for now, let's focus on your current thought patterns so we can create a game plan for success. What are you thinking about these interviews so far? I've been watching them from the sidelines, but you might have caught something I didn't."

"So far, I've noticed a faint pattern among them. They all seem to have the same reaction whenever I mention Blake's name."

Jed searched his mind, trying to remember each of the six interviews thus far in detail. His head tilted as he thought.

"You mean that they all sort of have an amused reaction, or outright laugh, when you bring him up?"

Christie nodded. That was exactly what she had been noticing. Their amusement only seemed to show up when Blake's name became part of the conversation. It was morbid, the way they just launched into laughter so easily, as though Blake had been a bird they had shot down during hunting season in the forests of upstate New York. She wasn't sure what exactly was so funny about the questions she was asking, but she had already begun to work through a pattern in her mind that was related to the issue.

She was trying to analyze the questions she had asked. For a number of them, the question about Blake had been simple. *What was your connection to Blake?* That had earned her couple of chuckles and a lot of silence. Blake had definitely been doing something for them, but the gang refused to say what it was. A couple of them had laughed outright when she asked them what their motive was for attacking Blake.

Regardless of what triggered their laughter, one thing was certain. None of them had denied the accusation that they had killed Blake, which was promising for the investigation. They would be indicted on charges of possession and distribution of drugs. That would give her time to keep grilling them. Christie sensed, without question, that their refusal to acknowledge or state their innocence when presented with an accusation of guilt was enough for them to continue investigations into them.

To support the case, they were looking for forensic evidence that linked the weapons seized from the men that morning to the bullet that was used to shoot Blake. Based on the forensic analysis of the crime scene, Christie knew that the bullets that had led to Blake's death had come from a .44 pistol. At the scene of the take-down, at the end when all the men had been in handcuffs on the ground, their officers had conducted searches of the men and vehicles. The men had been stripped of five .44 pistols and additional rounds of ammo were discovered in hidden places in their cars that had been engineered to hold any substances they would want to hide. The rounds of ammunition found in their cars and guns matched the wounds Blake sustained, which strengthened their connection to the murder. The guns were being tested now against the bullets that killed Blake to see if they had a match.

"My plan, you say?" Christie asked, still staring at her desk.

Jed hummed, watching her expression change, a smile pulling on her lips as her thoughts solidified.

"It's actually quite simple. I don't know how I didn't think of the solution before now."

"Christie…" Jed replied in warning.

Her smile widened, and she raised her head to look over at him.

"Yes, yes, I know. No more beating myself up." She shook her head, amused by Jed's playful glare. "All I have to do is play the role they're playing with me."

"Which is…?" Jed prompted.

"Their amusement is likely because of their internal code. They laugh when I ask about Blake because they all know that no one among them would even dare to expose the truth. Their loyalty is sworn to their group. They wouldn't betray each other. Betrayal means certain death in their culture."

Jed nodded. Christie's grin seemed to grow larger the longer she spoke, and Jed couldn't help the smile that began to form on his face. Her joy was contagious.

"But what if one of them did begin to break down? That would fracture the uniformity of the whole thing. Once someone has betrayed their pact, they will feel less and less secure in their lies."

Jed nodded. "But no one has broken down so far. They're all still confident in their group."

"They don't have to know that," Christie finished, reaching for her pen and notepad. "They're all being held in different spaces. They have no contact with each other. They are laughing at my question about Blake because the fact that I have to ask them means I have been unsuccessful in getting their fellow gang members to crack."

Jed suddenly understood where Christie was going.

"You're the one in control here, and its your turn to hold the laughter. We plant the seed of doubt so that their defense begins to break down—so that they each think they are being betrayed by a member who broke," Jed added.

Christie's hands flew across the page before her as she made notes. "And in the meantime, we'll run gunshot residue tests on all the men in custody to further gather evidence that will connect them to the murder. With the evidence, and with some manipulation, we'll crack the case before the day is done."

Jed grinned. "Brilliant, Detective. Simply brilliant."

Christie grinned wickedly. "I also have an extra trick up my sleeve to help our case. We'll bring in one of the other suspects while we're interviewing their lead guy—Dredge—by 'accident'. If he thinks his men are weak, or have betrayed his trust, he'll come crashing down. That'll really seal the deal. They'll both think the other is about to give them away."

"I couldn't have thought of anything better myself."

Thirty minutes later, they were back in the interview room, standing before one of the gangsters in their custody. And by 'they', Jed meant Christie. After their conversation, she had issued the request for the residue testing to be done, and all the seven men had been collected, one by one, from their respective holding cells. After their testing was complete, they were returned to their holding cells without ever coming into contact with or seeing another one of their gang members. None of the seven knew whether they were the only one who had been selected to be put through the test or why the test was being done, which would undoubtedly increase their suspicion about what the other gang members had led the detectives to believe.

Christie had also clued Carter and Graham in. They were set to bring the other gang member into the room 'on accident' in the middle of Christie's interview with Dredge. It was perfect—almost too perfect.

It was all working in Christie's favor. The man Christie was now standing before was known by his street name, Dredge. Now, after he had been through the residue test, his mood was not so lighthearted and confident anymore. Now, it was Christie who was smilingly gloating over him.

"So," she began, in a pleased voice, "you all gave us quite the hard first round of interviews, but you guys are not so foolproof as you let on, are you? The cracks are already starting to show." Her eyes shone with victory, and her lips curled with amusement.

For a long moment, his expression never wavered. But then Christie spotted the tiny smidgen of doubt that scurried across his features like a squirrel rushing between two bushes. It was there for hardly a moment, but she had caught it. Christie's smile widened even further as she watched the man's indifferent façade begin to crumble. That was all the confirmation she needed that her words were already beginning to work. She shook her head, rubbing her hands together and looking down at the paper in front of her, making a show of delaying until she had to speak again.

"Not quite so confident this time?"

He was staring at her. Now there was rage in his eyes, rage at what he knew she was doing to him and what he knew he would soon succumb to.

"Nothing to say?" Her smiled stretched further, revealing her pink gums and the pearly white tops of her teeth. "Hmm," she continued, "what a shame. Not that we need you to say anything. Your friends have already ensured that we have exactly what we need for now."

The man still refused to speak, but now there was more doubt creasing his face, more squirrels darting through the underbrush which were not quite so hidden anymore.

Christie sighed theatrically, continuing unbothered, as if she were simply talking to herself, as if his input wasn't even needed. "You guys evaded the police's attention for a while. I'll give that to you. You had a good run. Since your run-in with that drug dealer that a couple of your guys were charged for murdering a few of months ago, you've been doing all your business without the use of violent force, haven't you?"

The man continued to maintain his stony silence. But the storm of confused uncertainty raging within him was so palpable it could now be felt in the room. Christie could practically sniff the stench of his dissolving loyalty.

She shook her head. "But manipulation tactics only work for so long, huh? Tomorrow, next week, sooner or later, someone doesn't uphold their end of the deal, and you have to, you know… take care of them."

Jed recognized what she was saying as the information she had received from Blake's best friend in his interview.

"It's irritating how quickly guys like Blake start to think they're part of the core of the gang, huh? That they can't be punished. It's tragic." Christie clicked her tongue regretfully. "A tragic story but one we hear often. It was just his time," she cooed, as though sympathizing with the gang's motive for what they had done to Blake.

"What the fuck are you on about?" Dredge eventually snarled, his eyes now narrowed to slits.

Christie tilted her head at him, her voice suddenly condescending. "As though you don't know what I'm on about." She waved a hand toward his face. "Oh, come on. We've already got enough information out of your boys to move forward. You don't even have to worry about saying anything incriminating."

Through his window of observation, Jed noticed the beads of sweat gathering on the man's forehead. His hateful expression had still not changed. Christie shuffled her papers around, dragging her finger down the page until she got to what she was looking for.

"You guys are known for using a .44. Why that one? Seems a little too specific… a little too traceable." She turned the page, letting her finger down until she got to another point of information. "And why do you guys love drive-by shootings so much? Aren't you ever worried you'll miss your target?" Christie laughed as though she found the question, and the whole interview, intensely amusing. "I admit it is impressive that so far you guys have reasonably impressive accuracy. Very efficient process you guys have. I'll give you that".

The man's chest was rapidly falling up and down now. His baleful eyes were locked on Christie like he intended on devouring her. But it was all just pretend now; Jed could clearly see it. The man's resolve was a dam marked with a spider-web of thick cracks, and any moment, now his true emotions would come flooding through the crumbling wall.

Christie sighed as though she was bored.

"Either way once, we have the results of the residue tests you guys will be seeing the lock up."

"What?"

Before Christie could manage to respond, the door behind them opened. She whipped around in time to see Carter and Graham leading in another of the gang members—he was called Vero. He was a short, stocky man with tanned skin and hair that was long on top and cropped at the sides. From her peripherals, Christie spotted Dredge's eyes bulging. Graham and Carter looked confused for a moment before Carter spoke up.

"Sorry, Detective. We had one willing to talk, so we brought him in. Didn't realize you were still speaking with this one."

Shock and dismay filled Vero's features, and he whipped around to face Carter. Christie was glad the man's arms were handcuffed behind him and that both Carter and Graham had a firm hold on each of his arms. If he had been free, she was sure he would have lunged for Carter's throat.

"That's alright. We should be wrapped up in about fifteen. Nothing much left to say after all. We've already got what we wanted."

Vero looked frantic. "She's lyin', man. I didn't say shit!"

As the officers retreated with their quarry, Christie turned back to Dredge, determination and satisfaction set in her features. Her plan was going off without a hitch.

Dredge's hate was gone now. That mocking confidence had drained from his body. His eyes nervously flitted left and right like the gaze of a cornered animal. His mind was in disarray, scrambling to deduce what possible information Vero could have supplied to the police.

"What's the matter?" she asked, picking up their conversation as though it had never been interrupted. "Like I said at the start, your group is not nearly as solid as you think." Christie dramatically crossed her arms as though doing him a favor with her explanation. "Gangs are all the same. They start off hard, they laugh, they pretend as though they aren't interested in investigations, as though the police have no idea what they're talking about... but then, once you get them alone, and you talk to them one-on-one," she tutted softly with disappointment, "they get to talking. And it's not like any of you know who it was that finally cracked under pressure and spilled the beans."

Then, she shrugged and said with a sinister smile, "But the first guy to spill, gets the best deal."

Returning to her casual demeanor. "Like I said I don't even know why you guys bothered. It always comes down to every one of you looking out for yourselves and trying to make the best deal. Your loyalty is always an illusion."

"That's impossible!" Dredge cried, hands balling into fists on the steel desk.

Her plan was working. His chest was heaving so hard that he might as well have been running a marathon.

"They wouldn't tell you anything," Dredge repeated firmly, but now it sounded like the words were spoken more to convince himself than the detective in front of him.

Christie smiled apologetically. "Of course they wouldn't," she said. "That's exactly what they want you to believe."

Jed was watching her work, hanging on her every word, every inflection in her tone. Watching her drill him and influence his reactions was extremely attractive.

"Since you will be seeing the inside of lock-up very soon, you may as well get acquainted with your accommodations here. Prison isn't nearly as hospitable."

Dredge's eyes went wide. His lips quivered once, twice, and then it finally happened. He broke.

"Listen, you," he hissed, doubt flashing in his eyes, "he had it coming. We gave him enough chances. It's not like we're terrible people. We're just doing our job the same way everyone else has a fucking job in this city. We have our job, and we have a responsibility to the people we serve. Anyone who gets in our way is fucked. That's why we give so many chances, and he had as many chances as we could give him. But he was so confident after we saved his ass from the people who were after him."

The confessions were pouring out of him. Christie acted as though she had already had this information, like what he was saying was exactly what she had expected and already heard.

"I mean, I can't tell you how to run your business, and you clearly know the law, which is why you're trying to convince me that you did the right thing."

Dredge narrowed his eyes at her and cursed under his breath. "You'll never get all of us in any case. There's nine of us here, and there's three times as many still out in the city. Your police force is fucked. We will never be stopped. And the more you mess with us, the worse it'll get. They'll start pulling off shit you never even knew was possible—then you'll see how many police officers it takes to take down our whole team."

Christie wasn't the slightest bit phased by his threats of larger retaliations.

"The NYPD will always catch and dismantle any plans your gang could have," she said with a grin. "You nine just won't be around to see it happen. We'll see you in court."

Jed couldn't contain his smirk. They would definitely need to have an office party tonight, with the way things were going. As per Christie's plan, when Carter and Graham came to retrieve Dredge and take him back to the holding area, Carter not so subtlety directed a 'thank you for your cooperation' at Dredge, just within earshot of the others so the seed of fear and doubt could spread.

In Christie's second interview, with Vero right after, all the rest of the story came out. He confirmed that it was Dredge who had pulled the trigger on Blake. Fingerprints on the bullet casing at the scene matched Dredge's fingerprints.

Amongst all the other interviews they did with the other seven men, no one confessed to any association with Joel and Ethan's murder. None of them even seemed to know who he was. No matter how Christie phrased her questions, at the end of the day, the answers were a resounding 'no'. Blake's murder was solved, but for Ethan and Joel, they were back at square one.

CHAPTER 16

"CONGRATULATIONS ON CRACKING THEIR collective hardened mask," Jed offered to Christie as he watched her pack her things before they left the station together.

Christie smiled at him in response, but he noticed it didn't quite reach her eyes.

"Thank you," she remarked. "It was a bit nerve-wracking at first because I absolutely did not know what the hell I was talking about. But he didn't know that. And that was enough for me to keep pushing."

Jed's head tilted to the side, appreciation and something coy written all over his face. Christie's heartbeat picked up as she watched Jed's eyes trail down over her body, lazily, before their eyes met again.

"In the end, it worked out well," she finished.

"You did amazing in there," he said, the heat now clearer in his eyes.

Christie flushed. "Thank you."

The silence stretched between them until she had secured all her belongings into her purse and picked it up to head for the door. Jed was blocking her path.

"At the risk of putting too much on your plate, Detective, I do want to have a serious conversation with you about the way you undermine yourself and your own capabilities." His eyes narrowed down at her. "Call it a free therapy session."

Christie hesitated, unsure of how to respond.

"There's no pressure, of course," Jed continued, stepping aside so that she could get to the door if she preferred. "I just want to talk to you about it. That's all. I find it interesting the way you exude so much confidence and expertise but simultaneously knock yourself down."

"I'm open to talking about it," Christie said, looking up at him. "Your place or mine?"

Jed laughed aloud, reaching for the knob on the door and pulling it open. "Yours. I don't want you to get tired of my apartment so soon."

Christie joined him in laughing as they headed down the hallway.

Walking home with Christie was a new experience. His rule of protection for her was that she shouldn't leave the police station without an accompanying officer or him by her side. Tonight, for the first time, he was the one upholding his own rule for her. The journey from the station was short, just a fifteen-minute walk. But as they chatted about the case and the lighter things in life, like the traffic they were walking by and the full restaurants and the wonderful smells seeping out of their open doors and into the city air, Jed couldn't help but feel his heart squeeze painfully.

Her route was as safe as safe could be, especially for New York. But the dark sky, and the people walking by, made him more and more queasy with the realization of how quickly things could go south if she were walking home alone.

He wanted to protect her more than he had initially realized. Setting the regulation in place that she was with someone at all times was easy. It was for her own good, after all, and had nothing to do with his male ego. But now that he was the one walking her home, he felt himself grow more and more protective. She had already bristled at his attempts to protect her a few times. It was subtle, not an outright rejection that made him concerned that he was being overbearing. Apart from their miscommunication, she had been largely open to his offer of protection. But now, as they were approaching her apartment, her on the inside of the sidewalk chattering away about how much she wanted a kitten and how she had one growing up, Jed was realizing that apart from wanting her to be protected and safe in general, *he* wanted to be the one to protect her and keep her safe.

Relationship. It came to mind again as they stepped into the elevator from the lobby and rode it to her floor. It was always on his mind when he was around Christie. He wanted to be the one to protect her, and there was no way for him to do so, or even propose to do so in their current working relationship. She hadn't bristled outright at his imposition on her movement and her independence, but if he were to suggest that he be the only one to accompany her to and from work, Jed knew he would risk her feeling imposed upon. He didn't want to do that. But on the other hand, he did want to do that. He wanted to be with her at all times. He wanted to protect her full-time. He wanted her to be his.

As the elevator doors opened and they walked down the hallway to her door, her leading the way, him behind her watching her hips sway, the memory of Jason's pushback on her boundary came to mind. He didn't even want to entertain the thought of what could have happened if Jason hadn't backed off. What if Christie hadn't closed the door? Or what if he had forced himself into the apartment with her? The thought made his blood boil within him. When Christie opened the door and turned to invite him in, he knew his expression was stony.

Christie's brows creased as she watched him close the door behind him.

"Everything alright, Jed?" she asked, setting her purse and keys down on the counter.

Jed watched her lean down to pull her shoes off. He nodded. "Everything's just fine, Detective."

Her eyes narrowed at him as she put her shoes into the shoe organizer next to the door.

"I don't believe you." she said, walking up to Jed and standing in front of him with her arms crossed.

He looked down at her in the dim light of the kitchen, letting his eyes run over her figure, down to her toes and back up to her face. She was a delicious little thing. And he loved the way her lips pressed into a line when she was trying to pry the truth out of him.

"Just... worried about you, Detective. And trying not to overstep my boundaries in my zeal to protect you."

"What boundaries might those be?" she asked. "I don't recall us having a conversation about where the line is for you protecting me."

Jed looked at her for a long moment before nodding.

"You're right," he conceded. "Let's have that conversation right now. Where is the line, Detective? Because if you let me, I'll walk you to work and walk you back home every night."

Christie blinked. "Are you that worried about me?"

Jed's expression darkened. "I am, Detective," he murmured, reaching out to push a strand of her hair behind her ear. "Especially since the most recent interaction you've had with an officer taking you home was him pushing back on a boundary you set. Now, I'm wondering if I can even trust the NYPD to protect you, even though I know those men care about you."

"Are you saying you care about me more?" Christie asked, pressing him for response.

Jed tilted his head down at her, wondering at the curiosity and hesitancy in her voice. Did she think he would back away from her question or answer her with anything except the whole truth?

"Without question."

Her eyes flashed with surprise. She looked down at his chest for a moment, thinking.

"I don't have a problem with you taking me to and from work," she finally answered, "but I don't think it's the best decision. I do go out with my friends quite often, and they tend to take me home. My best friend, Roman, always brings me home. He did the same when we were back home. He moved here a couple of months before me for a job opportunity." Christie laughed to herself. "And then I got one, too."

Christie didn't miss the way Jed's eyes darkened when she mentioned that her best friend was a man.

"And he takes you all the way up here?" he asked, keeping his voice neutral.

Christie nodded. "Yes, but I don't tend to invite him in. He's never wanted to anyway. He usually waits for me at the elevator until I get inside, and then he goes back down into his car."

Jed nodded, but then, his eyebrows scrunched together at the thought occurring to him.

"So, you told Jason no, and your best friend, Roman, doesn't come in either." He stepped closer. "Am I to infer that I'm the only one you've let into your apartment?"

Christie took a deep breath in, suddenly feeling a little flustered from his closeness. She nodded. Jed hummed deep in his throat, satisfaction flowing through his body.

"Good." Raising his head away from her, Jed looked into the living room. Then he looked back down at her. Christie's arms were still crossed over her chest, and her breathing was slightly faster than it had been when he had initially asked the question. He guessed it was because he was now closer to her, close enough to see the way her pupils dilated and contracted with her various expressions. "So, Detective, where's the line?"

"Well," Christie began, "since we've already established a routine of you coming to the office after your workday ends, you could take me home."

"I'll settle for that for now." His tone made it clear that this conversation would come again up later. "Now," he said stepping around her and into the kitchen to open her fridge, "should I cook you dinner, or should we order in? We might be here a while." He glanced over at her over the top of the door of the fridge. "I want to make sure I get into all the details of that mind of yours."

"In that case, we should order in," Christie replied, her voice soft in the large space. "We don't want to waste any valuable time".

His eyes ran over her again as she turned to head into her room.

"Indeed, we don't."

When Christie had come back from her shower wearing a tank top and sweatpants, Jed had their dinner laid out on the table, ready and waiting. He had ordered pizza, thinking it was the easiest option and the fastest thing for them to get through before their conversation. For some reason that he was still trying to identify, he was nervous. There was no reason for him to be nervous, but because of the nature of the conversation and the dynamic of their relationship, it felt a bit strange. He shook his head to himself. It was so interesting how the dynamic of a relationship could change in such a short time.

In the three or so weeks between their previous case and Joel's murder, their relationship had deepened. Initially, as they had been settling into their partnership, and particularly while he had been away at the cottage, Jed had had no trouble being objective in his conversations with Christie—in holding her accountable for some of the emotional patterns that he had noticed in her behavior. Now however, for some reason, he was struggling to maintain the same level of objectivity.

He closed his eyes. Ever since the first day of the retreat, when he had really opened up to her, he struggled more and more every day to keep his feelings at bay. Now, watching her bite into a slice of pepperoni pizza, the cheese dripping down her lip, Jed steeled himself for the conversation about to begin. In between bites, Christie looked over at him.

"What's on your mind, Gray?" she asked.

Jed smiled ruefully. He shook his head. "We'll talk about it in a second. After you've eaten your fill."

"Are you sure?" she pressed.

When he nodded, she returned the gesture, and they went back to eating in silence. When they were seated on the couch together, Christie turned to him. "Now, Jed, tell me what's going on. What do you want to talk about? My self-sabotage, you said?"

Jed nodded, giving her the space to initiate the conversation.

"Well," Christie sighed, "it all started when I was born."

Jed threw his head back as a laugh barked out of him. He had not seen that one coming. "Forgive me, Detective," he said as he regained control and his laughter faded.

Christie was smiling at him.

"Continue your story."

Christie shook her head. "I think it has to do with my parents." she said under her breath, looking up at Jed nervously. She found no judgment in his eyes and managed to continue. "My dad was a cop, the best one in his town. Everyone loved him, and he was great at his job. He never had any strikes on his profile, he obeyed the law even when it was inconvenient, and he never took advantage of the power he had. Still, sometimes I felt like he held me to a bit of an unrealistic standard. I don't think he did it on purpose," she mused, "but that's what happened. He was always on me about my grades. If I brought home a B+? Oh, please. That was beneath me.

It was straight As or nothing. And with sports, every time I missed a pass, or missed being the gold medalist, even if I placed second, his response was the same. *You're better than that Christie,*" she managed to mimic his voice, tears filling her eyes as the memory of the loss of her father bubbled to the surface and she remembered his voice. "*You're better than that.* That's what he always said. That's the standard he held himself to. And that's the standard he transferred to me."

She sighed, letting her head fall against the back of the sofa. Her eyes fluttered closed.

"My mom did the same, only in a different way. When it came to chores, or anything I did around the house, I could never get it right. If I did the dishes, she would complain about a single spot in the sink. If I vacuumed the rug, she would complain that the lines weren't done correctly. If I cleaned my room, she would find something that was out of place to mumble about. I could never get things just right." Christie's voice grew quiet as the memories came back to her. "I don't think they meant any harm by what they did. They just wanted the best for me."

She looked over at Jed, whose eyes were already fixed on her. Kindness shone out of them.

"Well, Christie," he began, "you don't need to be better. You are perfect as you are"

Christie stared at him, blinking more and more rapidly as tears formed in her eyes until, eventually, they spilled down her cheeks. Jed resisted the urge to pull her into his arms. He wanted to give her the emotional space she needed.

"I can understand your feelings of empathy toward your parents' actions and the way they chose to teach you how to work hard. They did the best they knew how to. But the impact of their actions and words cannot be denied, regardless of what they intended. Their actions and their words caused you pain. They led you into a false belief that you need to be perfect to be good enough. Your output has nothing to do with your value."

More tears.

"Your output has nothing to do with your worth."

Christie swiped at her eyes.

"And your output certainly has nothing to do with how the people around you see you."

Silence stretched between them for a while as Christie struggled to compose herself.

"One of the difficulties with how your parents chose to try to teach you that lesson about hard work is that they never acknowledged the good things you did. It sounds like they only focused on the areas where you messed up, the small areas where you weren't perfect."

Christie nodded. "I do believe they only wanted the best for me. And if I'm being honest, it did work. I was at the top of my class and have a reputation for being a great detective. So, I guess it isn't all bad."

Jed tilted his head at her. "Well, you should know that the people around you see more than just the minute things you focus on. When we were at the Chinese restaurant waiting for you to give your cue, I knew for sure that all the officers were confident in whatever you decided. We discussed it at the station before we moved out and initiated the plan, and everyone knew that there was a chance that if we got there and there were too many members of the gang for our numbers to take, you would have called it off. Everyone agreed that would be best, instead of risking our plan going south because we decided to take on something that was bigger than we could handle."

Jed paused, watching as she swiped at her cheek again.

"No one would have held that against you. Yet at the last minute, you were consumed with worry about how you would be perceived if you decided to call it off—as though it would have equated to a personal failure on your part. Meanwhile, everyone else was entirely confident in whatever you would decide."

Christie sniffled.

"While you were at the station today, I was watching you beat yourself up about something you have no control over. None of our officers, and surely not the chief, would hold you to blame for not being able to crack the defenses of a hardened group of gangsters in the first 10 minutes of talking to them. Yet, you were lost in your mind, drowning in those thoughts of yours, beating yourself up."

Christie swiped at her eyes again.

"No one is looking at you through a lens of criticism. Do you automatically do that when you look at the people that you work with? Do you immediately start calculating what they could do better?"

Christy shook her head 'no' immediately. "No, of course not," she said. "That would be ridiculous. Everyone has imitations. I know that my team is working hard to help us succeed as a unit."

"Hmm," Jed hummed as he formed his reply. "So, you have empathy for other people but not for yourself."

Christie blinked, suddenly realizing the connection Jed was going after with his question about the way she saw and thought of others.

"Yeah," she replied, her voice defeated, "I guess so. Kind of stupid, isn't it?" She let out a weak laugh that sounded more like a huff.

Jed smiled. "No. I don't think it's stupid. I think it's *human.* And I don't think you're stupid either. I think you're brilliant. I think you have a wonderful, analytical mind. Like you said when we first met, I think you're the best wherever you go, and I hope you stay. New York City is better because of you. Two cases cracked in two months. Do you understand the statistical glory that is?"

Christie didn't reply. She was looking down at her hands. She was never sure what to do in situations where people were complimenting her.

"Something just went through your mind," Jed observed.

Christie raised her face to his, confusion clear on her features.

"Your expression changed while you were looking at your hand. What went through your mind?"

Christie's brows pulled together. "How are you so perceptive?"

"It's easy to be perceptive when I care about you so much."

"So, you're not being paid by the NYPD to psychoanalyze me?" Christie inquired, a tease in her voice.

"No, I'm not. For you…"

"I would do it for free," Jed and Christie said in unison, and then burst into laughter.

Christie's mind returned to the question Jed had asked her. She sighed. "I'm not sure what to do when people compliment me. That's what I was thinking."

Jed nodded slowly. "Do you think that's because your parents only focused on the areas where you were weakest?"

Christie nodded right away. "Yeah, the people who I needed that kind of acknowledgement from the most completely failed to give it to me, so now whenever other people compliment me, it feels… empty."

Jed shook his head. "It's understandable how your experience would result in that kind of reaction. What that tells me is that I need to praise you more."

Christie's cheeks flushed pink. Jed's head tilted at her, and he chuckled.

"Of course," he whispered under his breath.

"Of course, what?" Christie asked, immediately on the defense.

Jed looked her dead in the eyes, a smile on his lips. "Of course, you would blush when I mention that I want to praise you more. Do you like the sound of that?"

The blush on her cheeks deepened, and she felt heat sneaking down her neck. Jed watched her, a strange mix of seriousness and amusement in his eyes.

"If you prefer, we could try another way of getting you used to compliments and making sure they mean something to you—not that I would mind singing your praises all the time. There are very many praises to sing, after all."

Christie pulled her eyes away from his as she thought about the question. Her cheeks burned nonstop. She knew what she wanted, but she wasn't sure how to say it without dying of embarrassment. Jed's eyes were on her, and as though he could sense her dilemma, he prodded gently.

"Use your words, Detective."

Her eyes flashed up to his. She still hesitated. Jed maintained his silence for a moment, giving her the opportunity to speak if she was ready. She didn't. He shook his head, smiling.

"We may also need to shift into discussing your aversion to expressing your emotions and feelings outright."

Christies' lips parted.

"What do you want?" Jed asked, his voice firmer now.

It was clear that he wasn't going to back down. She sighed, resigning herself to her fate.

"Praise me," she said under her breath.

Jed leaned forward, tilting his head down at her. "What was that?" he asked softly, "I'm not sure I heard you clearly."

Christie swallowed, cheeks once again burning under his attention. "I want you to praise me," she said louder.

Jed nodded, satisfied. Sitting back, he continued. "What we're going to try to do is counter all the years of having your shortcomings picked out with constructive, truthful, genuine applause for all you do right. And trust me, there is plenty that you do right. I don't think I'm ever going to run out of praise for you."

Christie was unsure what to say.

"I hope this strategy will help you feel more confident in your abilities moving forward. I never want you to feel like the people around you, your team, and even more particularly, me, are constantly evaluating you or that we're holding you to the impossible standard of perfection. And I want you to stop holding yourself to that standard of perfection," Jed said, his voice firm. "I want you to stop punishing yourself whenever you don't get things perfect. No one could live up to that standard."

Christie nodded again. Then, Jed smiled. "Now, on to your avoidance of confessing your feelings," he began, his eyes narrowing at her. "Where do you think that comes from?"

Christie sighed again, harder this time. "I think from the same place. Whenever I said how I felt, my feelings were always overlooked. It didn't really matter that I had been feeling sick on the morning of the test. All that mattered was that I didn't get 100%. And it didn't really matter that I didn't see the spot in the sink my mother was talking about. All that mattered was that I didn't do it correctly."

Christie's eyes were glossy once again, and Jed's heart was breaking for her.

"So, your feelings were always overridden on account of your performance?"

Her voice cracked. "My feelings don't matter."

Suddenly, Jed reached forward, taking hold of her by the knees and pulling her forward on the couch so that she was closer to him. And he tilted her face up to his, his expression serious—more serious than she had ever seen it.

"Your feelings matter. Even if you feel like they don't, or you don't have sufficient evidence that the people around you hold space for how you feel, your feelings matter. I'll also work on making sure you know that. But I don't ever want to hear you say that your feelings don't matter. Do you understand?"

Christie nodded.

"Use your words, Detective," Jed commanded, his voice lower.

Christie sighed, but she didn't pull away from his hold. "Yes. I understand."

They sat in silence for a few minutes, and Jed looked at his watch. It was already 9:30 at night. He said, "Well, this has been a very eventful and productive day. You must be exhausted. I will let you get some well-deserved rest after I help you clean up".

Jed helped Christie clean up the dishes and put the left-over pizza away in the fridge.

After Jed left, Christie bolted the door, turned off the lights, and headed into her bedroom. She was thinking about her conversation with Jed. She had never been so honest or raw with anyone before—not even with Roman. She felt twenty pounds lighter. She changed into her favorite t-shirt to sleep in and slid under the covers.

Christie couldn't even remember her head hitting the pillow or any thoughts or dreams she had that night. She had one of the best night's sleep she'd had in several years.

CHAPTER 17

"Hi, Mom," Jed answered. "What's up?"

It was Wednesday. Tuesday had come and gone in a blur. He had woken up, completed his morning routines, gone to work, gone to the station, walked Christie home, then headed home and crashed. Today, he felt a little more like himself.

"Hi, Jed. How are you?" Laurie asked.

"I'm alright, Mom. Just getting ready for work this morning."

"How are the cases?"

"Well, I've got good news and bad news," he told her. "We made significant progress in one area, in that we made arrests for the shooting that took place."

"That's wonderful news," Laurie exclaimed. She clapped her hands.

Jed smiled at his mom's enthusiasm. "Christie did a fantastic job in orchestrating and leading the execution of a stake out that mobilized a massive portion of the NYPD. That was what led to the initial arrests we made. Then she headed the interrogations and interviews, which brought forward the confession of guilt so we could move into formal arrests."

"Wow," Laurie commented, clearly impressed. "For sure, she is one hell of a detective."

Jed smiled wistfully. "Yeah, she is."

Laurie giggled at her son's vague response. "Is that all you're going to say?"

Jed sighed into the receiver, and his mom laughed even more. "There's a lot I could say," he began, grinning despite himself, "but what are you wanting to hear?"

"Well," Laurie answered, "I'm not actually sure. I'm not expecting you to give me a play-by-play of your relationship with her. After all, you are an adult. I'm just curious how things are going between you two."

Jed could hear the eagerness in her tone, and it only widened the smile on his face. *Oh, Mom. Where do I even start?*

"Well, she's just as beautiful as ever, her work ethic is even more impressive, and I'm learning more and more about the things she does and why she does them the way that she does them."

Jed looked down at his hands and adjusted the watch around his wrist. "One thing is certain, though, and it's that since the start of this case, we've grown a lot closer emotionally. We've both had to open up a bit to understand each other better so we can support each other throughout our working relationship. We worked on and through multiple murders in the span of a little less than two months, and even though it's only been two formal cases, we're both fighting our own emotional battles."

On the other side of the line, Laurie hummed softly. "Yes, I can understand that. It's definitely important that you two work through your own emotions and, perhaps, work through them with each other. You may be able to help one another with the benefit of an outside perspective. If you guys are going to be partners, you definitely need to have that connection."

Jed scratched his chin, wondering whether or not to make the admission lurking at edge of his mind. After a few moments of indecision, he just gave in and decided to blurt it out. "Having a closer connection with her has been helpful for our working relationship so far... but not so much with the struggle of keeping my feelings platonic."

"Oh?" Laurie murmured, trying to feign some surprise. Of course, she had already guessed this a long time ago. "Were your feelings for her ever platonic?"

Jed snorted at the question before biting his lower lip. "That's a good question," he mused.

"I know!" she replied in a sing-song voice.

A few moments passed, a few moments during which Jed's features were crisscrossed with a look of deep thought. When he finally spoke, it was in a resigned tone. There was no hiding from the truth once it was out. "They weren't. From the first moment I saw her, there was an instant glimmer of interest. Alas," he continued, "now that has grown into a massive, and sometimes overpowering, desire to be far more than just her work partner."

"And I take it you haven't brought that up with her?" Laurie asked.

"I mean, I kind of did... but still not in a straightforward manner. I don't want to make things weird. And I'm pretty sure things would get weird quickly if I started declaring my feelings."

"Do you think she feels the same?"

Jed hesitated. "I want to believe that she does, but I don't want to make it a habit of reading too deeply into her mannerisms and behavior. I don't want to make things up when things aren't there because that could impact the way I behave toward her."

"Yes, yes," Laurie agreed impatiently, "I know. Work boundaries and ethics. But you haven't actually answered the question."

Jed thought about the question for a moment. His heart had begun hammering inside his chest again, and he was feeling a bit woozy.

"I think it's a possibility," he admitted finally, sensing his throat turning dry with fear. Now that he had spoken it out aloud, he realized how much the idea of Christie not reciprocating his feelings terrified him. "I think there's a chance she does. Although I do think that I'm far deeper into it than she is, if she is interested in the first place."

Laurie nodded. "I can understand that. And I figure that for now, you guys are just going to continue working together. Your partnership is admirable though. It's remarkable what you guys have managed to achieve together in such a short time. You both will have New York City corralled in no time. In fact, I wanted to ask you a question about it all."

Jed snickered. "Now, Mom, I haven't suddenly become an expert in solving crimes, but sure. I'll take a stab at it."

Laurie laughed along at her son's tease. "You're more of an expert than I'll ever be. I wanted to know what you thought about this—it's for my story. The main conflict is that the detective hasn't been able to figure out a motive for the crime. I'm more than half-way through, and it's starting to feel a little unrealistic. The issue seems obvious. I feel like I'm dragging it out."

Jed laughed a little, then sighed. "No two cases are exactly alike, I've learned. And even if something seems straightforward when you first approach it, there are often a thousand small complications and nuances that make it miserably difficult to truly nail. Is the detective making any progress with evidence or clues?"

"Yes," Laurie answered after a moment. "There have been a few small patterns she has noticed that are beginning to add up."

Jed nodded. "Patterns are good. You have to remember that you know the end of the story already. So, it seems like she's lagging behind when, in reality, she's not seeing all the details and signs you're able to see. You control the story. She only knows what she can see."

Laurie hummed. "You're right. I have become a little impatient. I guess I just really want the story to be finished so I can celebrate that I've written a full novel."

Laurie giggled, and Jed smiled.

"Wait," she asked, jerking herself out of her reverie, "what's the bad news? We got distracted, and I forgot to ask."

"The bad news is that we're having a repeat of events like the last case we worked on. We've made advancements in one area of the case and have run into a block in another. We still know nothing about the chef's murderer. We don't have many credible leads in that area."

***

At the office, Jed let himself sink into his chair for a while. He had done a good job keeping the heavier of his thoughts about Hugh at bay lately, but sometimes, when he was alone in his office before he really got started in earnest, his past conversations with Hugh came to mind. Unlike his memories and thoughts about Ethan, Hugh's never seemed to get easier to bear. Jed wasn't sure if that was because he had spent most of his time actively avoiding thinking about the ruined friendship or if the hurt was just deeper.

He stared at the ceiling. He would need to confront the feelings that were bubbling up inside him every time he was alone in his office and remembered his old friend. Had they really been friends? Did he ever truly know Hugh? Well, at least he knew the answer to that question. He hadn't really known Hugh. They had just met, after all, and for as perceptive as he liked to think he was, Jed hadn't immediately noticed that the man had the potential to be a serial killer.

And, of course, he knew it was both unfair and unrealistic to hold himself to trial by fire because he thought he should have noticed. But even knowing this, Jed still felt partially responsible for what Hugh had done. He felt as though noticing the signs earlier in their interactions would have been beneficial in preventing him from murdering more homeless people. He felt as though, by associating with Hugh, even for as short a time as they had, he had personally played a part in the murder of three homeless victims.

Jed knew this thought was ridiculous. He knew it was logically unsound. But it was still how he felt, and there was no use lying to himself about it. In a way, this underlying sense of responsibility had begun to seep into his friendships—like during his time at the retreat. In their first group interaction, when the team of officers had arrived, Jed had found himself paying closer attention to their every move and word than he would have before

Hugh had turned out to be a serial killer. The whole ordeal had made him distrusting. And of course, he was trying to overcome it, trying to not let the bizarre circumstances drive him to erect walls around his heart that were unscalable. He needed to remain open to the people around him; he needed to remain open to his clients. If Jed did fall into the trap of erecting those walls, he knew that they couldn't keep track of who was who. Once he closed himself off emotionally, his heart wouldn't let in some people and keep out others. All his relationships would suffer. He had worked very hard through his recovery to deal with his trust issues because of being abandoned by his father. It was those feelings that led him to seek out the numbing effects of drugs. He didn't want to backtrack on all the hard work he had already done.

Jed was meeting with one of his clients today. Braxton was coming in for his second session. In their last conversation, he and Braxton had worked through some of the man's self-image struggles. Jed found it tragically interesting that even though Braxton desired so deeply to get married and start a family, and so intensely wanted to be a better father than his father had been to him, he had sabotaged himself so thoroughly.

It was incredible and terrifying what the human brain could do. Programmed to keep us safe, the human mind would sabotage even the purest and most wholesome of our desires if it perceived that we would need to put ourselves through any great risk to obtain it. This was what had happened with Braxton. He never approached women, and he spent most of his time being hard on himself, unnecessarily, for the way he looked.

Of course, one's appearance was a key factor in dating. Jed knew the horrors of online and modern dating well—from his friends' experiences, not quite from his own. He could never bring himself to try online dating. But he also heard his clients share some of their experiences. It was a hard road to walk, putting yourself out there. And he wasn't sure who had it harder, typically—men or women. There were struggles on both sides. Of that fact, he was sure. Still, Braxton's disappointment and insecurity about his appearance was a means of self-sabotage. They would need to continue talking through that today because Jed wanted to be sure that they were making progress in that direction.

Of course, his addictive behavior might be connected to this same self-sabotage. It was something he had been looking over as he reviewed the client notes from their previous meeting, considering options for how to mention it when Braxton arrived and was sitting across from him.

As it turned out, he wouldn't need to. Braxton brought it up himself.

"You know, I've been thinking about the last conversation we had. And I think you're right. I'm actually kind of... surprised I didn't notice a connection myself. I definitely think I've been extra hard on myself for how I look, and I'm not even sure why... or how it started." He scrunched up his eyes and paused, trying to focus his energy on remembering his childhood. "I was a pretty happy kid—up until I was teenager. You know how high school kids are. They are bullies. In high school, I was called all sorts of names, and I would just generally be given a really rough time. I spent most of my time alone. My middle school friends didn't really wanna be seen with me anymore. And the girls... the girls that I liked all liked, you know," he waved his hand through the air dismissively as though that would paint the picture perfectly, "the typical popular guys."

Jed nodded. "It's interesting that you brought up the fact that your friend group from middle school suddenly did not seem interested in being friends with you anymore. Do you have any theories as to why that was?"

"Everyone decided to suddenly get cooler over the summer break, and I guess I didn't get the memo."

"How have your relationships with friends been now, in your adulthood?"

For a long moment, Braxton didn't respond. Jed watched a myriad expressions form and disintegrate on his face as he foraged through his thoughts and memories for the answer.

"In order to answer how my relationships with friends have been, I would have to have relationships to begin with," he finally stated in a slightly bitter tone.

"Yes, that is true. Do you feel that you don't have any true friendships right now?"

The man shrugged. "I mean, given that I just got out of prison, no. But even before I got locked up, I found myself alone most of the time. I've never really had a group I felt like I belonged in. Having the wrong group would have been better than having no group at all. I was at bars alone; I went to the movies alone. I would just see groups of guys hanging out, you know, doing guy stuff—watching games, drinking beers, talking about cars. I just didn't have that."

The confession was made in an utterly casual manner, and that was what made it so heartbreaking. The most saddening people were the ones who spoke about the tragedies of their life with complete indifference, as if they had been pummeled to the ground so many times that they had even grown tired of complaining.

"I'm sorry that you didn't have a safe group of people that you felt seen by and could rely on in that period of time." Jed's voice brimmed with sympathy. "And I'm sorry that you don't have that now. I hope that, through our sessions, we can explore what it would look like for you to have close friendships and how you can begin to build those now. It's not too late to build friendships that will last." Jed immediately noticed the skepticism on Braxton's face. It broke his heart even further. His assessment had been right. Braxton had been living without hope of a better life for so long now that the very concept had become alien to him. He shied away from the prospect of a bright future as if it were some nasty disease.

"Lots of people pass a certain age," Jed continued in a firm voice, "and suddenly start thinking that it's too late to make friends. That couldn't be further from the truth. But I wanted to focus on building yourself confidence first."

Braxton nodded uncomfortably. This conversation was clearly not an easy one for him. It seemed he had grown too accustomed to his own lonely existence and wasn't receptive to change. Jed watched him fidget in his chair, his arms lying awkwardly limp in his lap. Then, after a minute or two, he raised his eyes back to Jed.

"This is uncomfortable," he confessed.

Jed smiled kindly.

"Is it always going to be like this?"

Jed actually thought about that question first, so that Braxton wouldn't think he was just saying things to make him feel better. "No," he finally answered. "It's not always going to be like this. In fact, most of the time, it might feel like pressure is being relieved. We will talk about what you've been through, what your experiences have been, and explore your motives, and you'll begin to feel lighter. Because the more you understand yourself, the easier it is for you to make improvements. You may also discover how exhausting it is to keep most of these things bottled up inside you. Once we uncover them and you are able to let them go, you will have more energy to focus on things you actually want."

Jed paused, gathering the rest of his thoughts. "It's uncomfortable right now because we're working on creating a plan of action. A lot of my clients start off believing that therapy is only about understanding themselves. In fact, it's about a lot more than just that. Information is a vital part of the process. Gathering information looks like me asking you hard, thoughtful questions, and us having conversations that can be scary sometimes but will never harm you. But the other part of the equation is that therapy is about creating plans of action for some things we can do in order to form new healthy habits and thought patterns and reinforce healthy ones you already have."

Braxton took a deep, shaky breath. Then, he nodded. "I understand," he spoke in a voice that once more seemed to be shining with the faintest ray of hope. "And I want to move forward. I don't want these same thoughts to keep drowning me."

"You feel like you're drowning?" Jed noticed quickly, his eyes suddenly homing in on the weary lines creasing Braxton's face. "Let's talk about that feeling in more detail."

"You know, I've just been thinking about my time in prison—how much time I lost, how many opportunities I lost. There's just this feeling of sorrow, and it feels like I'm drowning in it. There's no getting rid of all the feelings of grief after you go through hard things. You know how that feels?"

Jed nodded. "Indeed, I do."

CHAPTER 18

"YOU KNOW, JED," CHRISTIE said while Jed was staring out the window, his mind half occupied by his conversation with Braxton, "I grow more and more discontented with this case by the day. It's ridiculous how many hours I've spent staring at these files, willing the answer to come to me."

Jed didn't respond for a while, his attention still out the window. Christie watched him for a moment before sighing and leaning back into her seat.

"What is it?" she asked, just a bit miffed. "Am I boring you today?"

Despite his sadness, a smile pulled at Jed's lips. "No," he told her quickly, "not in the slightest, Detective." He turned to face her. "Forgive me. What were you saying?"

"What's on your mind? That secret wife and kids you still haven't told me about?" A smile tugged at the corners of her lips.

Jed tilted his head at her. "Actually, the wife sends regards. The kids are happy and healthy, and our little kitten is doing well, too."

Christie's mouth dropped open. Jed laughed.

"I'm just thinking about a conversation I had with my client today. He's going through a hard time and asked for strategies to process grief."

Christie's eyes softened.

"Of course, I gave him all the strategies I know. And I made sure to explain the unpredictable nature of grief—that it comes and goes, waxes and wanes, how sometimes no matter what strategy you employ, it crushes you under its weight. He seemed to take it all in stride." Jed's sudden sigh was loud in the room. "But I know that's because he's already been dealing it on his own for a while. He seemed relieved that I didn't bombard him with questions about why he was only just mentioning it and that I wanted to help him. And most of all, I think that's what really broke my heart. There are so many people hurting, everywhere. And for as much as I pour my soul into all my clients, there are so many people that I will never be able to help. It's… crushing."

Christie's frown was evidence that Jed's confession had caught her off guard. "I didn't realize you felt that way about your work." She looked down at her hands for a moment. "Of course, I knew that you cared deeply about your clients. I guess, well, not many people expand their desire to play the role of helper in their community outside of their job descriptions. Unless they're billionaire philanthropists who have the money to throw at large causes and foundations, most people just do what they can. But they never really think about the bigger picture."

Even though she felt like she was making a mess of her explanation, she watched as Jed nodded. Christie sighed in relief. She could always count on him to make sense of what she was saying.

"I'm constantly thinking about the bigger picture," Jed supplied. "Even before our partnership. I always wished I could do more… reach more people. But especially when we started working together, and the murders started happening to the homeless people—the same people I work with—it made it so much more real. All the lives we were losing that I hadn't been able to reach. All the people I wanted to help. It just… it makes it so much more painful. Our conversation today really reminded me about the different types of grief. There's grieving for things you've lost, there's grieving for things that should have happened but didn't, and there's grieving for things that you still have; you just haven't lost them yet. It's all heavy, and we all experience it."

Christie nodded. "Grief is, indeed, a universal experience."

They were silent for a few minutes while Jed worked through some of the fog in his mind. Then, he took a deep breath and focused his attention on Christie.

"Now, what were you saying about being discontented?"

Christie grinned. "I thought you weren't listening to me."

"We've talked about this before, Detective," Jed replied, not smiling. "I'm always paying attention when it comes to you."

"I was just saying that Joel's case is starting to weigh even more heavily on my mind now that we've wrapped up Blake's case. The checks that I had done on the military connection and politician connection of the family that threatened me also came back as inconclusive. We have no reason to believe that the Brooks family would have access to VX, whether by their own doing or by some connection they have."

She glanced over the notes before her. "I went as far as having checks done into what kind of connections the military connection in this situation has and what kind of access to weapons of warfare he might have. In the end, those came back with a long list of weapons—bombs, guns, heavy artillery, tankers, everything you can imagine the US military has access to. But there was no chemical agent in sight. Not that it would have been readily declared in the initial stages of a police investigation."

She was sifting through the papers in front of her as she spoke, pulling each one to the forefront as she recounted the relevant information. Jed admired how organized she was.

"No chemical agents in sight," she replied as she leaned back into her chair. "I said this before, but now I feel even more certain."

Jed nodded. "This makes me even more nervous. We don't have a plausible lead for Joel's murder, and we don't have anything we could reasonably consider to be a motive. I'm still worried about your safety. The rules concerning you traveling alone still stand."

Jed's eyes were level with her, and Christie nodded.

"My client did mention something that I thought was interesting when he first brought it up. I've been thinking about it all this time, knowing how perceptive he is. But, still, I haven't been able to figure anything out."

"Mind telling me what it was he mentioned?" Christie asked, reaching for her pen.

"He said something about nervous agents on the ground. And opps. He said he knows who his opps are."

"Which implies that we don't know who ours are," Christie finished his sentence.

Jed nodded.

"It's a cryptic message for sure," she remarked after a moment of silence. "Very cryptic, very coded. I have no idea what he's trying to say."

Jed smiled. "Yeah, he tends to do that. He drops something casually, weaves it into the fabric of the conversation we're having, and then he just moves on as though nothing happened. In our previous case with the homeless men, he made a couple comments that I sort of... pushed to the side instead of paying attention to them. It was at the very last minute, when I had exhausted all the other options, that I recognized his meaning. I don't want to make the same mistake. Not this time."

The two looked at each other across the table, understanding the unspoken.

"But so far, nothing. There's clear innuendo to the nerve agent—VX—for sale, and that's a clear indication that we don't know who this nervous agent is. And the ethical battle in my mind, constantly, is whether I should ask him outright what he means or if I should let it slide. I don't want to get my wires crossed. I don't want to endanger my clients just to potentially get ahead on a case. And especially not this client. I just... sometimes, I wish he'd speak more clearly."

A smile was overtaking Christie's face, and she shook her head. "Kids these days, huh? It is like they are speaking a different language."

Jed joined in with a grin of his own. "Yeah, kids these days."

Friday rolled around. Another day passed in a blur. Yesterday had been much like every other day this week—arrive at work, work until lunchtime, take a quick break to eat a homemade meal, then get back to work until it was time to go to the station. Then, he and Christie spent a couple hours discussing the latest leads and trying to figure out a new lead for Joel's murder. So far, much like in Ethan's case, they were coming up short. All they knew was the way in which the murder had been committed. They still didn't have a suspect or motive.

Jed sighed and leaned back in his seat, allowing his thoughts to swarm over him while he stared out the window. Outside, the bustling city life was moving with its same chaotic incoherence, unchanged by all the murders and arrests and drug peddling taking place within it. Kids were still briskly walking on the sidewalk, their faces set in concentration, their colorful schoolbags bouncing on their shoulders. Flocks of pigeons floated in the air like billowing gray curtains, waiting for the next kind soul to throw some food their way. No matter what happened, no matter what the stakes were, the city moved on. *Life* moved on. Jed let his eyes take it all in for a few more seconds, and then he returned his thoughts to Max.

They had met once while Max was still in juvie to set their expectations for therapy and set up the first few appointments. He already knew that Max knew how he looked, how Hugh looked, and how Christie looked. It was incredible how perceptive he was.

If Jed hadn't personally experienced this heightened level of perception when he had been on the streets as a youngster, Max knowing so much about him would have been frightening. But the boy was just checking him out. And Jed didn't blame him. If he were talking with a therapist every week, he would also try to figure out what kind of person they were. Either way, his perceptiveness was of great benefit. Max was the one who had recognized that Hugh was the murderer in their previous case and had given Jed clue after clue, everything to lead Jed to the conclusion without actually saying anything. It was admirable how he volunteered whatever knowledge he had about the murders that were happening.

It wasn't his job to do so, and he was under no obligation. Jed didn't want to get to the point where his ethics were put to the test, but he was prepared for it. With Max, the line was sometimes blurred.

The phone rang. 4:30.

"Hello?"

"Mr. G, what's up?" Max's voice came through the phone.

"I'm doing well, Max, I was just waiting on your call."

"Damn. My bad. I'm a little bit late today."

Jed's eyes narrowed down at the notepad in front of him on which he was preparing to make notes about their session. This was the first time max had ever acknowledged that his calls were later than the 4:00 time they were scheduled for. Jed had never complained about it, knowing that Max would eventually call—though it did make him worry at times, especially since the boy was constantly getting into altercations with other men on the streets.

"That's okay", Jed continued. "I'm happy to wait."

He heard Max sigh before the boy continued on, his chirpy attitude returning.

"So," he said dryly, "I hear personal chefs are expensive."

Jed started at that choice of words and barely held back the surprise that crept into him.

"Yep," he answered carefully. "Upwards of hundreds of dollars for an evening. It all depends on how experienced and in demand that chef is."

Max agreed with a soft grunt.

"Yeah," he drawled, "switching the subject, Mr. G. Do you know where I can get a dart gun?"

Jed grimaced. Now they were really crossing the line between legal and illegal.

"No," he replied calmly.

Max laughed aloud, amused by Jed's sudden shift in tone. "I know what that tone means. Come on, man, don't start lecturing me. I just wondered because," Max took a long gulp from his recently-opened drink, "I keep hearing people talking about them. That they're getting popular, you know? What with it being impossible to trace darts like you can bullets or whatnot."

Another parallel to the case, this time to the tracing test they had done on the gang that had killed Blake.

"In any case, I think it's kind of weird that people are transitioning into darts versus guns. I mean, if you shot a man right through the head, he'd be immediately dead."

Jed was clearly concerned about the direction of the conversation and was steered back into that direction by Max, who didn't seem to share this same level of hesitation.

"So, it's kind of weird," the youngster continued without hesitation, as if entirely unaware of the parallels he was drawing... or feigning unawareness. "I dunno, man. What kind of psycho would go as far as loading a dart with poison to kill somebody?"

Jed breathed slowly and softly, trying not to let Max know how close he was to dangerous territory.

"Honestly, Max," he answered with casual indifference, "I wish I knew. It's definitely an interesting concept that I'm not sure what to make of. Do you know someone who's using darts instead of other means? This is a very interesting turn of conversation."

Jed was hoping that Maxwell would shrug the question off and continue talking about it for a minute or two until they finally let the topic die. As was expected from his very relaxed client, Max laughed, entirely unphased.

"No," he answered. "I don't know anyone who's using darts in favor of the classic stuff. Word on the street says they're getting popular for some reason."

As per usual, Max then steered the conversation toward tamer things like his plans with his girlfriend for the weekend.

CHAPTER 19

THE GARAGE WAS STEEPED in an inky blackness. And then suddenly, like the ancient religious texts claimed, there was light. The door joining the garage to the house creaked open, skewing the darkness with a thin triangle of light. Footsteps came a moment later, the dull thwack of canvas shoes striking concrete. They moved in the direction of the same chest that had been opened just weeks before. Once more, the chest's lid was unlatched and sprung upward. Gloved hands reached forth into the chest's dimly-lit depths, pulling out another glass vial of amber liquid. They held the vial up in the scant light filtering into the garage from the open door, and the light revealed a figure dressed in a gas mask and a hazmat suit.

There was one more thing lying in the chest: an old cellphone that was powered off. Once those covered hands were satisfied with their inspection of the vial, they reached forth into the chest again and withdrew the phone. Then, they closed the lid with a soft thud. A moment later, the footsteps resumed, slowly disappearing beyond the open garage door and back inside the house.

There, the footsteps continued, following a path which led to a musty, beat-up couch in a cramped corner of the house. The vial was placed gently, almost reverently, into a test-tube holder. Then, one of the gloves was peeled off the hand. Pale fingers picked up the phone and powered it on. As the screen brightened after ages of sleep, the call log showed that there had only been one recorder call.

It was registered under a false name and was in no way connected to him, save the IP address the phone was attached to whenever it was powered on and connected to the main grid of New York City. His hand hovered over the call button, but he didn't click it. The phone was a battered, broken old thing that he had bought from a dealer he used to know.

The man had gotten shot recently, but that was all water under the bridge now. He had different plans. Going back into drugs had been his initial goal until he had accidentally crossed paths with that idiot from rehab when he saw him on the news. The reporter was talking about the city's attempt at combatting the increased crime, mental health epidemic, and the opioid crisis with a new investigative team. And then, all the anger and suppressed rage came barreling back into his life. Now, he was on a different path, one that would eventually lead to his demise. That was a risk he was willing to take as long as he could take this idiot down with him. He stared at the small LCD screen, thinking about what he should say. He knew who his next target was. The target he had chosen a few weeks ago didn't seem to be yielding the results he wanted. He hadn't planned to get this close or this personal so soon. Well, he might as well. He pressed the button, and the 'dialing' graphic popped up on the screen.

CHAPTER 20

"DETECTIVE. I NEED YOU. NOW."

Christie swung her legs over the edge of her bed, pushing herself to her feet. She had just been thinking about their most recent conversation and the dead end they had arrived at in their case. Now, here Jed was, saying things that were making her heart race out of her chest.

"Gray? What's going on?"

She rushed to her closet to pull on the first pair of sweats she could find.

"When I get there, we'll talk. I'm on my way to your place. You are home, right?"

Christie nodded, then remembered that Jed couldn't see her. She was so used to communicating with him nonverbally. He was always paying attention to her cues.

"Yes, I'm home."

"Good." His response came immediately. "I'll be there in three minutes."

Christie's heart did not slow down until Jed knocked at her door. And even then, when she opened it and found him standing there, it did not stop racing. It didn't help that he was dressed in all black and his dark brown hair was still wet at the ends. Evidently, he had been in the middle of a shower or had at least just finished showering before he left home. The silence was deafening, and the only break was an irritated sigh that came from Jed.

"I'm not trying to freak you out on purpose. Actually, I'm trying to keep myself calm as well. There's something that you need to see, something that you need to hear—something that I should have noticed."

It was just after nine on a Friday night, and Christie's apartment was dim, only ambient lighting in the corners of the room. When Jed had closed her door behind him, he leaned against it, breathing in and out deeply.

"I've been trying not to worry, but you're starting to freak me out," Christie said, her eyes searching his face.

Jed nodded, the shadows under his eyes bouncing up and down. "I know. And I'm sorry. I'm just trying not to spiral into a panic attack."

He straightened, then walked by her to the couch, calling her over with his arm. When they were seated, he reached for his phone. Christie watched him unlock the phone, open his call log, and dial voicemail. She waited while the robotic voice welcomed them and gave the prompts to listen to new voicemails, listen to saved voicemails, or change the voicemail greeting. Jed clicked the second option, and the robotic voice read out the date. Christie looked over at Jed then. The date and time of the voicemail was just half an hour ago. Reaching into her pocket for the small notepad and pen she had stored away, Christie opened it to a new page.

Jed glanced over at her, a smile pulling at his lips despite the severity of the situation.

A voice crackled through the phone. It was strangely gravelly, perhaps distorted by static. Or maybe the man it belonged to was terribly sick. As soon as it filled Jed's ears, he was overcome by a nauseating wave of fear. He swallowed it down, letting the voicemail play out like it had the first time, so that Christie could hear it.

"So, you couldn't figure out Ethan's murder. I'm not surprised. You haven't figured out Joel's murder either. Still not surprised. But I'm a little disappointed. I thought they said you were the best in the city. Shrill laughter popped through the phone. *This is embarrassing, and honestly, I'm getting impatient. So, I'm gonna make the next one easy for you. Like they say on the streets, keep your friends close and your enemies closer. Somebody's about to get dropped."*

The weirdly distorted voice huffed, and then there was static for a few seconds before silence engulfed the apartment.

Christie's pen hadn't moved an inch. She was staring at Jed's phone with wide, fearful eyes. Her lips were pursed tightly together, and a vein throbbed thinly at the base of her neck. Before she could say anything, Jed raised both hands and pressed the heel of his palms into his eyes to stop himself from crying. Christie tossed her pen and notepad onto the coffee table right in front of them and immediately reached over to wrap her arm around his neck and pull his face into the crook of hers.

His entire body was rigid, and she didn't know whether she had ever felt him so tense before. For a long moment, he didn't speak. He hardly even breathed. He didn't cry either. It seemed he had gotten his emotions under control fast enough to prevent the tears from falling down his face. That didn't stop Christie from worrying. In fact, his silence drove her heart rate up more and more as the minutes ticked by without him saying anything. Eventually, his arms relaxed and wrapped around her waist, then tightened. He sighed.

"Diffusing your own triggers is so painful," he commented. His voice was a mix of agony and weariness.

Christie ran a hand through his hair absentmindedly, nodding. "Yeah," she murmured, "it is."

Jed's eyes closed at the feeling of Christie's hand running through his hair. He suppressed a groan. Instead, he filled his lungs with air, pushing the teasing pleasure that was building in his body to the back of his mind. Eventually, he sat upright, separating himself from Christie's arms even though he did not want to.

"Let's talk about this voicemail before you comfort me."

Still in shock, Christie reached for her pen and paper.

"If I'm honest, I'm not even sure what to say. I'm not sure where to begin. There's so much to offload here. First of all, whoever this is, just confessed to murdering both Ethan and Joel. And he was so bold as to threaten to commit another murder. Actually, unfortunately, we got more than just a threat. It sounds like the plan is already in place, and it's about to be actualized," Jed began.

Christie sighed. "This is so loaded. And this person seems to know you; maybe not personally, but at the very least, they know of you. They said they thought you were the best in the city..."

Christie watched Jed's expression darken. She read a kind of determination in his features.

"This voicemail is sinister and concerning, and I want to figure out that stupid threatening clue he left. This confirms for me that I was not at fault for Ethan's murder. This same voice sent me a voicemail in our previous case, accusing me of being the reason why he was able to overpower Ethan. That was why when the murderer turned out to be Hugh, I felt so betrayed. I couldn't imagine why he would send a voicemail so hurtful. But even then, that doesn't feel like it makes sense because this is a serial killer we're talking about. Of course he would do something to hurt me."

Jed sighed, running a hand through his hair and wishing it was Christie's hand instead.

"When Hugh confessed to only three murders and not Ethan's, refusing to even acknowledge that part of the case, it felt like it all suddenly made no sense. It robbed me of closure completely. At the time, we could have been considering the gang. But that was so far from my mind, and I was so lost in grief that it didn't come up until very recently when we talked about it all."

Jed looked over at Christie, who was making notes and nodding along as he continued.

"Now, right when we started to consider the gang as a possible suspect in Ethan's case, and not so plausible in Joel's case, we get a message from someone who's claiming bragging rights to both those murders. The good thing here is that we now know that Hugh didn't do it and that the gang didn't do it. We don't know who did it. We also don't know their motive. And ... we don't know who they're going after next."

Jed paused for a moment, willing his mind to slow down. His thoughts were all racing, and it was hard for him to restrain them long enough to turn them into words. He looked over at Christie, watching her write.

"It doesn't miss me that the clue they left was to keep your friends close but your enemies closer. You do know what that means, right, Detective?" Jed asked, his tone suddenly much firmer than it had been before.

Christie recognized that he was slipping back into the protective energy he had been exuding over the past weeks. "That you're not going to let me out of your sight?"

Jed nodded the affirmative.

"You know, you may as well ask me to move in with you, Gray," Christie teased, trying to find some light in this situation, but her voice came out sounding heavy and forced.

Jed didn't laugh like she expected. Instead, when he angled his face toward hers, she saw that he was completely serious.

"That's not a bad idea."

Christie's heart skipped a beat.

"It does make me breathe a bit easier, though," Jed continued, pretending not to notice the storm he had stirred up inside his partner. "We have a direction to go in. We just have absolutely no idea which direction that is."

"I guess we need to spend some time breaking down the riddle?" she asked even though she already knew the answer.

"Yeah, we do. Clearly this guy is getting impatient and is already planning his next murder."

Jed's eyes narrowed again as he remembered Max's words to him in their session earlier.

"I'm not sure what to make of this potential connection, but it seems that my client understands how ridiculous it is to go to the extreme measure of using a dart instead of a gun."

"He brought that up to you?" Christie asked, her pen flying across a brand-new page she had turned to.

"He did. I'm not surprised that he did, but he was a lot more... bold about bringing it up than he usually is about these things. Usually, he'll talk in parables, giving me the vaguest hints possible. He did that on the last case. I'm not sure if it's because he's more confident now that I will not rat him out that's making him so forthcoming. In any case, what he said was, 'What kind of psycho uses darts instead of a gun?'. I was thinking about it all evening, long before this voicemail came in, and he's right. What kind of psycho does use a dart gun with poison as opposed to a gun? Guns are so easy to come by in this country. It's not even like you'd have to go out of your way to find one. It's so strange that this person, whoever they are, has a big enough ego that they want to stand out in their murders."

Jed paused, letting Christie catch up for a few moments as she focused on what she was writing.

"It tells me that this person's motive might be unique. It's not every day a murderer goes out of their way to choose and implement a method so far from normal. It's odd that they want us to figure it out, though. You'd think that most murderers would want their deeds to stay hidden for as long as they possibly could. It's strange that he's disappointed that we haven't figured it out yet," Christie surmised.

Jed nodded, thinking hard. Christie watched his brows pull together more and more until he eventually seemed to no longer be paying attention to what she was saying.

"Everything okay, Gray?"

He closed his eyes and pressed his thumbs against his temples, as if trying to stave off a severe migraine.

"No, I'm afraid not. I need to take a hard stop. My focus is trash right now, and I don't think I will be able to continue talking about this for much longer before I tap out."

"Should we break now and reconvene tomorrow?" Christie asked hesitantly. She wasn't sure what she should do. She had only seen Jed break down like this when Ethan was mentioned. All his wounds were reopening.

"I'll stay the night. I need to know you are safe." That was all he said.

He reached for her, his eyes still closed, not seeing what he was doing. Christie took his outstretched arm and pulled him closer, until he leaned down against her chest, his breathing ragged and strained from whatever it was that was going on inside his mind.

"Stay." And that was all she said.

The Saturday afternoon sun was showering its blistering wrath through the windows of Jed's apartment, turning the entire living room into a small preview of hell. And although Jed wanted nothing more than to head into the cool darkness of his room and sink into bed, he knew it wouldn't help. He had just arrived home from Christie's. He'd spent the night on her couch, if only to keep his mind at ease, so that his fear that the threat from the voicemail was about her would be abated. He had struggled to fall asleep, and that was understandable. Jed's mind had been racing with all kinds of theories and speculations about the threat's meaning. They spent a large portion of the evening together, talking through the recent development in the case. He had worried a little about whether she was sleeping well or if the news was affecting her already frayed sleeping habits, but in the morning, she had reported a good night's sleep. Relief had spread through him like cold water, and it was then that he had returned home to shower.

As it stood, he was already trying not to beat himself up about it. It wasn't very often that he went into meltdown mode, but the combination of the stress and worry about Ethan's case, Joel's murder, Christie's safety, and the smug threat that this murderer had just leveled at them had all combined and proven to be too much to handle. Their conversation had gone mostly without a hitch, except for the moments when all his thoughts seemed to expand in his mind and he could focus on nothing else but the fear he felt at the casual challenge from whoever had sent the message—and from the clear jab at his career and his reputation.

Whoever was behind these murders and messages, one thing was slowly becoming clear in Jed's mind: this was personal. The more he thought about it, and the more he mentally replayed that awful voicemail in his mind, the surer he became. This was not just a deranged serial killer or some lunatic who had escaped from the nearest psychiatric ward. No, this was someone who seemed to know Jed intimately. That distorted voice, dripping with such vicious hate that Jed had almost felt its toxic stench through the phone, was testament to that. Someone was out to get him and was willing to put his own life on the line to succeed. Who could it be? A past client who Jed had dealt with unsuccessfully? Some enemy he'd made without realizing it?

Who?

Again, he had the niggling feeling come up, the strange sensation that these cases were starting to revolve around him more than he was comfortable with. In the first case, a large part of his clientele and one of his previous clients were attacked. Now, on top of the young man who had been gunned down, Blake, and their ordeal with the mobilization, arrests, and interrogations against the gang members, and the threat that this same guy had directed at the entirety of the NYPD, someone else was taking credit for Ethan and Joel's murder.

The spiraling thoughts were part of the reason he wasn't able to get to sleep at Christie's as easily as he usually did. After he'd arrived back home, Jed had resorted to sitting on his couch, staring out into the dark night and eating ice cream. It had been half full when he pulled from the freezer, and some hours later, he had managed to make his way through the entirety of what had been in the container. He had been so lost in his own thoughts that he hadn't noticed the time flying by and hadn't noticed just so much of the ice cream he was eating. When he showered and dropped into bed, it was past midnight. And then, after all that, he had laid awake for three more hours, staring up at the ceiling.

He sighed under the covers, realizing that he would need to stop hiding from the reality around him sooner or later. He had groceries to take care of and some laundry to get done. This week had been as mundane as possible, if one could count major police mobilization and intense investigations as mundane. His life had become so synonymous with visits to the NYPD, murders, crime scenes, close calls, and bloodshed that even that was starting to feel mundane to him—like just another day at the office.

Jed forced himself to get up, resting his feet on the soft carpet beneath his bed. Then, standing up and heading into the hot shower, he tried to regain control over his thoughts. One thing was clear; he had thought of it all night and hadn't realized it then, but now he could see that it had been clear all along. His mental health was taking a hit.

After his workout routine and a quick breakfast, Jed picked up the phone to call his mom. He scrolled through the notifications. There were a couple of messages from the group chat he and his friends had created years ago. Then there was the usual mail in his email account, with news outlets highlighting the latest that was happening in the city. There was a message from Christie. She wanted to know how he was feeling this morning. Ignoring all of those, he dialed his mom.

"Hi, Jed! How are you?" Laurie called cheerfully into the phone.

Jed felt like sinking to the floor on his knees. "I'm not great, Mom. How are you?"

"What's going on?" Concern instantly flooded his mother's voice. "How can I help?"

Hot, salty tears sprung into Jed's eyes. It was just like his mom to drop everything to try to help him.

"I think I had a bit of a meltdown last night," he managed in a choked voice, suppressing all his burning emotions deep within him where they smoldered like a bed of lit coals. "We've had a pretty big development in the case recently that connects both the case we've not been able to solve with the darts and the case where I lost my previous client. Someone is taking credit for doing them and has, essentially. challenged us to figure out his next victim before he gets to them"

"Oh, my God! That's terrifying!" Laurie's voice was aghast.

In his living room, Jed nodded. "It is. I told you about the voicemail that I got while I was working on Ethan's case, remember?" The words of the first voicemail he had received came back to his mind immediately. They would be forever burned there.

"Tsk. 'Tis a fucking shame. Maybe you should teach your clients how to fight so I can't overpower them so easily next time? The voice laughed. *He'd already started using fentanyl again anyways, so your little therapy shit failed. You're a fucking loser, Gray. Always were, always will be."*

Laurie was silent as she thought about the question. "No, actually, I'm not sure if you've mentioned it to me."

Jed sighed. "Well, I guess now is as good a time as any. Near the end of my last case, I received a voice message from someone saying that Ethan's murder was my fault—that it was my fault they were able to overpower him so easily and that he had already started taking fentanyl anyway, so my therapy had failed. I had initially thought that it was the same person who had committed all the other murders. But when he only confessed to three of the four, excluding Ethan, we started to get suspicious. Then, when this case started, with all the immediate concern about the nerve agent and how potent it was, and the unusual method the killer used, I completely forgot about the voicemail. I kind of relegated Ethan's case to the back of my mind so I could focus on the urgency of what was happening right then. But here we are again, at the end of our second case, with one murderer solved, one unsolved with little leads, and yet another voicemail. This time, the voicemail was about an upcoming murder. He's getting bored with how long we're taking to figure out who he is and what his aim is, so he gave us a clue and told us to figure it out and try to catch him before he ends up being successful in killing whoever he's going after next."

Laurie's frightened gasp told Jed all he needed to know about how she was feeling about that information.

"This is so frightening!" She exclaimed. "I'm not even sure what to say. Well, at least let me start here. Last time we spoke, you expressed concern that Christie might be the target of the attack."

Jed closed his eyes, bracing himself for the flood of protectiveness that built up in his chest as soon as his mom finished
the sentence.

"Now that you have another voicemail in your arsenal of
evidence, are you still concerned that this person could be
after her? What was the hint that they gave?"

Jed suddenly paled. "Mom, I'm not sure whether it would
be wise for me to repeat what the voicemail said right now.
I'm still trying to process the whole thing. Actually, I raced
over to her apartment to make her listen to it herself as soon
as I got it. But the hint was to keep my friends close and my
enemies closer. I think there is wisdom in being concerned
about her safety, but he said something about street code that's
making me reevaluate whether the friends part of the clue is
what I should actually be focusing on. Because the client that
helped me figure out the first case said the same thing to me,
except he only said to keep my friends close. At that point, I
didn't realize that it was my friend who was the murderer, but
eventually, it helped me figure it out. Now, the same street
quote is coming up, except the killer said the full thing: keep
your friends close but your enemies closer. I'm wondering if
this time it's the enemies I'm supposed to be focusing on. Or
I wonder whether it's a warning that he could go either way.
It feels like I have to have eyes on every single area of my life.
And right now, even though I haven't been hanging out with
my friends for the past couple of months, and it's a bad habit
I've been wanting to break, I'm actually grateful that I haven't

been hanging out with them. Because if I had, and this threat did have something to do with my friends, they would get dragged in, and I'd have to warn them."

Laurie was nodding along, all the dots connecting as she listened to Jed explain his thoughts.

"So," she started, "Jed, since the circle of people you're connected to is smaller than it usually is, that lessens the potential for casualties?"

Jed gave his agreement. "I think it does. However, it simultaneously increases the odds that Christie will be the target. If the part of the hint I'm supposed to be focusing on is the friends part and not the enemies part, she's in danger."

"Right," Laurie sighed. "So, it reduces risk on one side but increases risk on the other side."

Jed nodded. "Yes, because instead of spreading the risk wide with multiple people, it becomes more focused on one person. The good news is that I can keep an eye on Christie more easily than I could keep an eye on all my friends at the same time."

Laurie nodded, "Yes, that's true. And we already know just how much you like to keep an eye on Christie."

Jed felt his cheeks warm and coughed as he tried to clear his throat. "The good news is that I've already talked about it with her. So, we should be good to go for the current circumstances. We've already established a system for getting her home from work when she would usually have to walk home alone. I don't want her doing that anymore," he continued under his breath.

"I understand," Laurie said.

Then the line was silent for a while as they both thought about the words that had been shared between them.

"It's a hard place to be in when someone so close to me feels like the focus of this whole thing, and the only way out of this situation is to really and finally figure out who is behind this voicemail. That will figure this out for good. Still, I get the feeling it will not be quite as easy as we would hope."

CHAPTER 21

CHRISTIE AND JED WERE at the station in Christie's office, except this time, things were far from normal. It was a wonder how a small thing like a voicemail could change the dynamic of a working pattern so thoroughly. They worked on criminal cases. There was constantly a murder, investigation, or some level of involvement with illegal activity going on. It never stopped. But now, right on the heels of them wrapping up Blake's case, another curveball flew at them. The pattern was clear.

"Have you noticed just how much of an almost seamless pattern this murderer's operations have? It's almost as if he watches and waits for our new cases to begin and end and to time his strikes," Jed finally broke the silence.

"I'm not sure I'm seeing that connection. We were already in the middle of investigations when Ethan was struck down. In Joel's case, it happened first, so I'm not sure I'm seeing the same pattern that you're seeing."

"The pattern doesn't necessarily concern itself with the timing of when the murder cases start, but more so when we finish solving the case. In Ethan's case, the voicemail came after my client gave me the clue, right before Hugh attempted the fourth murder. So, essentially, whoever this crazy guy is timed his voicemail to when we were at the end of our investigations—as if to throw us off from what we were focusing on and get our attention back on Ethan's case. This time, pretty much the same thing happened. Right as we wrap up Blake's case, here comes another voicemail trying to get our attention back to Joel."

Christie nodded. "Now I get what you mean. It's kind of like we're dealing with someone who wants the attention on him constantly."

"That is what I was thinking, and I think the voicemail itself backs that up—the way he said that he was not surprised that we weren't making the connections but that he was disappointed. And that he was getting impatient." Jed shook his head, a frown on his lips. "Whoever the guy is, he's a cocky bastard. A cocky, overly-confident bastard."

Christie was taking down notes about what they were saying. "You're right. This person is definitely confident in whatever they're doing, and though their motives are evading me right now, I know that they, for sure, want our attention."

"Do you think this is part of some elaborate ploy from this same gang? Because when we were doing the final interrogation, Dredge mentioned that their plans were just getting larger and larger and more and more intricate until we weren't able to handle them anymore."

Christie said, "That did cross my mind, and I think it's worth looking into. What I will say from the jump, though, is that if this turns out to be the gang also orchestrating these separate events on the side, their patterns are serious deviations from the norm. From what we know about their behavior, they work in a group, they have their army because they want to be easily-identified by the people of New York, and their main dealings are in drugs. Whatever run-ins with crime or with people they have, it's always about drugs and money."

"I think you're right, but like you already said it's worth investigating. You never know, and there's no point in trying to rule out people we know are already in the business of murder."

Christie then sighed. "The timing pattern you noticed is an interesting one also. I'll definitely need to chew on it more, but as you explained it, it definitely holds up."

"What I'd like to do, though," she continued, "since he's promised that someone else is about to get murdered, is to figure out whether there are any patterns with the timing of his attacks in terms of when he starts them. With Ethan, that was in the middle of our frame, when we were still trying to figure out who the perpetrator was and what the motive was. It threw us off the scent for a long time. Obviously, he wasn't happy about that. In the case of Blake, he killed Joel first. He was probably very annoyed that Blake's murder took our attention away from him. And even then, when he noticed we were beginning to wrap up our investigations without making any kind of significant progress on his case, he sent us another clue, demanding attention."

Jed didn't like the sick feeling settling into his stomach. "I think that's a pattern in itself," he commented, watching as Christie raised her head to him and waited for him to continue his explanation. "The deviation from the pattern is the pattern. Initially, while he was still confident in our ability to figure out who he was and why he was doing what he was doing, he slipped Ethan's murder into our main case. Then, when we didn't catch on, he initiated another murder. No one could know that another case was about to open up. Now that we're wrapping up the second case, the one that came after Joel's murder, without having gotten closer to figuring out who he is, he's pouting and throwing a hissy fit once again."

Christine nodded, but she still wasn't sure where Jed was going with his train of thought.

"What I think this means is that not only is he going to commit this murder to solidify his place in our attention, but he might already be working on it as we speak. He's irritated that we're not making progress with his case and annoyed that he isn't our only priority, which means he might go as far as to make sure that his case is the only one that can take up our attention."

"So, you think it's possible that he's going to make a repeat of initiating a murder before we have a chance to take on any new cases?"

Jed nodded. "Exactly. I think while we're here deliberating and trying to figure out patterns and motives, he has already selected the person he's going to focus his attack on. It could be happening as we speak."

They stared at each other, the silence stretching between them. Then, Jed broke into a half laugh, half groan.

"This is nuts."

Christie cracked a grin. "It is."

That was all she said.

Jed stared at her. "I hope you're not sitting over there beating yourself up over not being able to figure this out any faster than we realistically can, Detective."

Christie's cheeks warmed, but she nodded. "I've been working on not doing that since our conversation about it. I never did thank you for helping me to talk through those things. But forcing myself to really face where those habits came from and what started them has helped me be less critical of myself. It's incredible how quickly a change happens once you know what's causing the problem. But for the times when I've been struggling a little harder than usual to keep my thoughts under control, I have been relying a lot on my journaling."

Jed couldn't help the grin that was wide on his lips. Christie shook her head at him, a full smile now on her face. "You're feeling very smug, aren't you?"

Jed shook his head. "Smug isn't nearly the right word. What I'm feeling is a great deal of pride. I'm very proud of you, Christie. This is a massive step in the right direction, and

I'm really glad we had that conversation, too. Initially, I was worried that it might have been too much and that pushed too hard. Or that it might have been too intimate and ended up making you uncomfortable. Now, hearing this, I'm glad I trusted my gut and insisted that you have that conversation with me."

Christie fought the blush trying to bloom across her cheeks. "It was definitely a more intimate conversation than I would have with just anyone—or even with a friend. But I appreciate you pushing me the way you did. I did really need to confront those old wounds."

Jed agreed. "The old wounds tend to be the ones that hurt the most because they happen long before we ever learn how to tend to wounds. So, they stay there, they scab over, but weren't ever really treated. We think that just because we're not seeing the blood and the flesh that it's all healed and everything's perfect. That is, until we run into something that triggers the wound, and we find that it's still as raw as the first day we got it. Meanwhile, all the new wounds we've collected over the years since then have healed perfectly because we knew how to dress them." Jed considered his own words. "Have you ever had one of those feelings where you said something that suddenly seems to have an alternate meaning? I think I'm having one of those moments right now. Except I'm not sure what the second meaning even is."

Christie smiled. "I definitely know what you mean."

"Exactly. You get it. Not that I'm surprised," he smiled at her. "You always seem to get me." He looked back down at his lap. "I'm not sure what that niggling feeling in the back of my mind was just now, but I'll mark it down and come back to it later. It's always worth revisiting these moments where your brain is trying to point something out that you're not able to fully discern."

Christie nodded before looking up at the clock that was hung over the door behind Jed.

"Ready to get rid of me?" he asked with a smile.

Christie looked right at him, shaking her head 'no'. "I don't want to get rid of you. We've already had this conversation."

Jed stared at her, caught off guard. Christie set her pen down and reached into her drawer to pull out a candy bar she had brought to work with her.

"I'm not the only one who dumps on myself," she started. "You do it, too. I'm not tired of you, I don't want to get rid of you, and I don't think your thoughts are too far-fetched."

Jed's brow raised higher and higher, but she continued.

"I don't think you're taking too long to figure things out. I don't think that your decision not to pressure your client into giving you more direct information is wrong. I don't think you're overlooking anything. I don't think you're not being fast enough... shall I go on?"

For the first time in a while, Jed stared at Christie without knowing what to say.

"No," he finally answered. "Message received."

"Good," she answered, smiling. But then, her smile turned into a frown, and her eyes narrowed. "I've been meaning to ask you what's up with you and Jason."

Jed tried his best not to let his expression change at the mention of the officer. "Is there supposed to be something going on between us?" he asked, perhaps a bit too innocently. "Did you issue some kind of instruction that I was not aware of?"

Christie tilted her head at Jed, as though implying that he should know better than to try to play it cool with her.

"You know what I mean to say. You guys were never best friends, but since the mobilization last Monday, you guys have been on ice."

Jed shrugged, then ran a hand through his hair, his eyes level with Christie's. "I haven't said anything to him. He hasn't done anything to me, and I guess in a way, that's exactly the problem. Honestly, I don't have anything to say. We don't work together, we don't interact very often, and all the times we have interacted, you have been in the middle of the interaction. I'm not sure if he thinks I'm limiting his access to you." Jed couldn't help the way his voice tightened. "But in order for me to be blocking him, you would have to be interested in him in the first place." He looked at her for a long moment. "Are you interested in him?"

Christie shook her head. Jed nodded in response, a sly smile on his lips.

"So, I'm not blocking anything."

Christie narrowed her eyes at him. "I'm keeping an eye on you two. I don't want there to be any unnecessary tension between our team. We were in the middle of our retreat when this whole thing started anyway, and we didn't even get to the good parts of the team-building exercises. If I need to talk to him about it, then I will. For now," she sighed, "I need to focus all my energy on figuring out the hints this killer keeps dropping."

CHAPTER 22

ALONE AT HOME ONCE again, deep in thought, the words from the voicemail played over and over in his mind. Jed wasn't quite brave enough to actually play It again. He didn't even need to. He could hear the words in his mind.

"So, you couldn't figure out Ethan's murder. I'm not surprised. You haven't figured out Joel's murder either. Still not surprised. But I'm a little disappointed. I thought they said you were the best in the city? This is embarrassing, and honestly, I'm getting impatient. So, I'm gonna make the next one easy for you. Like they say on the streets, keep your friends close and your enemies closer. Somebody's about to get dropped."

Whoever this was wasn't surprised that they had failed to sniff out the connection between Ethan's murder and Joel's murder, but they were disappointed.

Disappointment was a curious emotion to feel, and a very strange emotion to profess in the face of such a strange scenario. Irritation? That was plausible given the circumstances. Since this murderer was so pompous, attention-seeking, and self-confident, it was understandable that he would be irritated that they had not yet figured out his motives or his next moves. Joy? That was even more probable. In that case, it would align this person more with what was considered the norm for murderers. They were often happy with their handiwork, going as far as making sure the people in their inner circles of illegal activities knew that they were the ones who had killed a particular person. It was like collecting trophies—a game. They often thought they were more intelligent than everyone else, making it difficult for the police to catch them. They felt invincible.

Jed remembered Max mentioning this when the murders of homeless people were starting to tick upward. 'Bragging rights' was what he'd called it. Everyone wanted bragging rights for the people they had attacked. That connected more closely with the emotion of joy, but even then, it would still be a strange emotion to feel. Jed sighed, annoyed. Strange as it was, though, joy would have been an easy connection to the fact that this person was happy the NYPD was struggling with their cases. That could then lead to a connection in the thought pattern that would lead them to believe this person was committing these murders for the hell of it. It was a basis for a motive, perhaps. Disappointment... disappointment was a strange one. Disappointment implied that this killer was being let down by the NYPD the longer they took to figure out who he was. And of course, it was understandable that bragging rights we're being tampered with because the crimes had gone unsolved.

In their last conversation before Jed had walked Christie home, she had requested call tracing to be done on the two voicemails Jed had received. Unfortunately, whoever the guy was had been smart enough to know not to keep his number visible whenever he made the calls. Blocked numbers were notoriously tricky to trace. It was also a problem that the killer was going through such an elaborate means of contacting them, giving them hints, and expressing disappointment at their slow pace. It meant he was also smart enough to have used a throw-away phone—something not connected in any way to him, so that his anonymity would be preserved.

Of course, he was smarter than that. He went as far as quite literally contacting the people who were supposed to be solving his case and offering them a hint. It didn't make sense. It was as though he had something to prove, something to show off. A cause to defend. He even made a jab at Jed's reputation, or at least the NYPD's reputation; Jed wasn't sure which it was. Somehow, though, when he had listened to the voicemail the first time, it had felt completely personal to him.

The first voicemail, the one he received concerning Ethan, had definitely been personal. He had accused Jed of being a poor therapist, going as far as telling him he should have trained Ethan better so that he would not have been over-powered. It was clear that he knew Jed was a therapist, and it was also clear by extension that he knew Jed did not do physical training. Yet he had seemed to imply that he should have encouraged Ethan to work out so that he would have been physically stronger.

Jed shook his head, trying to clear away the dark thoughts that were beginning to crowd in the longer he thought about Ethan. He spent three more hours sitting on his sofa, staring out into the night and trying to work through the thought that was hiding in the back of his mind.

He hadn't been able to work past what he had last told Christie and his mom. The hint felt as though it were a test, some sort of teasing homage to the streets. Max said the same thing when he was talking with Jed, particularly when he was saying anything he knew was related to Jed's cases. Street code. It was what he used to live by. It was what was haunting his days as time went by. He had thought he had left that part of his life behind. But, alas, the consequences of getting involved with drugs seemed never-ending. Even when you were completely sober and back to normal living, it kept rearing its ugly head in different places.

After all, Jed had chosen his career. He was the one who decided to be an addiction therapist. He had known that his work would eventually trigger some of his past experiences. It came with the territory. That's just how it was. Whenever issues reemerged for Jed, he used the opportunity to strengthen his resolve and sobriety. It was like strength training to build muscle. Every time he was forced to revisit something he hadn't fully worked through, he was able to handle it in the present and support his sobriety. But this, this particular area of his experience, kept coming up, more so than any other of the things he had gone through. Street code. He stared out at the crescent moon far above the city lights, almost invisible because of the glare of the buildings. After a quick shower, he dressed and tossed his towel into the hamper in time to see his phone light up with a notification.

Another voice message had come in. He must have missed the call while in the shower. Heart immediately racing, Jed sat up on the couch before putting the phone back down on the sofa beside him. His already distressed mind was begging him to believe that it was just Christie leaving him a message before she went to bed. But then, Christie would have called, or she would have sent him a text. His mind ran through the list of all the people he knew and all the people who knew him. No one would have left a voicemail. Everyone would have just sent him a message or called again. This was turning out to be too much of a coincidence to not be true. With a trembling hand, Jed reached for the phone, unlocked it, and clicked the button to play the voicemail.

There was static. His stomach dropped into his shoes. Then, the distorted voice.

Say hello to your father for me, will you?

Honest reviews of my books help bring them to the attention of other readers, who are more likely to read something from a new-to-them author if it has more reviews. Reviews are the lifeblood of little authors like me. I would be grateful if you can find the time to leave a review. Thank you!

Here is the universal link to this book to leave a review: https://bit.ly/JedGray2

Or you can scan this QR code with your phone to take you to the universal book page:

ACKNOWLEDGEMENTS

I am truly grateful for all of my wonderful family and friends who have stood by me during the difficult times and are still here to help me celebrate the good time now!

I Love you all!

ABOUT THE AUTHOR

Jodi Walter was born and raised in the Western Prairies of Canada. She spent her childhood enjoying nature and animals on the family farm. She continues to volunteer with animal rescues and has adopted two rescue dogs that she shares her home with today.

Jodi went through some difficult times in her early thirties when her marriage broke down and she became a single mom of a fantastic young son. After picking herself back up and succeeding in whatever challenge she faced, she became a firm believer that "we are never put in any situation we can not handle". Her newest endeavour is to write mystery thriller stories for you to enjoy. Delving into her subconscious, she creates characters she hopes will connect with you. Jodi has experienced a profound amount of catharsis by putting her pen to paper and releasing her characters into the world.

Jodi's website: jodiwalter.com or https://thirteen-pages-btxdiq.mailerpage.io/

Jodi's Facebook: https://www.facebook.com/jodiwalterauthor

Jodi's Email: author@jodiwalter.com